D0964342

Hesitantly, she pressed her lips to his. Just barely a touch, but it was like a streak of lightning. Hot. His toes even tingled as if they'd been dipped in fire.

It took every bit of his restraint not to roll her onto the bed and kiss her senseless. His newfound patience and desire to not frighten the daylights out of her was one of his more stupid decisions.

She drew away immediately, her eyes wide, a touch of pink suffusing her soft cheeks. Then she slid one hand up his chest and over his shoulder, staring warily at him the whole while as if she expected him to bite her for daring to touch him. Jesu, but he was nigh to the point of *begging* her to touch him.

Her fingers wandered to his neck and then she put her mouth carefully to his again. This time she remained there as she tentatively explored his mouth. With her tongue. Sweet mother of God, this was killing him.

She stirred restlessly against him as she pressed closer, her mouth hotly fused to his.

A surge of lust rolled through his body, but he held back, not wanting to destroy the sweetness of her offering. She was an innocent for all her warrior ways and attempts at acting like a man. She deserved all the gentleness and wooing he could muster, though God only knew he'd deserve sainthood before this was over with.

"'Tis not unpleasant, this kissing," she whispered.

By Maya Banks

In Bed with a Highlander
Seduction of a Highland Lass
Never Love a Highlander

Books published by The Random House Publishing Group
are available at quantity discounts on bulk purchases for
premium, educational, fund-raising, and special sales use.
For details, please call 1-800-733-3000.

Never Love a Highlander

Maya Banks

BALLANTINE BOOKS • NEW YORK

Sale of this book without a front cover may be unauthorized. If this book is coverless, it may have been reported to the publisher as "unsold or destroyed" and neither the author nor the publisher may have received payment for it.

Never Love a Highlander is a work of fiction. Names, characters, places, and incidents are the products of the author's imagination or are used fictitiously. Any resemblance to actual events, locales, or persons, living or dead, is entirely coincidental.

A Ballantine Books Mass Market Original

Copyright © 2011 by Maya Banks
Excerpt from *In Bed with a Highlander* copyright © 2011 by Maya Banks
Excerpt from *Seduction of a Highland Lass* copyright © 2011 by Maya Banks

All rights reserved.

Published in the United States by Ballantine Books, an imprint of The Random House Publishing Group, a division of Random House, Inc., New York.

BALLANTINE and colophon are registered trademarks of Random House, Inc.

ISBN 978-0-345-51951-1
eBook ISBN 978-0-345-51952-8

Cover illustration: Alan Ayers

Printed in the United States of America

www.ballantinebooks.com

9 8 7 6 5

Ballantine Books mass market edition: November 2011

For Telisa

Never Love a Highlander

CHAPTER 1

The weather for her first wedding had been a splendor of nature. An unseasonably warm day in January. Quite balmy with nary a breeze to ruffle her carefully arranged hair. It was as if the world stood still to witness the joining of two souls.

A snort rippled from Rionna McDonald's throat, eliciting a raised eyebrow from her soon-to-be husband.

The weather for her second wedding? Gloomy and dank with a winter storm pushing in from the west. Already a brisk chill had set in and the wind blew in fierce, relentless sheets. As if the world knew just how uncertain she was about the man who stood beside her, ready to recite the vows that would bind him to her forever.

A shiver skirted up her spine despite the fact that they stood in front of the huge fire in the great hall.

Caelen frowned and stepped closer to Rionna as if to shield her from the draft blowing through the furs at the window. She took a hasty step back before thinking better of it. The man made her nervous, and not many people intimidated her.

He frowned harder, then turned his attention back to the priest.

Rionna cast a quick glance around, hoping no one

had witnessed that particular exchange. It wouldn't do for people to think she was afraid of her new husband. Even if she was.

Ewan McCabe, the oldest McCabe brother and the first man she was supposed to have married, stood by his brother's side, his arms crossed over his broad chest. He looked anxious to be done with the whole thing.

Alaric McCabe, the man she'd very nearly wed after Ewan got himself married to Mairin Stuart, also looked impatient and kept glancing toward the stairs as if he might run out at any moment. Rionna couldn't blame him, though. His new wife, Keeley, was above stairs recovering from a wound that had nearly ended her life.

Third time was a charm, right?

King David wasn't standing for the occasion. He sat regally by the fire, looking on with approval as the priest droned on. Around him, also sitting, were the many lairds from neighboring lands. All waiting for the alliance between the McDonalds and the McCabes. An alliance that would be sealed upon her marriage to Caelen McCabe, the youngest—and last—McCabe brother.

It was important to denote last because if anything went amiss with this wedding, there were no more McCabes for her to marry, and at this point, her pride couldn't withstand another rejection.

Her gaze skittered from the king and assembled lairds to her dour-faced father who sat away from the assembled warriors, an unmanly, sullen pout twisting his features.

For a moment their stares locked and then his lip turned up into a snarl. She hadn't supported him in his bid to keep his position of laird. It was probably disloyal of her. She wasn't sure that Caelen McCabe would be a better laird, but surely he was a better man.

She became aware that all eyes were on her. She glanced nervously toward the priest and realized that she'd missed her cue to recite her vows. Even more embarrassing, she had no idea what the man had said.

"This is where you promise to obey me, cleave only unto me, and remain faithful all your days," Caelen drawled.

His words stiffened her spine and she couldn't call back the glare as she speared him with her gaze.

"And what exactly are you promising me?"

His pale green eyes stroked coolly over her, assessing and then lifting as if he found nothing of import. She didn't like that look. He'd all but dismissed her.

"You'll gain my protection and the respect due a lady of your station."

"That's all?"

She whispered the words, and she'd have given anything not to have let them slip. It was no wonder she'd been left wanting, though. Ewan McCabe clearly adored his wife, Mairin, and Alaric had just defied king and country to be with the woman he loved—effectively casting Rionna aside in the process.

Not that she was angry. She dearly loved Keeley, and Keeley deserved happiness. That a man as strong and handsome as Alaric had publicly proclaimed his love for Keeley gladdened Rionna's heart.

But it also brought home how sterile her own marriage would be.

Caelen made a sound of exasperation. "Exactly what is it that you want, lass?"

She raised her chin and stared back at him every bit as cool. "Nothing. 'Tis enough. I'll have your respect and your regard. I won't be needing your protection, though."

His eyebrow rose. "Is that so?"

"Aye. I can see to my own protection."

Caelen chuckled and more laughter rose from the assembled men. "Say your vows, lass. We don't have all day. The men are hungry. They've been waiting a feast for nearly a fortnight now."

Agreement rumbled through the room and her cheeks burned. This was her wedding day and she wouldn't be rushed. Who cared about the food and the men's stomachs?

As if sensing that she was working herself into a righteous fury, Caelen reached over, snagged her hand, and pulled her up next to his side until his thigh burned into hers through the material of her dress.

"Father," Caelen said respectfully, "if you'll tell the lass what she needs to say again."

Rionna fumed the entire way through the recitation. Tears pricked her eyelids but she couldn't even say why. It wasn't as if she and Alaric had been a love match any more than she and Caelen were. The entire idea of wedding one of the McCabe brothers had been hatched by her father and embraced by the McCabes and the king himself.

She was but a pawn to be used and discarded.

She sighed and then shook her head. It was ridiculous to be this maudlin. There were worse things. She should be happy. She'd rediscovered the sister of her heart in Keeley, who was now happily married even if she faced a long recovery in the days ahead. And Rionna's father would no longer be laird of their clan.

She chanced another look only to see her father throw back yet another goblet of ale. She supposed she couldn't entirely blame him for being so deep into his cups. His entire way of life was gone in a moment's time. But she couldn't muster any regret.

Her clan could be great—*would* be great—under the right leadership. It had never been her father. He'd weakened the McDonald name until they'd been reduced to begging for the aid and alliance of a stronger clan.

Her free hand curled into a tight fist at her side. It had been her dream to restore their glory. To shape the soldiers into a formidable fighting force. Now it would be Caelen's task and she would be relegated to a position of observation rather than the participation she craved.

She gasped in surprise when Caelen suddenly leaned in and brushed his lips across hers. He was gone almost before she registered what he'd done and she stood there staring wide-eyed as she raised a trembling hand to her mouth.

The ceremony was done. Even now the serving women were flooding into the hall, bearing a veritable bounty of food, much of which came from her own stores after her father's foolish wager several months ago.

Caelen watched her a moment and then gestured for her to walk ahead of him toward the high table. Rionna was gratified to see Mairin join her husband. In a sea of gruff, indistinguishable faces, Mairin McCabe was a ray of sunshine. Tired sunshine, but warm nonetheless.

Mairin hurried forward with a bright smile. "Rionna, you look so beautiful. There isn't a woman here who can hold a candle to you today."

Rionna's cheeks warmed under Mairin's praise. 'Twas the truth Rionna was a little ashamed to be wearing the same dress she'd worn when she nearly married Alaric. She felt wrinkled, rumpled, and worn through. But the sincerity in Mairin's smile bolstered Rionna's flagging spirits.

Mairin gathered Rionna's hands in hers as if to offer further encouragement.

"Oh, your hands are like ice!" Mairin exclaimed. "I

did so want to be present for your joining. I hope you'll accept my regrets."

"Of course," Rionna said with a genuine smile. "How is Keeley fairing this day?"

Some of the worry lifted from Mairin's gaze. "Come, sit so we may be served. And then I'll tell you of Keeley."

It irked Rionna that she first looked to her new husband only to catch his nod of permission. She gritted her teeth and moved to the table to sit beside Mairin. Already she was acting like a docile nitwit and she hadn't been married five minutes.

But in truth, Caelen frightened her. Alaric hadn't. Even Ewan didn't intimidate her. Caelen scared her witless.

Rionna slid into the chair beside Mairin, hoping for a brief reprieve before Caelen joined her. She wasn't so fortunate. Her husband pulled out the chair next to her and scooted to the table, his leg so close to hers that it pressed to the whole of her thigh.

Deciding it would be rude—and obvious—were she to slide toward Mairin, she decided instead to ignore him. She couldn't forget that it was acceptable for him to be so familiar now. They were wed.

She sucked in her breath as the realization hit her that he would of course exert his marital rights. Indeed, there was the whole wedding night, virginal deflowering. All the things women tittered about behind their hands when the men weren't around.

The problem was that Rionna was always with the men and she'd never tittered in her life. Keeley had been separated from her at a young age, long before Rionna had grown curious over such matters.

With a lecher for a father and Rionna's constant fear for Keeley, the mere thought of coupling nauseated her. Now she had a husband who'd expect . . . Well, he'd expect certain things, and God help her, she had no idea what.

Humiliation tightened her cheeks. She could ask Mairin. Or one of the McCabe women. They were all generous to a fault and they'd all been kind to Rionna. But the idea of having to admit to them all just how ignorant she was of such matters made her want to hide under the table.

She could wield a sword better than most men. She could fight. And she was fast. She could be ruthless when provoked. She didn't suffer a gentle constitution nor did she faint at the sight of blood.

But she didn't know the way of kissing.

"Are you going to eat?" Caelen asked.

She looked up to see that the places had been set and the food was on the table. Caelen had thoughtfully cut a choice piece of meat and placed it on her plate.

"Aye," she whispered.

'Twas the truth, she was fair to starving.

"Would you like water or ale?"

'Twas also true she never partook of spirits, but somehow today ale seemed to be the wise choice.

"Ale," she said, and waited as Caelen poured a gobletful. She reached for it but to her surprise, he put it to his mouth and first sniffed and then drank a small portion of the ale.

"'Tis not poisoned," he said as he slid it toward her place.

She gaped at him, not comprehending what he'd just done.

"But what if it *had* been poisoned?"

He touched her cheek. Just once. It was the only affectionate gesture he'd offered her and it might not even be construed as affectionate, but it was soft and a little comforting.

"Then you wouldn't have partaken of the poison, nor

would you have died. We already nearly lost one McCabe to such cowardice. I'll not risk another."

Her mouth fell open. "That's ridiculous! Think you that *you* dying somehow makes it all better?"

"Rionna, I just took sacred vows to protect you. That means I'd lay down my life for you and for any future children we have. We've already a snake in our midst trying to poison Ewan. Now that you and I are wed, what better way to prevent the alliance between our clans than to kill you?"

"Or you," she felt compelled to point out.

"Aye, 'tis a possibility. But if McDonald's only heir is dead then his clan effectively crumbles, which makes it easy pickings for Duncan Cameron. You are the heart of this alliance, Rionna. Whether you wish to believe it or not. Much rides on your shoulders. I guarantee you it won't be easy for you."

"Nay, I never imagined differently."

"Smart lass."

He piddled with the goblet before sliding it toward her. Then he solicitously lifted it and held it to her mouth, just as a new husband would do for his bride during the wedding feast.

"Drink, Rionna. You look exhausted. You're on edge. You're so stiff that it can't be comfortable. Take a drink and try to relax. We've a long afternoon to endure."

He hadn't lied.

Rionna sat wearily at the table as toast after toast was given. There were toasts to the McCabes. Toasts to the new McCabe heir. Ewan and Mairin were the proud parents of a newborn lass, who also happened to be the heir to one of the largest and choicest holdings in all of Scotland.

Then there were toasts to Alaric and Keeley. To Keeley's health. Then the toasts to her marriage to Caelen began.

At one point they degenerated into lewd toasts to Caelen's prowess, and two lairds even began a wager as to how fast Rionna would find herself with child.

Rionna's eyes were glazing over and she wasn't entirely sure it was due to the lengthy accolades being tossed about. Her goblet had been refilled more times than she remembered but she drank on, ignoring the way it swirled around in her belly and made her head swim.

Laird McCabe had decreed that despite the many issues that bore discussion and the decisions that must be made, today would be spent in celebration of his brother's marriage.

Rionna suspected that Mairin had everything to do with that decree. She needn't have bothered, though. There was little cause for celebration in Rionna's mind.

She glanced sideways to see Caelen sitting back in his chair, lazily surveying the occupants of the table. He tossed back an insult when one was flung his way by one of the McCabe men. Something to do with his manhood. Rionna shuddered and purposely blanked her mind to the innuendo.

She gulped down another mouthful of the ale and put the goblet back down on the table with a bang that made her wince. No one seemed to notice, but then it *was* unbearably loud.

The food before her swam in her vision, and the idea of putting it to her mouth, despite Caelen having cut the meat into bite-sized morsels, turned her stomach.

"Rionna, is anything amiss?"

Mairin's soft inquiry jolted Rionna from her semi-daze. She glanced guiltily up at the other woman and then blinked when Mairin suddenly became two people.

"I should like to see Keeley," she blurted.

If the laird's wife thought it odd that Rionna would

wish to visit with Keeley on Rionna's wedding day, she didn't react.

"I'll go up with you if you like."

Rionna sighed in relief then started to rise from her seat. Caelen's hand snapped around her wrist and he tugged her back down, a frown marring his features.

"I wish to see Keeley since she wasn't able to attend my wedding," Rionna said. "With your permission, of course."

She nearly choked on the words.

He studied her for a brief moment then relaxed his grip on her wrist. "You may go."

It sounded so imperious. So . . . husbandlike.

Her stomach heaved as she excused herself to the laird. Married. Jesus wept, but she was married. She was expected to submit to her husband. To obey him.

Her hands shook as she followed Mairin toward the stairs. They walked quietly up, one of Ewan's men tagging along behind, but then Mairin went nowhere without an escort.

Merciful heaven, would she be expected to be led about by the reins now that she was married to Caelen? The idea of being unable to go anywhere or do anything without someone breathing down her neck suffocated her.

At Keeley's door, Mairin knocked softly. Alaric answered, and Mairin spoke in low tones with her brother by marriage.

Alaric nodded and stepped out but then said, "Try not to be overlong. She tires easily."

Rionna glanced at the man who would have been her husband and couldn't help a silent comparison between him and his younger brother. The man she now found herself wed to.

There was no doubt both were fierce warriors, but she

still couldn't help but feel she would have preferred marriage to Alaric. He didn't seem as . . . cold . . . as Caelen. Or indifferent. Or . . . something.

She couldn't quite put her finger on it, but there was something in Caelen's eyes that unsettled her, that made her wary, like prey poised to flee a predator. He made her feel tiny, defenseless. *Feminine.*

"Rionna," Alaric said with a nod. "Congratulations on your marriage."

There was still a hint of guilt in his eyes, and truly, she wasn't resentful. Not of why he hadn't married her. His falling in love with Keeley hadn't quite managed to banish her humiliation of being jilted, though. She was working on it.

"Thank you," she murmured.

She waited until Alaric passed her and then she entered Keeley's chamber.

Keeley lay propped on an abundance of pillows. She was pale and lines of fatigue etched grooves on her forehead. Still, she smiled weakly when her gaze met Rionna's.

"So sorry I missed your wedding," Keeley said.

Rionna smiled and went to her bed. She perched on the edge so she wouldn't cause Keeley pain and then gingerly reached for her hand.

"'Twas not of import. I barely remember it myself."

Keeley snorted and a spasm of pain crossed her face.

"I had to see you," Rionna whispered. "There was something . . . I wanted to seek your counsel on something."

Keeley's eyes widened in surprise and then she glanced beyond Rionna to Mairin. "Of course. Is it all right if Mairin stays? She's completely trustworthy."

Rionna cast a hesitant glance in Mairin's direction.

"Perhaps I should go down and fetch us some ale," Mairin suggested. "'Twill give you time to speak freely."

Rionna sighed. "Nay, I'll wait. 'Tis the truth I could use the counsel of more than one woman. Keeley is newly married after all."

A soft blush suffused Keeley's cheeks and Mairin chuckled. "I'll send for the ale then, and we'll talk. You have my word, naught will pass the doors of this chamber."

Rionna looked gratefully at Mairin, and then Mairin went to the door and conversed with Gannon, the warrior who'd accompanied them up the stairs.

"How easily is sound carried through the doors?" Rionna whispered to Keeley.

"I can assure you that nothing can be heard from the halls," Keeley said, a twinkle in her eyes. "Now what matter would you like to discuss?"

Rionna dutifully waited until Mairin returned to Keeley's bedside and then she licked her lips, feeling the worst sort of fool for exposing her ignorance.

"'Tis about the marriage bed."

"Ah," Mairin said knowingly.

"Ah, indeed," Keeley said with a nod.

Rionna blew out her breath in frustration. "What am I to do? What am I supposed to do? I know nothing of kissing and coupling or . . . anything. 'Tis a sword and fighting I have knowledge of."

Mairin's expression softened and the amusement fled from her eyes. She covered Rionna's hand with her own and squeezed. "'Tis the truth that not too long ago, I was in your same position. I sought out the counsel of some older ladies of the clan. 'Twas an eye-opening experience to be sure."

"Aye, as did I," Keeley admitted. "It isn't as though we're born with such knowledge, and none of us had mothers to guide us through such things." She cast an apologetic look to Rionna. "At least I assume your mother never discussed such delicate issues with you."

Rionna snorted. "She despaired of me from the time I grew breasts."

Keeley's eyebrows rose. "You grew breasts?"

Rionna flushed and glanced down at her bosom. Her flat bosom. If Keeley—or anyone—actually knew what lay beneath the wrappings . . . Her husband would know soon enough, unless Rionna figured out a way to consummate a marriage fully clothed.

Mairin smiled. "'Tis not so difficult, Rionna. The men do most of the work, as they should in the beginning. Once you learn your way around, well, then you can certainly do all manner of things."

"Alaric is wonderful at loving," Keeley said with a sigh.

Mairin colored and cleared her throat. "'Tis the truth I didn't think Ewan overly skilled at first. Our wedding night was hastened by the fact that Duncan Cameron's army bore down on us. 'Twas an insult Ewan took exception to and made great effort to remedy. With very satisfying results, I might add."

Rionna's cheeks warmed as she glanced between the two women. Their eyes became all dreamy and soft as they spoke of their husbands. Rionna couldn't imagine ever having such a reaction to Caelen. He was simply too . . . forbidding. Aye, that was an apt description.

A knock at the door interrupted the discussion and the women went silent. Mairin issued a summons, and Gannon stepped inside, a disapproving look on his face.

"Thank you, Gannon," Mairin said, as he set the flagon and the goblets on the small table beside Keeley's bed. "You may go now."

He scowled but backed out of the room. Rionna glanced up at Mairin, curious as to why she accepted such insolence from her husband's man. Mairin simply smiled smugly as she poured the ale into the goblets.

"He knows we're up to mischief and it's killing him to say nothing."

She handed Rionna a goblet and then carefully placed one into Keeley's hand.

"'Tis the truth it will dull the pain," Keeley said.

"I'm sorry, Keeley. Would you like me to go? I have no wish to cause you further distress," Rionna said.

Keeley sipped at the ale and then leaned back against her pillows with a sigh. "Nay. I'm about to go mad being sequestered in my chamber. I welcome the company. Besides, we must ease your fears about your wedding night."

Rionna gulped at her ale and then extended the goblet to Mairin for it to be refilled. She had a feeling she wasn't going to like this conversation.

"'Tis no reason to fear," Mairin soothed. "I've no doubt Caelen will take care with you." Then she wrinkled her nose. "Give thanks you don't have an army bearing down on you. 'Tis the truth I had no liking for my wedding night."

Rionna felt the blood drain from her face.

"Hush, Mairin. You aren't helping," Keeley chided.

Mairin patted Rionna's hand. "All will be well. You'll see."

"But what do I *do*?"

"Exactly what is it that you know?" Keeley asked. "Let's start there."

Rionna closed her eyes in misery and then downed the entire contents of her goblet. "Nothing."

"Oh dear," Mairin said. "'Tis the truth I was ignorant, but the nuns at the abbey did see fit to provide me cursory information."

"I think you should be honest with Caelen about your fears," Keeley suggested. "He'd be a brute to ignore a maiden's worry. If he has half of Alaric's skill, you'll not be left wanting."

Mairin giggled at the boast, and Rionna held out her goblet for another round of ale.

The very *last* thing she wanted was to talk to Caelen about her maidenly fears. The man would probably laugh at her. Or worse, give her that cool, indifferent gaze that made her feel so . . . insignificant.

"Will it hurt?" she strangled out.

Mairin's lips pursed in thought. Keeley's brow wrinkled a moment.

"'Tis the truth it's not overly pleasant. At first. But the pain passes quickly and if the man is skilled, it's quite wonderful in the end."

Mairin snorted. "Again, as long as there isn't an army bearing down on you."

"Enough with the army," Keeley said in exasperation. "There is no army."

Then the two women looked at each other and laughed until Keeley groaned and went limp against her pillows.

Rionna just stared at them, never more certain that she had no desire to indulge in this marriage bed business. She yawned broadly and the room spun in curious little circles. Her head felt as though it weighed as much as a boulder, and it was harder and harder for her to hold it up.

She stood from her perch on the edge of Keeley's bed and started for the door, disgusted with her cowardice. She was acting . . . Well, she was acting just like a woman.

To her utter dismay, she ended up at the window and she blinked in confusion as a blast of cold air hit her in the face and the corner of the furs blew up.

"Careful, there," Mairin said in her ear.

She guided Rionna to a chair in the corner of the room and eased her down.

"Perhaps 'tis best if you sit here awhile. It wouldn't do

for you to navigate those stairs, and we don't want the men to know what we've been about."

Rionna nodded. She did feel a bit peculiar. Aye, it would be best if she sat awhile until the room stopped spinning in such spectacular fashion.

Caelen looked toward the stairs for what seemed like the hundredth time, and Ewan looked impatient as well. Rionna and Mairin had been gone for some time. It was late into the night and Caelen was ready to have done with the entire wedding celebration.

Some celebration. His bride had been stiff and distant throughout the entire ceremony, and afterward she'd sat silent while the room celebrated around her.

If her demeanor was anything to go by, she was even less thrilled than he with the match. It mattered naught. They were both bound by duty. And right now his duty was to consummate his marriage.

His loins tightened, and the surge of lust took him by surprise. It had been a long while since he'd had such a strong reaction to a woman. But it had been thus since the day he'd laid eyes on Rionna.

He'd been shamed by his reaction to his brother's betrothed. It was disloyal and disrespectful to feel such a keen burning in his gut.

But no matter that he damned himself, it didn't change the fact that she had only to walk in the room and his body leapt to life.

And now she was his.

He searched the entrance to the stairs one more time and then sent a pointed stare toward Ewan. It was time to collect his wife and take her to bed.

Ewan nodded then stood. It didn't seem to matter that the king was still heartily enjoying himself. Ewan merely announced that the festivities were at their end and that everyone should seek their beds.

Everyone would reconvene in the morning and talks would begin. Ewan had a legacy to claim on behalf of his daughter and there was a war to wage against Duncan Cameron.

Caelen followed Ewan up the stairs where they were met by Gannon.

"Lady McCabe took to her chamber an hour ago when the babe awoke for feeding," Gannon said to Ewan.

"And my wife?" Caelen drawled.

"Still within Keeley's chamber. Alaric is in Keeley's old chamber, but he's losing patience and fair itching to get back to Keeley."

"You may tell him Rionna will be gone within the minute," Caelen said as he strode toward the door.

He knocked, only because 'twas Keeley's chamber and he had no wish to alarm her by barging in. 'Twas an insult for Rionna to have spent so much time above stairs, missing most of their wedding celebration.

Upon hearing Keeley's soft summons, he opened the door and entered.

His expression eased when he saw Keeley propped haphazardly on her pillows. She looked as though she was about to slide off the bed, and he hurried to prop her up. Exhaustion ringed her eyes and she grunted as he positioned her better.

"Sorry," he muttered.

"'Tis all right," she said with a small smile.

"I've come for Rionna." He frowned when he realized she wasn't present.

Keeley nodded toward the far corner. "She's there."

Caelen turned and, to his surprise, saw her propped in a chair against the wall, sound asleep, her mouth open and her head tilted back. Then as he took a closer look around the room, he saw the tankard of ale and the empty goblets.

With a suspicious frown, he peered into the tankard only to find it empty. He glanced back at Keeley, whose eyes looked precariously close to rolling back in her head, and then back to Rionna, who hadn't stirred a wit. He remembered all the ale she'd consumed at the table below stairs and how little she'd eaten.

"You're soused!"

"Maybe," Keeley mumbled. "All right, probably."

Caelen shook his head. Foolheaded females.

He started toward Rionna when Keeley's soft entreaty stopped him.

"Be gentle with her, Caelen. She's afraid."

He stopped, stared down at the passed out woman in the chair, and then slowly turned to look back at Keeley. "Is that what this is about? She got herself soused because she's afraid of me?"

Keeley's brow wrinkled. "Not of you particularly. Well, I suppose that could be part of it. But, Caelen, she's frightfully . . . ignorant of . . ."

She broke off and blushed to the roots of her hair.

"I understand your meaning," Caelen said gruffly. "No offense, Keeley, but 'tis a matter between me and my wife. I'll be taking her now. You should be resting, not consuming ridiculous amounts of ale."

"Has anyone ever told you that you're too rigid?" Keeley groused.

Caelen leaned down and slid his arms underneath Rionna's slight body and lifted her. She weighed next to nothing, and to his surprise, he liked the feel of her in his arms. It was . . . nice.

He strode toward the door, barked an order to Gannon whom he knew to be standing on the other side, and the door quickly opened. In the hall Caelen met Alaric, who raised his eyebrow inquiringly.

"See to your own wife," Caelen said rudely. "She's probably unconscious by now."

"What?" Alaric demanded.

But Caelen ignored him and continued on to his chamber. He shouldered his way in and then gently laid Rionna down on his bed. With a sigh, he stepped back to stare down at her.

So the little warrior was frightened. And to escape him, she'd drank herself into oblivion. Hardly complimentary to Caelen, but then he supposed he couldn't blame her. He hadn't been . . . Well, he hadn't been a lot of things.

With a shake of his head, he began peeling away her clothing until she was down to her underclothes. His hands shook as he smoothed the thin linen garment over her body.

He could see nothing of her breasts. She was a slight woman and she didn't have much in the way of a bosom. Her body was lean and toned, unlike any other woman he'd ever encountered.

He ached to lift the hem of her underdress and pull it away from her body until she was naked to his gaze. It was his right. She was his wife.

But he couldn't bring himself to do it.

He could wake her now and assert his husbandly rights, but he had a sudden desire to see her eyes flame with the same want he felt. He wanted to hear her soft cries of pleasure. He didn't want her to be afraid.

He smiled and shook his head. When she woke in the morning, she'd likely have a raging headache, and she'd wonder what the hell happened the night before.

He might have a conscience about taking what was rightfully his until she was prepared to surrender herself body and soul, but that didn't mean she had to know it right away.

He slid into bed beside her and pulled the heavy fur over the both of them. The scent of her hair curled through his nose, and the warmth from her body beckoned to him.

With a muttered curse, he turned over until he faced away.

To his utter dismay, she murmured in her sleep and then snuggled up against his back, her warm, lush body molded so tightly to his that he hadn't a prayer of sleeping this night.

CHAPTER 2

Something or someone was sitting on Rionna's head. She moaned softly and batted at the offending object only to find herself swatting at air.

She forced her eyelids open and promptly regretted that action. Though it was dark, just the air sliding over her eyeballs made her twitch in agony.

As she lay there she became aware of other peculiarities. Such as the very warm, very hard body next to her, and the fact that she was clad in only her underdress.

Her hand flew to her bosom and she felt the linen binding around her breasts. It was still in place, which meant her husband hadn't been too invasive, nor did he realize the fullness of her breasts. Not that she cared if he knew. He was her husband after all. He'd know soon enough. It wasn't as if she could hide them forever.

She searched her memory but couldn't summon a single image of what had happened the night before. The last thing she remembered was standing in front of Keeley's window.

Now she was lying in bed next to her . . . husband.

Did it count as consummation if she couldn't remember it? Shouldn't she have shed more clothing than she had? Keeley and Mairin hadn't gone over specifics such as that. Then she realized that if she had no memory of the event, it couldn't have been so bad, could it?

Humiliation burned her cheeks and tightened her chest. What on earth was she to say to him? How could she face him? What if she'd acted like a harlot? What if she'd disappointed him, or worse, what if her lack of skill had disgusted him?

Despite the throbbing in her head and the nausea boiling in her stomach, she eased from the bed and shivered as the cold slid over her body. The warrior put off a lot of heat and it had been toasty warm in the bed.

Thank the good lord she couldn't see him. She'd been close enough to him to know he hadn't worn a tunic. What if he . . . What if he were completely naked?

She was torn between wanting to run from the room with all haste and succumbing to the absurd urge to peek under the covers.

Close on the heels of that dilemma came the realization that this was his chamber, not the one afforded to her as a guest.

She stumbled over her wedding finery that lay on the floor and heat singed her cheeks all over again. Had he undressed her? Had she?

She yanked on the gown and held it up as best she could before cracking the door open to peer into the hall. It was dimly lit by half-burned wall candles and, as best she could tell, empty.

Thank God.

She pushed out of the chamber and fled down the hall to hers. She stripped off the dress and donned what she was more comfortable in. Warm trews, a worn tunic, and leather boots. She needed to clear her head despite its horrendous ache, and the only way she knew to do that was with a good fight.

Caelen awoke to find his bed empty and a cold draft blowing over his privates. He yanked up the furs with a muttered curse and then searched the room for his wife's whereabouts.

She was nowhere to be found, which irritated him. He was always the first one up and about in the keep. Even Ewan, who rose early and retired late, never managed to rise earlier than Caelen.

It was a time he had grown to crave for its solitude. While the rest of the keep slept, he began the day, sometimes with a swim in the loch and other times honing his fighting skills.

He tossed aside the furs and stood naked as he stretched and allowed the first brush of cold to blow over his skin, awakening him. His blood surged to life, throwing off the lethargy of sleep.

He poured water from a pitcher into the washbasin and then splashed his face and washed out his mouth. Either his wife was mortified or she was sending a clear message about her feelings on the marriage. Either way, parameters had to be set, and there was no time like the present to let his new bride know the way of things.

After he found her.

After dressing, he slipped into the hall. Normally he'd not worry about being quiet, but the king was in residence and everyone had stayed up late into the night, plus he had no wish for anyone to know his wife had fled his bed.

He scowled as he stopped outside her chamber door. To hell with knocking. He pushed open the door and was greeted by darkness and . . . cold. No fire was lit.

It occurred to him that he hadn't lit a fire in his own chamber, a practice he was accustomed to, but Rionna was a slight lass and no doubt she'd woken with chattering teeth.

He wasn't used to accommodating others. Particularly in his private rooms. But he was married now, and he supposed some concessions would have to be made. He'd show his wife that he could be a reasonable man.

He strode inside but found the bed empty and undisturbed. Slung over a chair was her wedding dress. The one he'd taken off her the night before.

Where had she gotten off to at this hour?

Suspicion nipped at his gut until his belly clenched. Surely the lass wouldn't be fool enough to sneak to a lover's bed on her wedding night. What other reason would a woman have for leaving the warmth of her bed in the middle of the night?

If there was a problem, she should have awakened him. He was her husband now, and it was his duty to solve any issues that arose.

The more he pondered, the angrier he got. Old betrayals still soured his belly, despite his best effort to put them behind him.

It was hard not to dwell on all that Elsepeth had done when she'd changed the entire course of the McCabe clan. His current marriage was the result of her betrayal. His attempt to remedy the foolishness of youth and allowing emotion to cloud his judgment.

For years, his clan had struggled to survive its near decimation at the hands of Duncan Cameron. Only in recent months, with Ewan's marriage to Mairin and the birth of Isabel, were things finally looking up for his kin.

How could he refuse to do the one thing that would solidify a union that would bring about the destruction of a man hated by him and his brothers above all others?

By God, he may have had no choice but to wed Rionna McDonald, but it didn't mean he was going to be made a cuckold, or that he'd let his wife run wild as her father had done for years.

He was now her laird whether she liked that fact or not, and if she did nothing else, she'd obey him.

The sound of steel striking steel drifted through her window. He frowned and strode over to lift the fur. Her room overlooked the courtyard, but who would be sparring so early. And why?

He leaned out to see torches surrounding a small area in the middle of the courtyard. Two men were sparring furiously. One of the fools was going to get himself killed. As one turned, Caelen caught the flash of golden hair and the decidedly feminine set of the lips pursed in concentration.

Hell.

One of the fools was his wife.

He let the furs fall back to cover the window and he turned to stalk from her chamber. Shaking his head, he descended the stairs only to have Cormac fall in next to him when he strode into the great hall.

"Did you know that Rionna was out sparring?" Caelen bit out.

Cormac's eyes widened and he looked abashed—and uncertain as to what to say.

"Nay," he finally muttered. "I only just arose."

Caelen glanced at him in disgust. "Are you growing soft and lazy on me?"

Cormac grinned, undisturbed by Caelen's censure. "I find now that I have a soft, warm lass in my bed every night, 'tis hard to find motivation to rise so damn early."

Caelen grunted.

"The question is, why your lass is out of your bed the morning after she wed with you. One might draw some interesting conclusions."

Caelen sent him a chilling glare.

Not in the least bit worried over Caelen's mood, Cormac continued. "Why, the very fact that she has the strength to spar suggests that you did something . . . well, not right."

Cormac's smug teasing made Caelen's lips turn up into a snarl. "I'd wager that Christina wouldn't care too much for a toothless husband."

Cormac held up his hands in surrender, but he wore that stupid grin all the way outside.

Caelen welcomed the brisk chill. It was a reminder to him never to get too comfortable. Never let his guard down. When men became too ensconced in their own comfort, it was inevitably their downfall.

That wouldn't happen to him. Not if he could help it. Nor would it happen to his clan—both new and old.

"She has skill," Cormac noted.

Caelen scowled again as they approached the area lit by the torches.

"Rionna!" he barked.

Her head yanked in his direction just as the other man's sword flew. Directly at her exposed neck.

Caelen thrust his sword forward to deflect the blow, and Rionna's eyes widened as the tip of her sparring partner's blade stopped within an inch of her flesh.

With a flick of his wrist, Caelen knocked the sword from her opponent's hand and sent him a look that had him backing away in a hurry.

If he expected his wife to be frightened, abashed, or grateful that he'd prevented her death, he was wrong.

She was bloody furious.

Her eyes sparking with demonic light in the glow of the torches, she turned on him, reminding him of a spitting kitten. The comparison would probably only make her angrier, but it was an amusing enough thought.

"What did you think you were doing?" she yelled. "You could have gotten me killed! You don't bellow at someone when they're sparring!"

His nostrils flared and he advanced on her, furious that she'd address him thusly in front of others.

"Think you that distractions don't exist on the battlefield, Rionna? Think you that no one will ever shout at you? A warrior is strong, not just physically but in the mind as well. *Allowing* yourself to become distracted during battle will get you killed."

She flushed and looked away, her sword lowered toward her feet.

"Nor do you ever lower your sword. You're now completely vulnerable to attack."

Her lips twisted in anger. "You've made your point, husband."

"Have I? I think not. I'm only about to begin to make my point. You will take yourself inside at once. You'll not indulge in such activities again. Do I make myself clear?"

Her mouth dropped open and those golden eyes flashed with rage—and humiliation.

"When you present yourself to the table to break your fast, you'll do so as a credit to the McCabe clan, and you'll show respect due the king and the laird of this clan."

Her lips snapped shut and formed a mutinous frown. He took another step forward until there was no space separating them. He'd never admit it, in a thousand years, but the sight and smell of her, all disheveled from swordplay, had his cock about to split at the seams.

He couldn't have her running about in this manner of dress or doing battle with the men because he'd be naught but a walking erection.

He waved a hand to dismiss her and to let her know she was dismissed. As she turned away, he called after her.

"Oh, and Rionna? Take a bath. You stink."

CHAPTER 3

Stink. He'd told her she stank! Rionna slid farther down in the tub until water lapped at her ears. They still burned with mortification, and she could still hear the men's laughter ringing in her ears as she'd all but fled into the keep.

He'd humiliated her. Not just with words but by actions. He'd proven her inept and she'd committed the sin of allowing herself to become distracted.

She knew all of this. She wasn't an idiot. She could hold her own with a sword, and yet from the moment she'd become aware of his presence, all sense had flown right out of her mind.

She'd become nothing more than a bumbling fool playing at being a man. Her disgust knew no bounds.

A knock sounded at her door. She frowned and sunk so low in the tub that only her nose and eyes stuck out of the water. A moment later, the door opened and Maddie stuck her head in.

"Ah, there you are, lass. Caelen thought you might be needing help. He wants you below stairs to break your fast in half an hour's time."

"Oh he does, does he?" Rionna muttered.

"Let me help wash your hair. 'Twill take some doing

to get it all dry in such a short time. You have such long, thick hair. 'Tis as beautiful as a sunset over the loch."

The woman's praise bolstered Rionna's flagging spirits. She knew she wasn't beautiful. Keeley was beautiful. Rionna . . . Well, part of it was her fault. She could have practiced being more feminine when she was younger.

Now her body had lost some of her youthful softness and she had muscles that no lady should ever have. Her arms were firm. Her waist slender. Her legs were hard with muscle, and no flab gathered at her hips. In fact she was quite narrow.

The only womanly place on her was her breasts, and she despaired of them. They simply didn't match the rest of her.

Which is why she kept them bound. They simply got in her way and they were a great distraction.

There were occasions when her father insisted she dress as a woman, the few times the McDonalds hosted honored guests. Her mother's gowns had been altered, but the bodice had still been too tight. Her breasts had strained the limits of the bodice, and the result was men making twits of themselves as they stared lasciviously at her cleavage.

Men were ridiculous. Show them a breast and they became slobbering fools.

And one man was a fool above all others and 'twas him she feared the most. As long as she remained boyish in figure, she didn't have to worry about drawing unwanted attention.

"Well, lass? Are you going to sit there all day while the water grows cold or are you going to let me wash your hair so we can get you ready to go below stairs?"

Rionna shook herself from her thoughts and then nodded. Maddie briskly fetched a wooden bucket from the window and then motioned for Rionna to sit forward in the tub. As Rionna sat up, Maddie's eyes widened.

"Well now, where have you been hiding those?"

Rionna looked down and flushed as she became aware that Maddie was staring at her exposed breasts. They bobbed in the water and Rionna laid her arm across her chest to push them down.

"I'm cursed," Rionna muttered.

"Oh, Lordie, no you're not cursed. Lasses would kill to have a shape like that. Does your husband know what he's got?"

Rionna scowled.

Maddie let out a chuckle. "I'll take that as a no. Oh my but is he in for a surprise."

"He won't be seeing them for a while if I have my way."

Maddie hooted again and then poured a bucket of water over Rionna's head. "Surely you aren't going to hide them forever."

"Nay. Not forever."

"You think he's not going to want a peek at your treasures when he beds you?"

Rionna frowned. "How do you know . . ."

Maddie made a *tsk*ing sound. "Oh come now, lass. You were as drunk as an old warrior put out to pasture and there was no stain on your bed. Unless you're going to tell me you weren't a maiden."

Another flush crawled over Rionna's face. Maddie was as forward as they came, and Rionna wasn't used to the counsel of other women. It made her distinctly uncomfortable.

"There'll be plenty of time to warm your husband's bed," Maddie advised. "Until then you need to give him a taste of what he's missing so far. The lad's tongue will be hanging out his mouth if you show those breasts to their best advantage."

Rionna shook her head. "'Tis not my husband's reaction I'm concerned with."

"Think you Caelen would allow another man to get near his wife? Come now, lass. You may have worried before about untoward advances, but if a woman can't look her finest at her own wedding celebration, then when can she? A man would be a fool to approach you with your new husband there beside you."

"What do you have in mind?" Rionna asked warily.

Maddie shot her a smug smile as she began rinsing away the soap. "You leave that to me. I think I have just the thing."

Caelen was growing more irritated by the minute. The king had already sat down to break his fast and yet they still awaited Rionna's presence. Even Mairin, who was still weak from childbirth and nursing a babe, was seated at her husband's side, waiting for the meal and the talks to commence afterward.

He was about to go drag her down the stairs himself when a hush fell over the room. Indeed, the silence was so pronounced that unease prickled over his nape.

When he saw all attention focused on the entrance to the hall, he turned to follow the stares. His first reaction was one of aggravation, given that she'd made them wait so long. But then he took in her appearance, and he was puzzled by what was different.

He was slower to catch on than those around him, maybe because he was more focused on the fact that she was late. But realization, when it hit him, made his mouth drop open. He snapped it shut and glanced hastily around to make sure no one had caught his reaction.

Then he jerked his gaze back to his wife.

There had never been a doubt that she was a comely woman. She had eyes of an unusual shade. Amber and golden. Much like her hair. Not red or even auburn, but not exactly blond either. Depending on which way the sun hit her, the locks were golden, sometimes russet, lighter and darker. A fascinating blend of the sky at sunset.

Aye, she could even be considered beautiful, if she weren't always dressed as a man with dirt on her face and hands.

But now . . .

Jesus wept. The woman had breasts. Who knew? He swallowed back the instant knot in his throat. He wouldn't be expected to have such a reaction. By all accounts, he should have discovered this most interesting detail last night. When he was supposed to have bedded his new bride.

Where the hell had she hidden such a bounty of femininity?

And furthermore, why?

She was attired in a fine gown, one that seemed familiar to him. He glanced in Mairin's direction, realizing that it had been made for her. On Mairin it had been handsome enough, but on Rionna it was spectacular.

Rionna looked . . . dainty. Not a word that would have ever come to mind before. Fragile and feminine. Her hair was swept up atop her head, and strands slid down her neck like little sips of sunshine.

She also looked extremely uncertain.

He arched an eyebrow at his little warrior as fear crowded into her eyes. He would have thought she'd cut her own throat before allowing anyone to see her fear.

But now, twice in less than a day, he'd seen fear and vulnerability in his bride's eyes and it made him want to do daft things.

Like lie beside her all night because he worried he'd frighten her more if he bedded her.

He almost snorted. Of all the stupid things, that was

probably the most. If his men knew of his sudden patience, they'd laugh him out of the keep.

Which was why he had to pretend he'd already seen the feast of feminine flesh that his wife now had on display.

He scowled at the ogling men and then stepped forward to assist his wife into her seat. He was still scowling when he greeted her, which was likely why tight lines appeared around her eyes and mouth.

He meant to tell her that she looked nice and he wholeheartedly approved of the change. What came out, however, was not what he planned.

"Why don't you cover yourself properly? 'Tis indecent."

She yanked her arm from his hand, fixed him with a glare that would shrivel a man's cods, and then elegantly seated herself, leaving him to feel like the worst sort of tyrant.

He glared again at his men when they continued to stare with their tongues wagging about like they'd never set eyes on a lass.

"You look beautiful, Rionna," Mairin said from across the table.

Guilt crept up Caelen's neck. It should have been him who acknowledged how regal and, yes, beautiful, his wife looked. It shouldn't be left to others to comment in order to remove his insensitive remarks.

And yet he couldn't open his mouth to remedy his error.

"I've never seen a finer bride," the king said with a broad smile.

Caelen scowled at the king and ignored Ewan's look of reprimand.

David merely laughed and dug into his food.

"'Tis a good thing we've done, Ewan," David said heartily as he wiped his mouth with the back of his arm.

Caelen wished he could be so sure this alliance was necessary. Still, his brother looked more at ease than he had in many months spent worrying over Mairin and Isabel and Duncan Cameron. And Alaric looked . . . content. For too long Alaric had been tormented by an impossible choice. The woman he loved or his loyalty to his clan. Having chosen wrong before, Caelen didn't feel qualified to decide on such matters.

With everyone so bloody happy around him, it was hard to make the argument that the right thing hadn't been done. The only problem was that he and Rionna seemed to be the only ones *not* happy.

Ewan cast a glance in Caelen's direction before turning back to the king. "Aye, we've done a good thing."

"As soon as the babe is well enough to sustain the journey, you must make haste to claim Neamh Álainn. 'Tis important to secure the last link in our stronghold."

The king turned to Caelen. "'Tis the truth a winter storm is nigh, but 'tis also important that you travel back to McDonald keep. The alliance has been made, but I do not trust the former laird not to stir up dissension. It will be your task to bring the McDonalds under control and to honor the alliance with the McCabes."

Rionna stiffened at the insult, and her head jerked up as she shot daggers at the king. Caelen's hand shot out to grasp hers and he squeezed a warning.

"Forget you that I am a McCabe? Think you I would betray my kin? My brother?" He fought to keep his own anger under control. He and Rionna were sacrificing much for the good of their clans. He wouldn't allow the insult to pass. "Just because the McDonald laird is without honor does not mean that his people are lacking as well."

Rionna eased back into her chair, her rigid shoulders sinking as she relaxed the tiniest bit. When she turned her liquid golden stare on Caelen, he saw gratitude for his defense. And grudging respect.

"I meant no disrespect," David said. "'Tis the truth, you'll not have an easy time of it. The McDonalds won't readily accept you as their laird. You'll have to be on guard at every turn. Duncan Cameron will use any means to weaken our alliance. He's a viper who must be disposed of."

"I have no doubt that my brother will do all that is necessary to shape the McDonalds into a formidable fighting force," Ewan said. "He is largely responsible for the McCabes' invincibility. 'Tis the truth I'll be sorely disappointed to lose him even if by doing so I gain a strong ally."

"You'll not lose me, brother," Caelen said with a smile. "We'll be neighbors now."

Alaric, who'd been silent until now, frowned and glanced between his two brothers. "What will you do, Ewan? You cannot be in two places at once. Neamh Álainn will have to be defended well and Mairin and Isabel must be protected at all costs. But neither can you neglect our keep. Our clan."

Ewan smiled and exchanged conspiratorial glances with the king. "Nay, Alaric. 'Tis the truth you speak. You are the only McCabe without land and holdings to call your own now. It only seems fitting that you will defend McCabe keep when Mairin and I take up residence at Neamh Álainn."

Alaric appeared stunned. He looked between his brothers and shook his head. "I don't understand."

"I cannot be laird any longer," Ewan murmured. He turned to Mairin, his eyes full of love. "Surely you see that. Upon the birth of Isabel, my destiny—all our destinies—changed as soon as she took her first breath. 'Tis my duty to protect my daughter's legacy. I cannot split my duties between my clan and my wife and daughter and be fair to either. Which is why you'll become laird. I cannot think of a better man for the duty."

Alaric dragged a hand through his hair and stared at Ewan in disbelief. "I don't even know what to say, Ewan. *You're* the laird. Since our father died. It's the way of things. I never considered that I would take over."

The king arched an eyebrow. "Are you saying you have to think on it?"

"Of course not. I'll do whatever is necessary to ensure the safety and future of my clan."

"Except marry me, apparently," Rionna muttered under her breath.

But Caelen heard and he glanced sharply at his wife. He hadn't considered that perchance she harbored tender feelings for Alaric. Surely they hadn't been together for long enough. But then how did anyone explain the workings of a woman's mind?

Alaric wasn't as cold as Caelen, and Caelen knew he could be unforgiving. Harsh even. Alaric seemed more in tune with the lasses. They adored him. Found him bonny.

Was she upset over the fact that she found herself married to the wrong McCabe? 'Twas something Caelen hadn't considered, and now that he was he didn't like the thought at all.

"'Tis settled then," the king announced as he put down his goblet. "We'll gather the lairds and Ewan can name his brother the new laird of the McCabe clan."

"What of our men?" Alaric asked Ewan.

Caelen leaned forward, for he had need to hear this as well. The McCabes had an awesome fighting force, but it would have to be split, which benefitted no one.

Ewan grimaced. "I'll take a large enough contingent

with me to see to the protection of Mairin and Isabel. Once we've arrived at Neamh Álainn, I can afford to send some back provided I am well satisfied with the king's guard there."

He looked to Caelen. "I thought to leave Cormac here since he is newly married and 'twould be more difficult for him to relocate to the McDonald holding with a new wife. I can't spare men to give to you but I can send Gannon with you to aid in the training of the McDonald soldiers."

Caelen viewed his brother with surprise. "But Gannon is your most senior man, your most trusted. He has protected you and your wife and child faithfully."

"It is why I would send him with you," Ewan said quietly. "You'll need an ally, someone you can trust without question." He glanced apologetically at Rionna as he spoke.

Rionna stared stoically past the men to the tapestries hanging over the fireplace. You could have broken stone on her face. No hint of emotion. Her eyes were guarded, no betrayal of her thoughts.

Then she turned as if deigning to acknowledge the men sitting around her. She gave a delicate, feminine sniff, but somehow Caelen knew it had cost her not to let out a decidedly male snort.

"It's a wonder you allowed yourself to consort with people such as the McDonalds. Why bother with an alliance when we're so clearly inferior and untrustworthy?" Rionna said.

Caelen nearly crushed her hand in his. His nostrils flared and he would have chastised her for speaking to the king and his brother thusly, but something in her gaze held him back. It wasn't so much the anger, but hurt lurked where before she'd allowed no hint of what she was feeling to show.

It was gone so quickly he wondered if he'd imagined it. The king chuckled while Ewan grimaced.

"I realize this isn't easy for you to hear, Rionna. You have my apologies. I would not send my brother into a hostile environment without support."

"He is more protected by being my husband than he is by your man," she pointed out. "Perhaps you should concern yourself more with not insulting *me*."

At that Ewan's eyes narrowed. He was angry at the implied threat. Caelen was merely amused.

"Now, Rionna. You'll have him worried you're going to split my gullet while I sleep," Caelen drawled.

He leaned over, wrapped his hand around her nape, and did what he'd been dying to do ever since she floated into the room. His lips mashed against hers. It was no kiss of seduction, accompanied by sweet gestures and honeyed words.

It was a command to be silent. To cede to his authority. It was a reminder of whom she belonged to.

The feisty little wench nipped at his lip. He tasted blood but he also tasted her sweetness. He didn't rear back as she likely expected. He deepened the kiss until his blood was forced onto her tongue. When she tried to pull away, he hauled her against him until she was flat against his chest, her ample breasts straining at her bodice.

Only when she went slack against him and the fight leeched from her body did he pull slowly away. He wiped at his mouth with the back of his hand, all the while staring into her eyes.

"See, Ewan, she's perfectly harmless. You just have to know how to handle her."

She sprang to her feet, her eyes flashing furiously. "You are the worst sort of braying ass!"

He battled a grin as she turned and flounced dramatically from the room. She'd be insulted to know that her usual long, mannish stride was completely ruined by the yards of material flowing at her feet. She looked like a woman in a pique.

And wouldn't that infuriate her.

Chapter 4

"Jesu, Rionna, where did those come from?" Keeley exclaimed.

Rionna shut the chamber door with a scowl and then looked down as she realized what Keeley referred to.

"They're breasts!"

"Well, I can see that. The question is how you grew them overnight."

Rionna stared at Keeley for a moment and then burst into laughter. It was either that or cry, and she'd poke her own eye out before she let that happen.

Keeley's eyes were full of mirth as Rionna walked over to collapse on the bed next to her.

"He's a . . . He's a . . ."

"Yes, Rionna? He's a what?"

"He's a dolt! A pompous, overstuffed . . . windbag!"

"I can see your education is sorely lacking in the area of insults," Keeley said dryly.

"I was trying to be circumspect," Rionna muttered.

"I assume you were referring to your new husband?"

Rionna sighed. "It's never going to work, Keeley. I look at you and Alaric. I see how Ewan is with Mairin. And then I look at Caelen."

Keeley's face filled with sadness and worry. "Do you think you'll be so very unhappy?"

Rionna felt immediate guilt. Here Keeley lay recovering from a terrible injury. She'd married the man Rionna was supposed to marry and she likely felt horrible that Rionna was unhappy.

"'Tis the truth I'd be miserable with either McCabe, so you needn't feel guilty for marrying Alaric. At least one of us is happy and I'm delirious with joy that you have someone who loves you so very dearly."

"How was last night?" Keeley asked carefully.

Rionna's eyes narrowed. "I wouldn't know. The last thing I remember is standing by your window. I woke up next to Caelen in naught but my underdress. Surely it couldn't be so bad if I don't even remember it?"

"You say you were still dressed?"

"Aye, well, I wasn't completely naked if that's what you're asking."

Keeley giggled. "Nothing happened, Rionna. He didn't bed you. You were passed out in the chair over there. He came in, picked you up, and carried you out. He must have undressed you and put you to bed."

Rionna gave a mournful sigh and her shoulders slumped. "'Tis the truth I'd hoped it was over and done with. Now I have to dread the deed all over again."

Keeley patted Rionna on the hand. "You worry over much. 'Tis naught but a pinch and then it feels very nice."

Rionna wasn't convinced but she wasn't going to argue.

"Now tell me why you suddenly have such a generous . . . bosom."

Rionna rolled her eyes. "I've always bound them. 'Tis the truth that when I began to grow more womanly, my breasts got way ahead of the rest of me. I can't wield a sword and dodge and be quick when I have these things bouncing at my chest. 'Tis obscene, to borrow Caelen's word."

Keeley gasped. "He said that?"

"He muttered something about covering myself and mentioned the word *obscene*. I'm inclined to agree with him."

"You're right. He's a dolt."

Rionna grinned and then sighed. "'Tis the truth this dress is driving me daft. I'm going to go change and maybe take in some fresh air. The walls of the keep are closing in on me."

"You always were more comfortable outside," Keeley said with a smile. "Go then. I'll not tell Caelen I've seen you if he asks."

Rionna leaned forward to kiss Keeley's cheek. It was on the tip of her tongue to relate all that had been said below about Alaric being the new laird, but she wouldn't ruin the news for Alaric. 'Twas the truth the new couple needed all the good moments they could manage. They'd been through hell already.

"I'll come to see you later. Rest now, sister of my heart."

Keeley shot her a mischievous grin. "When you return, I'll tell you all I've learned about matters of the flesh. 'Tis the truth you can tame the gruffest of men with a few touches and a most inventive use of your mouth."

Rionna's face burst into flames. She clapped her hands over her ears with a groan.

Keeley leaned back into the pillows and smiled. "I'm so glad you're here, Rionna. I missed you so."

"I missed you, too."

Rionna hurried down the hall to her chamber where she all but tore the frothy confection of a gown from her body. She embraced her anger because the alternative wasn't bearable. What she really wanted was to curl into a ball on the bed and shut out her humiliation.

It was stupid of her to allow Maddie to interfere. Playing dress up was for beautiful women who knew all the social niceties. How to talk. How to walk. How to be quiet and deferential. All the things Rionna wasn't.

All Rionna had accomplished was making an even bigger fool of herself. And she'd given Caelen yet another opportunity to humiliate her.

She hated him.

It was bad enough he thought himself some noble self-sacrificer for taking on his brother's discarded bride, but he had to be a smug, overbearing jackass to boot.

If only she'd had a sister to marry off. Then Rionna could have dressed the way she wanted, acted as she wanted, and she could damn well pick up a sword when she wanted.

Realizing she was standing in the nude and it was quite cold, she pulled on the scruffy trews and then pulled her favorite tunic over her head. Her boots were old. There was a hole in the heel, but they fit her like a glove and they'd never let her down.

Taking only a few extra moments to plait and secure her hair, she slid her sword into the scabbard and enjoyed the comfort of being herself once more.

Then she turned and strode from her chamber.

To hell with Caelen McCabe. To hell with the lot of them. Her clan might not be the mightiest or the cleverest. They might not have the fighting skills of another clan. But they were hers and she wouldn't allow them to be spoken poorly of. Her father had done enough of that. Self-righteous bastard.

She slipped silently down the stairs, hoping the men would still be involved in talks. She cocked her head when she reached the base of the stairs and heard the sound of voices echoing through the great hall.

She hurried the opposite way and out one of the side exits into the courtyard.

Soldiers from the various neighboring clans sparred.

They jested and laughed. The smell of sweat filtered through her nose, and the sounds of metal banged in her ears, welcome and familiar.

Still, she moved away from the assembled soldiers and made her way through the trees toward the loch.

"Rionna!"

She turned hastily, seeing her father standing in the direction she'd just come from. He was frowning, his arms crossed over his chest. Then he loosened one hand and motioned her to come.

She contemplated ignoring his summons, but 'twas not the time. He was still her laird, albeit for not many days longer. Her new husband would take over the mantle of leadership and, God help her, she didn't know who she dreaded in the position more.

Her jaw tight, she walked back to her father and stopped a short distance away. "Yes, father?"

"I want to have a word with you. We cannot allow Caelen McCabe to take over the McDonald clan."

"We have little choice in the matter," she said carefully. "'Tis either ally ourselves with the McCabes or face Duncan Cameron on our own."

"Nay, 'tis not our only choice."

She raised an eyebrow. "Think you that you're a little late to be saying such? You couldn't have come to me with this solution *before* I married Caelen McCabe?"

"Silence that mouth of yours before I do," her father roared. "I am still your laird and, by God, I'll not tolerate your insolence."

Rionna stared defiantly at the man she'd lost all respect for over the years. He was a pathetic excuse for a man, even if he was her laird—and her father. She couldn't help the circumstances of her birth. Would that she could.

"Tell me, father. What is this plan you've hatched to save us all from the McCabes and Duncan Cameron?"

He smiled then and Rionna shivered. "If you can't beat a man, you should consider joining with him. I've a mind to strike a bargain with Cameron. He allows me to remain laird of my clan and I'll aid him in his endeavors."

Rionna paled, all the blood draining from her face. "You speak of treason!"

"Quiet!" her father hissed. "Lest we be overheard."

"You're a fool," she bit out. "I'm married already. There is naught to be done. Duncan Cameron is a man without honor. You can't seriously think to ally ourselves with one of his ilk."

He slapped her across her cheek, shocking her into silence. She stumbled back, her hand cupping her jaw.

Then she regained her footing, her rage so fierce that she feared exploding.

She drew her sword and flew toward him, the tip notched against his neck. His eyes bulged and sweat beaded his forehead as he stared back at her.

"You'll not ever touch me again," she ground out. "If you ever raise your hand to me, I'll carve out your heart and feed it to the buzzards."

Her father raised his hands slowly, his fingers shaking like leaves in autumn. "Don't be rash, Rionna. Think what you're saying."

"I speak the truth," she said in a harsh voice she didn't recognize. "You'll not lead our clan to dishonor. Nor will you drag me into the mire you've created. We'll not ally ourselves with Cameron. We'll not betray our bond with the McCabes."

She took a step back and lowered her sword.

"Get out of my sight. You sicken me."

Her father's lip curled into a grimace of distaste. "You were always a sore disappointment, Rionna. You play at being a man and yet you're neither a man nor a woman."

"Go to hell," she whispered.

He turned and stalked away, leaving her standing, shivering in the cold.

Slowly she turned back toward the loch and walked closer to the water's edge. Today the water was dark and ominous. The wind whipped along the surface, boiling the water into waves that beat at the shoreline.

Her face throbbed. Her father had never struck her. She had always feared him but for another reason entirely. In truth she'd avoided him when at all possible, and until she became a valuable pawn, her father had ignored her as well.

She stared sightlessly over the water, and for the first time since this whole mess began, felt a wave of despair slide over her shoulders, weighing her down.

What did she know about being a wife?

She glanced down at her attire as shame tightened her cheeks and swelled in her chest. Caelen McCabe had managed to do what no other person had ever managed. He'd made her ashamed of who she was, and it infuriated her.

She rubbed her hands together and then tucked them under the hem of her tunic. She hadn't donned gloves—an oversight. She'd been in too big a hurry to leave the keep and the walls closing in around her.

But even the brisk wind and the biting chill couldn't drive her back toward the warmth of indoors. Back to her future with a man as cold as the mist blowing off the loch.

"Rionna, you shouldn't be out in the cold."

She stiffened but didn't turn around as her husband's terse reprimand reached her.

"You'll take ill."

He came to stand beside her and stared over the loch in the direction of her gaze.

"Have you come to make your apology?" she asked as she glanced sideways at him.

He jerked in surprise and turned to stare at her, eyebrow raised. "Apologize for what?"

"If you have to ask, 'tis not a sincere apology you'll issue."

He snorted. "I'll not apologize for kissing you."

She flushed. "It wasn't the kissing I was referring to, but you had no right to do something so intimate in front of others."

"You're my wife. I'll do as I like," he said lazily.

"You humiliated me," she said in a tight voice. "Not once but twice this morn."

"You humiliated yourself, Rionna. You have no discipline. No restraint."

She whirled on him, her fist balled. Oh, she'd love to hit him. But she'd only bounce off and probably break her hand in the process.

She opened her mouth to let him have it, when his expression stopped her.

It was positively murderous.

His eyes went flat, and his jaw twitched.

His roar nearly flattened her. "Who struck you?"

Her hand flew to her cheek, and she took a step back. But he was having none of that. He pushed forward and reached up to pull her hand down. With his other hand he touched a finger to the still sore spot.

"Who dared raise their hand to you?"

She swallowed and dropped her gaze. "'Tis not of import."

"The hell it's not. Tell me and I'll kill the bastard."

When she finally dared to lift her gaze back to his, the terrible rage in his eyes puzzled her. He was furious.

"Did your father do this?"

Her lips parted in surprise and his lips tightened.

"I'll kill him this time," Caelen muttered.

"Nay! He isn't worth your anger. He won't touch me again."

"Damn right he won't."

"I took care of the matter. I don't need your protection."

Caelen gripped her shoulders. "No one touches what is mine. No one does harm to one of my own. You may not think you need my protection, but by all that's holy, you'll have it. You may be used to going your own way, Rionna, but that's done with now. You and I have a responsibility to our clans."

"Responsibility. And what is my responsibility, husband? So far I only see that you wish me to dress and act feminine, never gainsay you, and pretend I'm a witless ninny in front of others."

His eyes narrowed. "Your responsibility is to be loyal to me first and foremost. You're to be a credit to your clan and mine. You'll give me heirs. Do that and you'll find I'm an easy man to get along with."

"You want someone I'm not," she whispered in a fierce voice tinged with tears. "You want a woman I cannot be."

"Do not engage me in a battle of wills, wife. You'll only suffer for it."

"Why does it have to be a battle? Why can you not accept me the way I am? Why must I change while you go on as before?"

His nostrils flared and he dropped his hands from her shoulders. For a moment he turned away from her and stood, legs apart as he stared over the water. When he glanced back at her, anger and impatience simmered in his eyes.

"Think you that nothing changes for me? I'm married, Rionna. I had no wish to be married. I certainly didn't prepare for it and certainly not so soon. I'm a warrior. Fighting is what I do. I see to the protection of my clan. Now I'm to be uprooted and must go away from my clan and bind myself to another. I'm expected to lead a people I've never met, who won't trust me any more than I'll trust them. On top of that, Duncan Cameron wants my brother dead. He wants Mairin for himself, and now Isabel's life has been in danger since the moment she was set in her mother's womb.

"He's tried to kill Alaric. He's sent traitors into the very heart of our clan. I should be *here*. Where I can protect my family. Not playing laird to a people who have no more desire for me as their laird as I have to be one."

"It wasn't my choice," she said fiercely.

"Aye, I know it. 'Tis no matter, though. We are both bound by duty. We have no choice in the matter."

She closed her eyes and turned away so that they stood side by side, gazes fixed anywhere but on each other.

"Why did you do it then, Caelen? Why did you really do it? You could have remained silent. Why did you step forward to marry me if 'twas such a distasteful chore?"

He was silent for a long moment before he finally acknowledged her question.

"Because I could not bear to see my brother wed to you when he loved another."

Pain tightened her chest again.

"I hope one day your answer will be different," she said quietly as she turned to walk back toward the keep.

CHAPTER 5

It was late when Caelen mounted the stairs to go up to his chamber. He and his brothers had planned late into the night, and on the morrow, he would make his journey to McDonald keep with his new wife to take over his duties as laird.

Not surprisingly, Gregor McDonald had taken his leave, and a dozen of his best soldiers had departed with him—men that Caelen couldn't afford to lose.

The former laird had slunk away like a defeated coward. He hadn't even bothered to bid his daughter goodbye. Not that Caelen ever wanted him close to Rionna again.

Aye, 'twas a good thing for the McDonald clan. The question was whether they'd recognize that fact and embrace Caelen as their new laird. Of course they would not. Maybe a few. But Caelen could only imagine how he would feel if he was suddenly presented with a new laird he had no knowledge of.

He'd never considered that he'd have the duties of laird. That had always fallen to Ewan and then to his heirs. Caelen was a third son and his duty had always been to support his laird. To be unfailingly loyal and offer his life for Ewan and his wife and children.

It was a daunting task before him. He didn't know if

he was up to it. What if he failed not only his new clan, but his brother and his king? Not to mention his new wife.

Caelen hated the insecurity that plagued him and he'd never admit it to anyone save himself. He may not be convinced that he was the best man to lead the McDonalds, but they'd never know that. Any show of weakness would be a clear sign to them that he was not worthy of the mantle of leadership, and he'd die before he'd allow that to happen.

Nay, he must be strong. And show no mercy right from the start. It was imperative that Caelen have their respect, for he had much work ahead of him in order to shape them into as formidable a force as the McCabe warriors.

To his surprise, when he opened the door to his chamber, Rionna was inside, still awake. She was sitting by the fire, her hair unbound and streaming to her waist. The tresses reflected the glow of the flames and shone like spun gold.

He'd fully expected her to retreat to her chamber and avoid him at all costs.

She didn't hear him at first, and he took the opportunity to study her slender shape. It amused him that she'd re-bound her breasts. It was quite remarkable how well the binding hid her lush curves. 'Twas a sin to hide such beauty.

As if sensing his stare, she turned slowly, her hair sliding over one shoulder.

"You should be asleep," he said gruffly. "'Tis late and we depart in the morning."

"So soon?"

"Aye. We must make haste."

"'Tis snowing. The storm has set in."

Caelen nodded and sat on the edge of the bed. He

pulled at his boots and tossed them aside. "'Tis likely to snow the night through. The going will be slow, but if we wait for the weather to break, we'll be here until spring."

Rionna went quiet. Confusion mirrored in her eyes. But she hesitated, her lips drawn as if she battled indecision.

He waited, not wanting to do any more that would put them at odds. He seemed to have the ridiculous habit of shoving his foot into his mouth every time he opened it.

"Will you be wanting to get on with it tonight?"

His eyebrows drew together and his forehead wrinkled as he stared back at her. "Get on with what, lass?"

She gestured toward the bed, color surging into her cheeks, painting them a dusky rose he found fascinating. Realization hit him, and again he was struck by how protective her hesitancy made him.

"Come here, Rionna."

For a moment he thought she was going to disobey him. Then with a sigh, she rose gracefully from her place by the fire and walked toward him, her hair shimmering down her back like a lighted torch.

When she was close enough, he drew her between his thighs and gathered her hands in his.

"If I expect you to mount a horse tomorrow, and 'tis obvious I do, then I'll not be doing anything tonight that would make you too tender for the ride."

Her blush deepened and she ducked her head.

He squeezed her hands so she'd look back at him. "However, when we do get around to consummating our marriage, you have nothing to fear, lass. I'll not do anything that frightens or hurts you."

She didn't look entirely convinced. She nervously licked her bottom lip, leaving it shiny and moist in the glow of the firelight.

Unable to resist the unintentional invitation, he tugged at her hands until she was perched on his thigh. With a gentleness and grace he didn't know he possessed, he stroked his hand over her cheekbone and then delved his fingers into the mass of hair behind her ear.

Warmed by her sitting by the fire for so long, it was indeed like caressing sunshine. Mesmerized by the feel and sight of the strands spilling and sliding over his fingers like liquid silk—he was sure he'd never touched anything so fine—he drew her closer until their mouths were just a breath away.

"Kiss me," he said in a voice he didn't recognize.

The directive unsettled her. She sat rigid in his lap, so tense she resembled a stone pillar. She looked at him, then at his mouth, and licked her lips again.

Ah hell.

His cock was as rigid as she was. He shifted his position, not wanting to alarm her, but every time he moved, he only became more aware of the fact that a beautiful, fiery woman was sitting in his arms. A woman he'd told he wasn't consummating their marriage tonight.

Idiot.

Surely he could put her on the horse with him so she experienced no discomfort.

Nay, that wouldn't work either because then he'd have to endure the entire ride in agony.

He sighed and resigned himself to a night of extreme discomfort. He had no intention of bedding her, but neither would he allow her to sleep in her own chamber.

His brothers never spent a night away from their wives. He'd give them no cause to think he was lacking.

Hesitantly, she pressed her lips to his. Just barely a touch, but it was like a streak of lightning. Hot. His toes even tingled as if they'd been dipped in fire.

It took every bit of his restraint not to roll her onto the bed and kiss her senseless. His newfound patience and desire to not frighten the daylights out of her was one of his more stupid decisions.

She drew away immediately, her eyes wide, a touch of pink suffusing her soft cheeks. Then she slid one hand up his chest and over his shoulder, staring warily at him the whole while as if she expected him to bite her for daring to touch him. Jesu, but he was nigh to the point of *begging* her to touch him.

Her fingers wandered to his neck and then she put her mouth carefully to his again. This time she remained there as she tentatively explored his mouth. With her tongue. Sweet mother of God, this was killing him.

She stirred restlessly against him as she pressed closer, her mouth hotly fused to his.

A surge of lust rolled through his body, but he held back, not wanting to destroy the sweetness of her offering. She was an innocent for all her warrior ways and attempts at acting like a man. She deserved all the gentleness and wooing he could muster, though God only knew he'd deserve sainthood before this was over with.

"'Tis not unpleasant, this kissing," she whispered.

"Nay, lass, 'tis not unpleasant at all. Who told you such?"

She paused and pulled farther away, her eyes faintly glazed as she stared back at him. "No one. I've never kissed anyone before. 'Tis the truth I don't know the way of it."

He nearly groaned. It pleased him that he was the only man she'd ever kissed—provided she told the truth—but such innocence couldn't be faked, surely, and what would she have to gain by such a falsehood? Nay, he was allowing past transgressions to color the present, which was hardly fair to his bride.

And that she said she didn't know anything of kissing made him want to snort. The lass was a born temptress. She kissed with a mixture of bold vixen and sweet innocence that inspired so many conflicting reactions that he was tongue-tied and cross-eyed.

"I think you have it just right," he murmured. "But just in case, perchance you could practice a bit more on me."

She shook with nervous laughter, the sound tinkling over his ears like little silver bells.

"Kissing can be wondrous if done correctly," he said. Even as he spoke, he thought on how long it had been since he'd truly enjoyed something as sweet as a simple kiss.

"Correctly?"

"Aye."

"Show me."

He grinned and pulled her lower, then bent and pressed his lips to the pulse at her neck. She jumped and then let out a breathy sigh just before melting against him. He nibbled a path to her ear and licked the lobe like she was a delicious treat.

Her fingers dug into his arms. She was turned in his lap so that her bound breasts were pressed tight to his chest. It was killing him, now that he knew what lurked behind that binding.

"Oh aye, kissing is nice."

There was no way in heaven or hell that he was going to content himself with lying beside her in the bed all night. He'd promised himself and her that he wouldn't do anything to hurt her or make tomorrow's journey uncomfortable, but that didn't mean he couldn't indulge himself in the feast of her silken skin.

He tugged at the sleeves of her gown until her shoulders were bared. She immediately went still and then pushed away from his chest, her mouth pursed as if to protest. She opened her mouth then sealed it shut as she continued to look at him.

"I want to look at you. Then I'm going to show you

that there's quite a bit more to kissing, not to mention a lot more places that kissing brings pleasure to."

"Oh."

The word slid from her lips with breathless excitement. Her pupils flared and a flush danced across her throat and cheeks.

"What do you want me to do?"

He smiled. "Not a damn thing, lass. I'll be doing what needs to be done. All you have to do is lie back and enjoy it."

CHAPTER 6

Rionna couldn't help her reaction to Caelen's husky drawl. It prickled over her skin, eliciting a feminine longing deep within. And then he stood, nearly carrying her upward as he set her away from him.

Before she could process the emptiness that suddenly besieged her at the loss of his touch, he began inching her gown up her legs, baring her ankles and then her knees.

She felt sinful and brazen and it perplexed her that she decided she quite liked it. Who would have ever accused her of being sensual? A woman to turn a man's head?

An indecent thrill sent chill bumps racing across her belly as the gown inched higher. She quite liked that, too. Panic scuttled through her chest about the time Caelen finally pulled the gown free of her head.

Clad now in her most intimate underthings, hardly barriers to his seeking gaze, heat scorched over her flesh and her cheeks tightened as she blushed furiously. He looked at her as though he wanted to devour her whole, like he was a beast closing in on his prey. She should be afraid, but what she really felt was . . . anticipation.

"I should do this slower so that I can savor the sight

of you, but I'm an impatient man, and I can't bear the excitement a moment longer. I simply have to see you, lass. I want to touch you so much, I'm shaking with it."

She'd never been a woman to swoon. She'd never fainted in her life, but her knees were precariously weak and she was so light-headed that she feared falling right over.

She had no sense of herself. She felt as though she were floating in some delicious dream she never wanted to awaken from. Only, her dreams had never been this erotic, and they certainly didn't include a magnificent warrior standing before her, trembling because he wanted her so. Staring at her like she was the only woman in the world.

With urgency he hadn't displayed so far, he quickly divested her of the last remaining material and suddenly she was clad in only the binding around her breasts. A shiver overtook her though she was far from chilled.

He stared at the binding for a long moment before lifting his gaze. "'Tis a travesty to hide such a wealth of feminine beauty. Are you ashamed?"

Her cheeks tightened in mortification. "Nay, I mean aye. Maybe. They're inconvenient," she finally managed. "They get in the way."

Caelen chuckled, his voice husky with amusement. "I'm torn between forbidding you to ever hide them and only allowing you to reveal them to me."

"You . . . You like them?"

"Oh aye, lass. We men are fond of such things. However, I'll like them more when I get this binding from around you."

He turned her around and gently untied the ends. Holding one of the strips of material, he walked around to the front and then began unwinding, transferring from hand to hand and reaching around her until her breasts pushed forward and at last, sprang free from confinement.

He stared unabashedly, though he didn't just focus on her breasts. Finally, she was completely nude, and he took his time, sweeping his gaze over her body from head to toe. Then he stared into her eyes. His breath came out in a ragged exhale.

"You are magnificent."

His palms glided over her, stroking reverently. Her breasts grew heavy. Aching. And so very tight. Her nipples puckered and became hard, pouty, begging for his touch.

She sucked in her breath when his fingers brushed over both of her nipples. Shards of exquisite pleasure streaked through her abdomen and down to her groin. Her womb clenched and her most intimate flesh grew damp. She was swollen and . . . hot.

Any idea that she could maintain her footing disappeared as soon as he lowered his head and his mouth closed around one taut nipple. She gasped and her knees buckled.

With a groan, he caught her against him, turned, and took a step to the bed. His arms wrapped tightly around her, he fell forward, coming down on top of her as her back hit the straw mattress.

His mouth melted over hers, taking until she couldn't draw breath. When he tore his lips away, they both gasped for air. Before she could regain her senses, he ran his mouth heatedly down her jaw then to her neck and lower until he shaped her nipple and suckled strongly.

With each pull of his mouth, she moaned and wave after wave of excitement tugged relentlessly at her womb. He swirled his tongue around each peak, one and then the other. He licked and teased until she squirmed in frustration.

He acted like a man starved. And yet he was exceedingly gentle and in turns rough. It confused her.

She wanted more. She needed more. But she wasn't at all sure what it was she wanted or needed.

He slid his tongue around and then up the underside of her breast until the bud balanced precariously on the edge of his lip. Then he sucked it inside, sweeping it past his teeth, pulling and tugging at it until she cried out and dug her nails into his broad shoulders.

"Caelen, please! Have mercy."

He raised his head, his eyes reflecting the dancing flames in the hearth. "Mercy? Lass, I have none. Furthermore, you won't want it. But you'll beg for more. Aye, you will."

He kissed the hollow between her breasts and murmured softly against her skin. "You're beautiful, Rionna. Never hide what God has given you. You are a woman blessed."

His words soaked into her heart, giving comfort she hadn't realized she needed. How could a man who was so harsh and unyielding speak with a poet's soul? He was a hard man. His words were harder. He was quick to offer criticism. He hadn't spared her feelings at any point. And yet now he wooed her as gently as a man wooing his lover.

He kissed a path down to her navel, moving his big body as his mouth moved lower. He tongued the indention, then grazed his teeth over the sensitive flesh.

More goose bumps scattered across her belly and still he moved lower, shocking her with his daring.

He parted her thighs and positioned his body so that his head was above her pelvis. Her eyes widened as he lowered his head. He couldn't. Surely he wouldn't.

Oh God, he did.

He slid his fingers through the patch of hair covering

her throbbing center and parted the swollen, aching folds. She was so mystified that she couldn't form a single objection as he pressed a kiss to her damp flesh.

She trembled uncontrollably. Her thighs shook. Her knees shook. Her belly quivered and her breasts strained upward, so unbearably taut that she wanted to writhe right out of her skin.

And then he licked her.

A long, positively sinful swipe of his tongue, from her opening to the hood of flesh where he circled the throbbing bundle of nerves at her very heart.

He followed it with a simple kiss and then he sucked ever so gently at the little bud until she was a sobbing mess of incoherency.

Oh aye, he'd certainly told the truth about kissing.

Her sense of urgency mounted. Her body tensed and coiled, tighter and tighter. Pleasure bloomed and became nearly painful through her breasts and her womb and centered at the pulsing nub that he so unmercifully teased.

It felt as though she'd simply break apart at some point, but each time she thought she'd surely split, the pressure and indescribable pleasure only increased, driving her further into the state of madness.

"Caelen! Please, I don't know what to do."

He kissed her center again and then raised his head, his eyes glowing with feral light. "Just let go, lass. You're fighting the inevitable. I won't hurt you, I swear it. 'Twill feel good. Relax now and let me love you."

His words soothed over her, sinking in and relaxing her tense muscles and frayed nerves. When his mouth touched her once more, she shivered and closed her eyes as the build began all over again.

"You taste like honey. Never have I had anything sweeter. You make me daft with wanting. You're all that a woman should be, Rionna. Never hide that or be ashamed of it."

Tears pricked her eyelids. She trembled from head to toe, not just from the onslaught of pleasure, but from the emotions welling from her chest. Emotions that he'd unleashed.

She felt like a woman tonight. She felt beautiful and desired. Like a bride should. How she should have been made to feel on her wedding day, instead of an inferior replacement.

His tongue circled her entrance and then slid inside, shocking her with the sheer intensity of the sensation. She arched upward just as she finally, *finally* broke free of the excruciating pressure building from deep within.

It was the single most bewildering, most powerful, most absolutely wonderful experience of her life. She flew. Soared impossibly high and then floated ever so gently back toward the ground.

She closed her eyes and melted into the bed, so boneless, so positively sated that she couldn't even imagine moving so much as a finger.

Her body quivered in the aftermath and tiny little shocks simmered through her blood, humming and buzzing. There was still a pulse between her legs, a slight ache and a throb, a reminder of the attentions he'd just given her with his mouth.

She'd never imagined such a thing. Surely this wasn't normal. She'd never heard other women speak of such. He hadn't just kissed her as he'd promised. He'd licked her. He'd suckled her.

Surely there was no more intimate act a husband could perform for his wife. Contentment warmed her entire body and she smiled in satisfaction, marveling at how happy she was at this precise moment. No matter what tomorrow brought, she'd always hold tonight close.

She felt Caelen leave the bed, but she couldn't summon the energy to open her eyes to see what he was about. A moment later, he pulled the furs up over her and climbed in beside her, his heated flesh a shock against her still quivering body.

Having no experience in such matters, she wasn't sure what she was supposed to do. Her mother and father never slept in the same chamber. Certainly not in the same bed. She knew Mairin and Keeley both slept with their husbands every night. Their husbands would allow nothing less, not that either woman wanted it any differently. Perhaps 'twas a McCabe thing. Maybe they were so possessive of their women that they couldn't bear to let them out of their sight. Or maybe they were just protective.

She decided she didn't care. What was the worst that could happen? She'd gain Caelen's censure? It wasn't as if she hadn't done that many times over the past few days.

She turned into his body and snuggled up tight against him. For a moment she worried she'd done something wrong because he stiffened against her. Gradually he relaxed and then he slid an arm around her waist and hauled her even closer until her nose was pressed against the hollow of his throat.

"Caelen?"

"Aye, lass?"

"You were right."

"What was I right about?"

"Kissing. 'Tis a most wondrous thing."

She could sense his smile.

"And you were right about another thing. There are so many other . . . places . . . where kissing brings much pleasure to."

This time he chuckled softly over her head. "Go to sleep, Rionna. We must rise early in the morn. We have a hard journey ahead of us."

She sighed and closed her eyes and just before she drifted off, she had the thought that this whole consummation thing wasn't so bad after all.

CHAPTER 7

Caelen was in a black mood. He hadn't slept a wink the entire night. He'd finally given up when he couldn't take the torture of Rionna's naked body wrapped around his a minute longer.

He had a raging erection, and even after prying himself from the bed and seeking privacy to take care of the matter, he was still hard and aching.

Her taste was still on his tongue. Her scent still filled his nostrils. Her lean body with her lush curves still haunted him. Whether he shut or opened his eyes, he couldn't rid himself of the images of her writhing beneath his mouth.

"Sweet Jesu," he muttered.

Panting after a woman had already caused him—and his clan—a lifetime of trouble.

He would bed her as soon as they arrived at McDonald keep and then he'd distance himself from her. A good tupping was what he needed. He'd been a long time without a woman. Aye, that was the issue. He needed relief and then he would regain his senses and he could function without being led about by his cods.

Knowing the others wouldn't be up for some time yet, he went below stairs and into the courtyard. Snow had blown into drifts, barring the usual walkways. He cursed as he stared around at the heavy blanket of freshly fallen snow.

At least it had stopped and the sky was clear above. The moon and countless stars shone and reflected off the snow until it appeared nearly daytime.

"Good morn, Caelen."

Caelen turned to see Gannon standing a short distance away.

"'Tis cold, Gannon. Where are your furs?"

Gannon grinned. "I don't want them wet before our journey. 'Twill be freezing on the ride to McDonald land."

Caelen studied the warrior who'd long served Caelen's brother. A more loyal man Caelen had never known. He was glad to get him, but he worried.

"What think you of Ewan sending you with me?"

Gannon stared around at the keep, the courtyard where they'd trained for so many years. At the still-crumbling walls that were even now being repaired, thanks to Mairin's dowry.

"'Twill be hard to leave the home I've known for so long. But things are changing. Ewan is newly married and he leaves for Neamh Álainn as soon as Isabel is strong enough for the journey. Alaric will become laird. Aye, things are changing, and 'tis the truth I'm looking forward to a new challenge. Going with you to McDonald keep will give me that."

"I'm glad to have you," Caelen said. "'Twill be a hard task to train the McDonalds to be warriors on par with the McCabes. We've not much time to whip them into shape. Ewan is impatient to be rid of Duncan Cameron once and for all."

"As is our king."

"Aye, for different reasons, but aye, David is eager to be rid of Cameron as well."

"Since we are both awake, perhaps we should ready

the horses for the journey. I had some of the men bring down the trunks last night to load into the carts. Will you wait for your lady wife to awaken before we depart?"

Caelen scowled. His lady wife had slept like a babe while he'd lain awake in pain. "I'll wake her once we've readied the carts and the men. I'll want to say my good-byes to my brothers and their wives."

"'Tis a new page in your life you're embarking on," Gannon said in a sage voice. "A fortnight ago, did you imagine that you'd be laird of your own clan, newly married to a beautiful lass and on your way to a life away from the McCabes?"

For a moment Caelen didn't acknowledge Gannon's question. It caused him too much discomfort. The truth was an ugly, unforgiving thing. Always there. Never changing.

"'Tis my fault we've struggled for as many years as we have," Caelen said quietly. "I owe my brothers more than I can ever repay. My agreeing to this marriage gives Alaric what he most wants in the world, and it aids Ewan in keeping his wife and child safe. It wouldn't matter if Rionna McDonald were a pox-riddled whore. I'd marry her for those reasons and never feel regret."

"How fortunate for you that I'm nay pox-riddled nor a whore."

Caelen swung around to see Rionna standing a short distance away, her face drawn into an impassive mask as she stared at him and Gannon. He cursed under his breath just as Gannon muttered "Uh-oh." Caelen was forever making a muck of things around Rionna.

"Rionna . . ."

She held up her hand to silence him and he did so before it sunk in that she was giving him a command and he'd meekly followed it.

"Don't apologize for speaking the truth, husband. 'Tis

the truth I had no more desire to marry you than you did me, but as you said last eve, neither of us had a choice. Perhaps it would be better to move forward rather than to keep rehashing the reasons why over and over."

He hated the hurt in her voice even as her gaze flickered coolly over him and Gannon. Her face had the perfect you-can't-touch-me expression, but her voice told the truth. He *had* wounded her.

"You shouldn't be outside the keep. 'Tis frigid this morn. What are you doing up at this hour?"

Her gaze was as chilled as the wind. She showed no reaction to the biting cold even though the clothing she wore was ill-suited for such weather.

"I woke when you rose and I knew you'd want an early start. 'Tis not an overlong journey but the snow will hinder us. I thought to aid you in preparing."

"'Tis a thoughtful gesture, my lady," Gannon said. "But 'tis my duty to assist your husband. I would feel better if you were inside where 'tis warm and you don't chance taking ill."

Caelen glared at Gannon for his well thought-out words. The sentiment should come from him, not his commander. He could see the effect it had on Rionna. Her eyes lost some of their frost, and her stance relaxed.

"I'll want to bid my farewells to Keeley as well as Mairin and the babe."

Caelen nodded. "I'll summon you when 'tis time to depart."

She gave a stiff nod of her own and then turned back into the keep. Caelen sighed and glanced over at Gannon.

"'Twill be a task to clear the pathways. We may as well begin now."

Rionna waited until she was certain Alaric had risen before she went to Keeley's chamber. Though all the

McCabe warriors were notoriously early risers—they somehow functioned on but a few hours' sleep every night—Alaric had devoted most of his time for the last weeks to Keeley's bedside.

After she saw Alaric reenter his chamber with food for Keeley to break her fast, she waited a few moments and then knocked.

Alaric opened the door and Rionna straightened her shoulders. "I'd like to say my farewell to Keeley if she's feeling well enough this morn."

"Of course. Come in. She's breaking her fast and grumbling about being held captive in her bedchamber."

Rionna grinned at Alaric's exasperated tone. She walked inside to see Keeley sitting up in bed, more color in her cheeks than had been there the day before.

"I've come to bid you farewell."

Keeley's lips turned down into an unhappy frown. "So soon? I had hoped to spend more time with you."

Rionna perched on the edge of the bed, taking Keeley's hand in hers and squeezing. "You'll come to visit when you're well. Perhaps I'll come back to visit you. We're married to brothers. We'll see each other often. I still expect you to attend me when I bear my first child, so make sure you do nothing foolish like injuring yourself again."

Keeley's eyes danced with merriment. "How went it last night with Caelen?"

Rionna's eyes narrowed. "I hate him. He has a wicked, silken tongue, but he turns into the worst sort of ass outside the bedchamber."

Keeley sighed. "Give him time, Rionna. He's a good man. You just have to dig below the surface to uncover that man."

Rionna made a face. "I don't have your faith, Keeley."

"I want you to be happy. Promise me you'll give him a chance."

"I can only promise not to stick my dagger in his gut while he sleeps," Rionna grumbled.

Keeley laughed. "'Tis all I can ask then. Be well, Rionna. And be happy. Send word when you're established at McDonald keep and let me know you've arrived safely. I'll be awaiting word on the news of your first child as well."

Rionna rose then leaned down to kiss Keeley's cheek. "'Tis the truth I'll never bear a child if he doesn't learn to close his mouth at the appropriate time."

Keeley grinned. "'Tis a skill I don't think any man has yet learned. But remember all I counseled you on. Use your skills as a woman and I guarantee he'll shut his mouth, for a time at least."

Rionna sat atop her horse surveying the line of McDonald men that was smaller than it had been when they'd arrived. Her chest ached for the men who'd chosen to side with her father. These were men she'd grown up around. Some of them were young and were probably swayed by her father's talk of loyalty and distrust of the McCabes. The older warriors were likely outraged over the ousting of her father as laird and had followed him without coercion.

There was no telling what would happen when Rionna and Caelen returned to her keep and announced that Caelen was their new laird. Not that the people hadn't been expecting Rionna to marry and for her husband to one day lead their clan, but it wasn't supposed to happen overnight.

She shivered as the wind knifed through her. The fur she wore was threadbare and the clothes underneath weren't suitable for traveling in such cold. When they'd made the trip to McCabe keep the weather had been unseasonably warm. That was no longer the case and she hadn't the wardrobe to withstand being outdoors in the biting cold for any length of time.

Caelen and his commander led the way. Rionna hung several horse lengths back, surrounded by four McDonald soldiers as they trudged through the crisp snow.

He hadn't once looked back, not that Rionna expected him to. She may as well not exist for all the mind he'd paid her since the journey began.

Apart from assisting her onto her horse, he hadn't acknowledged her at all since she'd overheard his words to Gannon earlier that morn.

"I don't like him, Rionna," James muttered beside her.

She jerked her head up to make sure Caelen hadn't overheard the disloyal remark and then she turned to the young warrior. Beside him, Simon, his father, nodded his agreement.

"I don't like him either, lass. The king and the McCabes have given us a bad turn. 'Twasn't right what they did to your father."

Rionna clenched her jaw until it ached. She could hardly reveal her true feelings. She couldn't very well say that she didn't like her new laird either, but she wasn't about to go as far as to defend her father.

"'Tis best to give him a chance," she murmured in a low voice, all the while keeping her gaze on Caelen's back. "He seems a good and fair man."

"He doesn't treat you with the respect you're due," Arthur said angrily from her other side.

Rionna turned in surprise and then surveyed all the men who rode back from Caelen and Gannon. None of them looked happy to have Caelen lead them back to their home. Their mouths were set in firm lines and their eyes were angry and hard.

"'Tis the truth neither of us wanted this marriage," she said. 'Twill be an adjustment for the both of us. He never considered that he'd be laird of our clan. Think you how you would feel if you attended your brother's wedding only to end up being saddled with his unwanted bride."

The men winced and James nodded his commiseration.

"Still, he has no cause to treat you as he's done," Simon argued. "The McCabe warriors have a reputation for being fair. Fierce but fair. You bring him much through your marriage. He should treat you gently as he would any other gently bred lady."

Rionna snorted. "Well, now, there's the rub. I'm no gently bred lady, remember?"

The men laughed around her and Caelen turned to look over his shoulder at the sudden noise. For a moment his gaze connected with Rionna's and she stared back, unwilling to let him cow her.

After a time, he let his gaze slide away and he turned away from her once more.

"He has to prove himself to us," Simon said. "I care naught what the king has decreed. If he is to be laird of our clan, he'll have to prove he's worthy of the mantle of leadership."

"May he prove more worthy than my father," Rionna whispered.

The others went silent, perhaps out of loyalty to the man they'd called laird for so many years. Rionna was through acting the dutiful daughter. She had plans for when she returned to her keep.

Whether her husband liked it or not, she intended to be a major force in the reshaping of her clan. For too long her people had suffered under the poor leadership of a greedy, belligerent fool.

Perhaps they'd traded one for another. She knew not yet. She hoped Caelen proved a good man and an even better warrior.

War was imminent. Ewan McCabe was preparing to fight Duncan Cameron and he was taking the whole of the highlands with him to battle.

Her clan wouldn't be the sacrificial lamb on the battle-field, if she could help it.

CHAPTER 8

It was nearing dark when Caelen called a halt to the procession. Rionna was so cold that she'd long since lost feeling in her hands and feet. Her cheeks were numb and she felt cold on the inside.

She was sure she'd never be warm again. The fires of hell would be welcome at the moment.

She pried her hands from the reins and tucked them under the fur, hoping to rub some feeling back into them. She dreaded dismounting. She had no wish to set her feet into the snow. She had no wish to do anything that required movement.

With a fortifying breath, she gripped the saddle and started to dismount. Caelen appeared by her horse and reached up to assist her.

She was so pathetically grateful that she nearly tumbled into his arms.

Somehow she managed to put her hands on his shoulders and allow him to lift her down. But when her feet made contact with the ground, her legs buckled and she went down into the snow.

Caelen immediately reached for her, but when his hands came into contact with her icy skin, he swore a string of blasphemies that singed her ears.

As he swung her into his arms, he barked out orders for fires to be built and for shelter to be constructed.

"Caelen, I'm quite well. Just c—cold."

She slapped her lips together as the last stammered out. 'Twas the truth she was so cold she burned.

"You're not well," he said in a grim voice. "God's teeth, woman, are you just trying to kill yourself? Why aren't you dressed for the cold? And why the hell didn't you tell me you were so miserable?"

She would have bitten her tongue off before complaining to him of anything.

As soon as the fires were laid and began to burn, Caelen carried her and perched on a log as close to the flames as he could without singeing their clothing.

He opened his fur and put her directly against his chest, where only his tunic and hers separated them. Then he wrapped her firmly into his embrace and allowed some of his warmth to seep into her body.

Oh 'twas wondrous. For a moment.

As soon as some of the numbing chill began to wear off, her skin began to prickle like a thousand ants were eating her flesh. She whimpered and struggled against him but he only held her tighter and wrapped his arms around her so that she was trapped.

"Hurts."

"Aye, I know it does, and I'm sorry for it, but 'tis the feeling coming back into your body. Be grateful you can feel anything at all."

"Don't lecture me. Not now. At least wait until I'm not feeling as though my flesh is being torn from my bones."

Caelen chuckled softly. "It must not be too bad if you still have your sharp tongue. I wouldn't lecture you if you weren't such a stubborn lass. If you didn't have adequate clothing for the journey, you should have said something before we left. I wouldn't have allowed you to travel in such bitter conditions without proper protection."

"You're lecturing again," she grumbled even as she snuggled closer to his body so she could absorb more of his warmth.

As more heat seeped into her body, she began to shake. Her teeth clattered so violently that she was sure they'd fall right out of her head.

She burrowed her face into Caelen's neck as she tried to still the shivers that quaked over her body. "C-cold. I c-can't get w-warm."

"Shh, lass. 'Twill be all right. Just sit still for a bit until I've warmed you."

She all but crawled inside him. Her hands clutched at his tunic and she kept her face tucked beneath his chin as she breathed the warmer air at the hollow of his throat.

Eventually her shaking diminished to occasional muscle spasms and she lay limp and exhausted in Caelen's arms.

"Are you warm enough to eat?" Caelen asked.

She nodded but the truth was she didn't want to move.

Carefully he got up and left her sitting on the fallen log. He tugged his fur tighter around her, sealing the opening against the wind. After he was satisfied she wouldn't teeter off her perch, he strode away, directing the men to finish erecting the shelters.

A few minutes later, he returned and offered her the heel of a bread loaf and a hunk of cheese. She stuck her fingers out of the fur and hunched over as she ate delicately at the offering.

She couldn't taste it. She was just too cold. But it felt good in her belly and it bolstered her flagging energy. As she ate, she watched with detached interest as snow was cleared in a wide arc around the fire. The tents were raised and snow was packed around the bases for extra stability against the stiff winds.

Extra wood was put on the fire until the flames soared skyward and the entire area glowed orange.

After she finished the cheese, she extended her fingers toward the fire, delighting in the intense heat that licked the tips.

Then Caelen was there, standing in front of her. He didn't speak. He simply hauled her up into his arms and carried her to the tent closest to the fire.

On the floor was a mound of furs made into a very comfortable-looking bed. He placed her in the middle of them and then pulled her boots off, frowning as he inspected them.

"These are a waste of good leather. It's a wonder you haven't lost your toes to frostbite. There are more holes than boot left."

She was too tired and cold to argue with him.

"Tomorrow we have to do something about these," he muttered. "You can't go about in the dead of winter with these miserable excuses for boots."

Still muttering under his breath, he crawled onto the furs beside her and lined his body up with hers so that she was flush against him. He rolled her to her side and then pulled the furs tight around them.

"Put your feet between my legs," he instructed.

She slipped her bare feet between his thighs and slid them down, moaning at the instant warmth. The man was like a fire himself.

She snuggled into his arms and pressed her face into his chest, sighing at how deliciously warm he felt. He smelled good, too. A mixture of wood, smoke, and his own natural scent. It was an intoxicating blend.

A groan of raw pleasure escaped her lips. He stiffened and then cursed softly under his breath. She frowned, unsure of what she'd done to gain his displeasure.

CHAPTER 9

It was mid-afternoon the next day when they neared the gates of McDonald keep. It was important to Rionna for her to ride to greet her people under her own power. It seemed just as important to Caelen that she appear the hapless female under his rule.

She sat before him in the saddle, cradled in his arms, as she'd ridden the entire day. He'd declared she'd ride with him since she wasn't adequately protected from the cold.

Rionna had insisted on returning to her own mount when they were a short distance from her keep, but he'd ignored her and kept riding.

'Twas the truth she dreaded facing her people. Much had changed since she'd departed some weeks before. She was returning with a different McCabe brother and without her father. And now she'd be introducing her clan to their new laird.

A shout went up as soon as the guard in the watch-tower spotted them approaching. Caelen frowned and glanced sideways at Gannon.

Gannon shrugged.

"What?" Rionna demanded, frowning at their silent communication.

"'Tis disgraceful that we got this close to the keep before we were spotted," Caelen said in disgust. "If Duncan Cameron gets this close, it will be too late to sound the battle cry."

"Perhaps 'tis best if you greet your new clan before you criticize them."

"I'm not worried about their feelings," Caelen snapped. "I'm more concerned over their safety. And yours."

Rionna turned as best she could when the gate began to swing open. As she'd feared, most of the clan had assembled in the courtyard, their curiosity great over Rionna's new husband.

"Put me down so that I may introduce you," she ordered in a low voice.

His grip tightened around her but he didn't look at her. He kept his gaze focused on the gathered men and women. He pulled up the reins when he was but a few feet away and then, without a word, he dismounted, his hand going up to steady Rionna so she didn't tumble from the horse.

"See to my wife," he ordered Gannon.

See to his wife? *See to his wife?*

Rionna gaped at Caelen as he turned away from her to address her clan. *Her* clan, damn it. Gannon dismounted then reached up and plucked Rionna from the saddle as easily as if she weighed naught.

He promptly wrapped her in a fur and stood back from Caelen, his hand at her shoulder to keep her in place.

"My name is Caelen McCabe," Caelen said in a calm, direct voice. "I'm Rionna's husband and your new laird."

There were gasps of surprise, exclamations rose, and then everyone began talking at once.

"Quiet!" Caelen roared.

"What happened to Gregor?" Nate McDonald called from the middle of the gathered clansmen.

Several others chimed in. "Aye, what happened?"

Caelen leveled a stare at the crowd. "He is no longer laird. That is all you need concern yourself with. From this day forward you will swear allegiance and loyalty to me or you'll leave. My word is absolute. We have much work and training to do if we are to stand strong against the might of Duncan Cameron's army. Our alliance with my brothers, Ewan and Alaric McCabe, as well as your neighboring clans will make us invincible. If you want to keep what is yours and raise your children in peace, then we must fight. And if we must fight, then we must be ready when the time comes."

Her clansmen exchange wary, suspicious glances. They looked at Caelen and then beyond to her as if they expected her to speak up. She would have, too, if for nothing else than to ease their fears, but Caelen turned and fixed her with a glare that momentarily kept her silent.

As he turned back, she pulled from Gannon's grasp and hurried forward to address her clan.

"'Tis an alliance that pleases our king. He blessed our marriage himself. The agreement was always for whomever I married to take over as laird of our clan. Instead of at the birth of my first child, Caelen McCabe takes the mantle of leadership now. We need him. We need his direction if we are to prove victorious against those who take our land and homes from us."

Caelen turned his furious stare on her but she calmly faced her clan, taking in their indecision and their confusion.

"My father was without honor," she said in a clear voice devoid of emotion. "'Tis my hope that under the leadership of a new laird we will regain what was lost. We will hold our heads high as we defend our legacy."

"You will be silent," Caelen said in a low, dangerous voice. "Go into the keep. Now."

The look in his eyes would have made a warrior tuck tail and run. But Rionna turned stiffly, her shoulders straight, and walked at a sedate pace toward the keep as if it had been her intention to do so all along after she finished with her speech.

As soon as she entered the keep, her legs sagged and she faltered her way into the hall. Sarah hurried to greet her, placing her gnarled hands on Rionna's shoulders with a grip that made Rionna wince.

"Tell me all, lass. What's this about you marrying Caelen McCabe and him replacing our laird? Where's your father? And our men!"

Rionna carefully pulled Sarah's hands away and then sank wearily into one of the chairs at the table. "'Tis a long story, Sarah."

"Well now, seems to me I've got nothing better to do than listen if I'm to know what's about here. How on earth did you find yourself married to Caelen McCabe? 'Tis common enough knowledge he's foresworn to never marry. He was a young lad when he made the vow. Fresh after a betrayal by a lass he loved."

Rionna emitted a gloomy sigh. Wonderful. Foresworn to never marry and yet he'd sacrificed himself for an emotion he had no use for. Love. Alaric's and Keeley's love.

Maybe he'd decided it mattered naught if he never had plans to give his heart to another woman.

"Do you know the story, Sarah? Why did his love betray him?"

"You're supposed to be telling me a story, lass."

"And I will," Rionna cut in impatiently. "Right now I'm more interested in this vow my husband made and why."

Sarah blew out her breath, then looked around. "All

right. I'll tell you what I know. Eight years ago Caelen McCabe fell in love with Elspeth Cameron. 'Tis the truth she seduced him. She was a wee bit older than the lad. More worldly, if you know what I mean."

Rionna didn't but she wasn't about to admit it.

"All along she was in league with her kinsman, Duncan Cameron. She drugged the soldiers and opened the gate for Cameron's men. 'Twas a horrible massacre. Caelen lost his father in the attack and Ewan McCabe lost his young wife. The brothers were away at the time of the attack, and when they returned, they found the keep in ruins and their kin murdered. 'Twas a terrible thing."

"Aye," Rionna murmured. "So the dolt now believes all women are evil and has vowed never to open his heart to another." She shook her head and rolled her eyes heavenward. "Why are men so stupid?"

Sarah threw back her head and laughed. "Well now, lass, that's the question, isn't it? You've a tough path ahead of you, but if anyone can convince the laddie that a woman's heart is true and loyal, you can. There's no more loyal or fierce a lass than yourself."

Unfortunately, Caelen thought her to be the price he had to pay for his brother's happiness and his clan's welfare.

"Now tell me what transpired at the McCabes and why your father has not returned nor all of our men."

Rionna quickly related all that had occurred while they had sojourned at the McCabes. Including Caelen's demand that her father cede the leadership of his clan to him and her father's subsequent departure.

"I wonder how many of the men would have chosen to follow my father had they not wives and children back home. The men who left with my father had no close kin to worry over seeing again."

"'Tis more a concern what they are about now,"

Sarah said carefully. "Your father is a vain man and not one to suffer insult lightly."

"He's a fool," Rionna hissed. "A lecherous old fool who placed his wants and desires above his clan's. He deserved to be removed as laird."

Sarah patted Rionna's hand comfortingly. "There, there, lass. No need to get worked up over a foolish old man. His time is over. 'Tis time to look to the future. The McCabes are a fierce clan. It took them long to rebuild but I believe Ewan to be honorable. I can only imagine his brothers would be the same. Perhaps Caelen is just what this clan needs if we are to survive the coming hard times."

Rionna didn't doubt that Caelen McCabe would be good for her clan. He was a fierce warrior with no equal on the battlefield. He commanded respect from the men around him. She knew the McDonald soldiers weren't the fittest. Nor were they the worst. But she'd seen firsthand the might of the McCabe warriors and she wanted that for the McDonalds. Aye, Caelen was a better choice than even Alaric McCabe.

She just wished that she could be equally sure that he'd be a good husband and father to her children.

If he'd already closed his heart, what chance did Rionna have of opening it?

CHAPTER 10

Rionna didn't see her husband for the remainder of the day. He didn't even come in to sup, and Rionna ate in the cold great hall alone.

She hated the feeling that she didn't know her place among her own clan. She'd remained in the keep ever since he'd ordered her inside. Not because he'd told her to, but because she simply had no idea what to do or what to say to her clan.

Her cowardice made her choke. The food she'd tried to consume stuck in her throat and she couldn't force it down no matter how hard she tried.

She alternated between wanting Caelen to put in an appearance so she could dress him down for humiliating her in front of her kinsmen and wanting him to stay as far away as possible so she didn't have to face him. Not until she regained her courage and decided her next course.

Disgusted with her sudden timidity, she pushed aside her food and backed from the table. She wasn't going to sit around arguing with herself about whether she wanted to see her husband. He could rot. She was tired. Beyond exhausted. It was past time she sought her bed.

She braced herself for the cold when she swung her door open. Her room lacked a hearth for a fire, but there were no windows so no wind blew through the chamber. She collected two candles and returned to the hall to light them from one of the torches lining the walls.

The meager light brightened the tiny chamber and the warm glow chased away some of the chill, although it was all in the perception. The half-burned candles could hardly provide enough warmth to make a difference. But still, they cheered her and made her feel a little warmer.

'Twas cold enough that she decided to leave her clothing on. All she did was remove her boots and then she donned her one luxury. A pair of wool stockings that Sarah had darned for her.

She sighed as the soft, warm material slid over her feet. She flexed her toes and then climbed beneath the furs on her bed.

Her eyes closed immediately but she didn't fall asleep. Her mind was too occupied with all that had transpired in the last fortnight.

If she were honest with herself, she'd admit to more than just passing trepidation. She was afraid of her future. Afraid for the future of her clan.

No matter that she'd always dressed as a man and indulged in swordplay while other girls dreamed of marriage and children. She harbored secret girlish dreams of her own. She imagined beautiful dresses and a warrior with no equal falling to one knee in front of her to pledge his undying love and loyalty.

She smiled dreamily and snuggled deeper into the covers. Aye, 'twas a nice fantasy. Her warrior wouldn't only love her beyond reason. He'd accept her faults and he'd be proud of her accomplishments in warfare. He'd boast to his men that his wife was a warrior. A warrior princess with unrivaled beauty and accomplishment.

They'd fight side by side and then return to the keep where she'd dress in fine gowns gifted to her by her husband. She'd serve him a fine meal directed by her own hand. Then they'd sit by the fire and sip fine ale before retiring to their chamber where he'd hold her and whisper words of love to her.

"You're an idiot," she muttered, self-loathing suddenly consuming her. No man would ever accept one such as her. A man wanted someone like Keeley. All soft and gentle with traits acceptable to a gentle lady. Like healing. Or needlework. Or a woman who could run a keep and always have a fine meal on the table.

All Rionna could do was cause injuries that required women of Keeley's skill to patch them up and send them back into battle. Rionna had neither a gentle touch nor womanly softness.

She frowned but kept her eyes shut. So what if she wasn't as other women? She wasn't lacking. Nor was she less. She was simply . . . different. Aye, she was different and a good man would celebrate those differences. If Caelen McCabe couldn't appreciate his wife the way she was, then he could sit on his sword and have a good spin.

The room was suspiciously warm. And the bed was softer and more luxurious than what she was accustomed to. She was aware that something was entirely different, but she couldn't force herself awake long enough to take stock of the situation.

Determined not to ruin a perfectly good dream, she snuggled deeper into the warm haven and sighed.

A soft chuckle intruded on her euphoria just as a lingering brush along the swell of her breast sent a shiver racing through her belly.

Her breast? She'd gone to bed with them bound. Indeed, she hadn't undressed. She'd fallen into bed fully clothed and had been asleep in a matter of minutes.

She cracked one eye open to see her husband undressing a mere foot from where she lay. She wasn't in her chamber. Nor was she in her father's. Best she could tell she was in one of the chambers reserved for honored guests. Not that there had ever been many of those at the McDonald keep.

Rather than bolt upward and demand how she'd gotten from her chamber to here, she silently observed Caelen as he removed his tunic.

His back was to her and his muscles rippled as he pulled the material over his head and tossed it aside. He spent a moment stretching before he began to divest himself of his trews.

Her cheeks burned when his buttocks came into view. Hard but with enough shape to appeal to her feminine senses. Paler than the rest of his body and supported by two tree trunks for legs. There wasn't a spare inch of flesh anywhere that she could see. All tight muscles, hair roughened and dark.

She shivered again but it had naught to do with being cold.

He was a beautiful warrior. All that a woman like herself admired. Not perfect. But beautiful still.

Scars ran the length of his body, from his ankles to his nape. She found herself eager to explore each of them with her fingers and her . . . mouth.

Would he enjoy the same attentions as he'd given her on their wedding night? The idea of kissing and tasting him so intimately tightened areas of her body that didn't bear mentioning.

She glanced down, once again cognizant of the fact that she was naked. Not a single stitch of clothing remained.

The furs felt sensual against her bare skin. Her entire body was in a state of heightened sensitivity. Her nipples were hard points, thrusting upward as if begging for her husband's mouth.

She almost groaned. He did indeed possess a wicked, wicked mouth. And tongue. She couldn't forget the wonders of that talented tongue.

Her most intimate flesh twitched and drew up until an ache bloomed deep in her womb. What was happening to her that merely viewing her husband and remembering his attentions wreaked such havoc with her body?

She stirred restlessly, no longer able to lie still. Caelen heard and turned to look at her, unabashed by his complete nudity.

Her eyes widened at the sight of his manhood, so rigid and . . . erect. It, like the rest of him, was hard and fierce looking. She swallowed nervously as her gaze finally lifted to meet her husband's.

"So you are awake."

She nodded dumbly. Of course she was awake. Any fool could see that.

"Why were you sleeping in that tiny, airless chamber? Were you hiding?"

His look suggested he was amused by that prospect. She scowled and sat up, realizing too late that the movement bared her entire upper body to his gaze.

"'Tis my chamber. Where else would I sleep?"

He cocked one eyebrow as if to tell her the absurdity of her statement.

She bared her teeth in frustration. "I don't see you once, not even at the evening meal. How am I to know what your *expectations* are?"

He curled his hand around the base of his erection and pulled upward, his gaze never leaving her. A faint smile hovered on his lips, one that told her whatever it was he'd say would infuriate her.

"Have I neglected my new wife?" he drawled. "And here I thought I was attending to important matters like the defense of your clan and asserting my authority."

She curled her fingers into the bedcovers until they

were bunched in her fists. "'Tis your clan now. Not only my clan. You speak as though you do us a grand favor, but 'tis the truth you gain much in this bargain."

"How fierce you look, wife. Have I told you how appealing I find you when you scowl at me?"

"'Tis not my purpose to be appealing!"

He grinned as he moved closer to the bed, his hand still doing curious things to his swollen shaft. She couldn't help but stare. It seemed it was all she could focus on.

"Whether 'tis your purpose or not, it doesn't change the way of things. I go as hard as a stone every time you open that saucy mouth of yours."

He loomed over the bed—and her—leaving her feeling small and vulnerable. The look in his eyes made her nervous. There was promise there, but of what she was unsure. She licked her lips and edged back, clutching for the furs to cover herself with.

"'Tis no use hiding your charms, lass. I'll find them soon enough."

"What mean you?" she asked breathlessly. 'Twas the truth it was becoming increasingly more difficult to draw air into her lungs. Her chest was tight and an odd squeezing sensation gripped her until she was light-headed.

He tugged the furs from her clenching fingers and tossed them down toward her feet.

"What I mean is that tonight I'm not going to stop short of my complete and utter satisfaction."

His eyes gleamed as his fingers stroked over one full breast to her nipple. He thumbed it gently until it puckered into a taut bud.

"And my satisfaction?" she asked crossly. The man sounded selfish and arrogant.

He smiled. "I don't think you'll be complaining, lass. You certainly weren't the night after our wedding night."

She had nothing to say to that because the man was certainly right.

Her legs trembled. Her fingers shook. Butterflies danced in her belly and up into her throat.

He bent over and then slid one knee onto the bed until he was over her, so close that she could feel the heat of his breath.

Instead of pressing his mouth to hers as she expected, he angled his head and brushed his lips over her neck.

It was like being caught in a fierce lightning storm.

She gasped and arched upward, her head falling back in an invitation for him to nuzzle below her ear.

"You have beautiful skin, lass."

His voice purred over her throat, vibrating and husky until her entire body tingled in anticipation of where he'd kiss her next.

His teeth sank into the column of her neck, light and grazing, a gentle nip and then one a bit harder.

"You taste as sweet as you look."

She sighed and closed her eyes. "You have a wicked mouth, husband."

"And to think I've only just begun."

CHAPTER 11

Rionna reached up to grasp Caelen's shoulders, her fingers digging into his hard muscles. She strained upward, wanting more of his mouth. Shivers of delight raced in patterns over her flesh, like raindrops on a warm summer afternoon.

"That's it, lass. Hold on to me."

Gently he lowered her until her back met the bed and she landed with a soft bounce.

"You're a feast for a man's eyes."

"Why is it the bed chamber is the only place you have a kind word for me?" she said with a twist of her lips.

He reared back, a faint smile curving his mouth. "'Tis the only time you're obedient, wife."

She balled her fist and hit him ineffectually on the shoulder. He captured her wrist and pulled it over her head, holding it there as he cupped one of her breasts and caressed the swell.

He stroked lazily with his fingers, tracing soft lines to her nipple. He captured the peak and pulled, gently at first and then sharper. Each tug sent a streak of pleasure straight to her core. Her womb clenched. She squeezed her thighs together and arched farther into his touch.

Then he lowered his head until his breath blew warm over the puckered bud. She moaned in anticipation, hardly recognizing the breathy, feminine sounds sliding from her throat.

Warm and rough, his tongue slid sensuously over her nipple, leaving a damp trail to the top of her breast. He released her wrist and lowered his hand to cup her other breast. He kneaded and massaged and then plumped them together.

He licked over one nipple and then pressed a tender kiss to the tip before moving to the other. She stared down at his dark head as he suckled. With each pull, her body tightened more until she was rigid beneath him.

Unable to resist, she thrust her fingers into his long, black hair. She stroked the braids at his temples, pulling when he stopped sucking. With a chuckle, he resumed and she relaxed her hold so that she threaded through the strands, enjoying the slide over her hands.

"I have a mind to taste you again, to feel your honey on my tongue," he whispered.

She closed her eyes and let her hands fall away as he kissed a path over her belly and lower to the juncture of her thighs.

He leaned over on his side, his big hand splayed over her pelvis. He propped himself up on his other elbow and idly toyed with the curls shielding her femininity. It mortified her and fascinated her with equal measure.

Part of her wanted to squeeze her thighs shut and turn away and the other part wanted to open them to give him easier access.

Carefully he delved inward and gently parted her flesh until she was open and damp to his touch. With one finger, he stroked down and then back up again to circle the tiny sensitive nub.

"I'm fair to bursting, lass. I want to bury myself deep inside your warmth."

Her eyes widened at the image his words provoked. She went still beneath his fingers and stared down at him. He tilted his head back so he met her gaze, and the intensity in his eyes made her mouth go dry.

His hand left her and slid up her belly to cup her breast and he leaned down to kiss the tip, forming it into a tight peak. Then he shifted his body and moved up so their lips were just a breath apart.

He touched her cheek with the back of one finger and trailed over her cheekbone to her jaw. "I won't hurt you, lass. You were afraid our wedding night. 'Tis why I didn't bed you. I'll be as gentle as a man can be when he's shaking with want for his bride."

She opened her mouth to refute his assertion that she was afraid of anything but the protest died as she blew her breath out and closed her lips once more.

Then he kissed her, his mouth moving with infinite tenderness over her lips. All the while his hands slid over her body, stroking, caressing. Soothing.

Somehow he managed to shift over her, his body covering hers like a warm blanket. One muscled thigh wedged between hers and nudged them farther apart.

She was so senseless from his kisses that she hadn't registered that his very large, very naked body was pressing tightly against hers, and another very hard, very large portion of his anatomy was prodding insistently at her most intimate flesh.

He found her opening and went still as she stretched around the tip of his manhood. Her startled gaze flew to his face. She tensed, unable to prevent the unease that gripped her.

"Relax, lass," he whispered against the corner of her mouth. "'Twill be easier if you give over. I'll give you pleasure. I swear it."

"Tell me what to do," she whispered back.

"Wrap your legs around me and hold on to my shoulders."

She lifted her legs and twined them around his, sliding

her calves up the hairy, muscled wall of his legs to lock them behind his knees.

Her hands felt small on his shoulders. Her fingers barely left dents in the hard flesh. She stared into his eyes and found gentleness there. It comforted her that he worried over frightening her. Surely she could find courage. How could she expect him to respect his "warrior princess" if she never showed her to him?

"Come to me, husband," she said boldly.

His hardness found her again, firm against her softness. Probing and insistent.

She gave a little gasp when he slipped the barest inch inside her body. She stretched to accommodate him but the fullness unsettled her.

It was an odd combination of hesitancy and urgency. She wanted him to stop and yet she wanted him to continue.

She bit her bottom lip and lifted her hips, urging him on.

"Ah, lass, how sweetly you beckon me."

He closed his eyes and a shudder rolled over his shoulders. Beneath her fingertips, he trembled and shook, so tense, as if he fought against his every instinct to hold back.

She ran her hands up and down his shoulders and arms, caressing as her heart softened. He truly was taking the utmost care with her.

"'Tis all right," she whispered. "I know you won't hurt me."

His lips were thin, white lines on a face etched in concentration.

"Aye, but I must, lass. I must break through your maidenhead and 'twill pain you no matter what I do."

He brushed a kiss across her mouth and then he wooed her gently, feeding and sipping at her lips. "'Tis sorry I am for it, but there is naught to do for it."

"Then be done with it. There is no sense in both of us being in pain. I can feel the tension in your body. 'Tis uncomfortable for you to hold back as you're doing."

He gave a soft laugh. "You have no idea, lass. You have no idea."

For the first time, she initiated an intimate gesture. Her hands framed his face, her thumbs feathering over his firm cheekbones. She caressed his angular jaw and then smoothed her fingers over his lips.

Raising her head, she framed his face once more and pulled him down into a long kiss. Their tongues tangled hotly. She had no breath but she refused to pull away. His kiss was intoxicating. The sweetest nectar she'd ever tasted.

Her body opened under his insistent push. 'Twas like having a fiery sword invade her depths. So hard and velvety. Her body resisted his intent to conquer but he held her in place, his hands grasping her hips as he thrust again.

"Kiss me, lass. 'Twill be over in an instant."

Just as their mouths met in a breathless rush, he thrust hard and deep. She was unprepared for the pain. Aye, she'd known what had to happen, but she'd expected a twinge. Maybe even a brief piercing pain. But not this tearing sensation that had her insides feeling brushed by fire.

She cried out and tears sprang unbidden to her eyes, burning as they trailed down her cheeks.

Caelen immediately stilled, his cock buried deep inside her passage. There was matching pain in his expression as he clenched his jaw tightly. His nostrils flared and he took in several deep breaths as he shuddered against her.

He kissed her forehead, her eyelids, each cheekbone, and even her nose. Then he kissed away the trails of moisture sliding over her cheeks.

"I'm sorry, lass. So very sorry."

The ache in his voice made her heart twist. A knot formed in her throat, swelling until she couldn't shape the words she most wanted to say.

He kissed her again even as a harsh groan welled from his chest.

"Tell me when 'tis better. I'll not move until you say me aye."

She clenched experimentally around him, testing the tenderness of her sheath.

"God's teeth, lass. Have mercy."

She smiled, relieved that some of the fiery pain had dulled to an odd ache deep in her womb. "'Tis much better now. The pain has dulled."

"Thank God," he muttered. "I cannot hold out much longer."

She swept a hand over his damp brow and then thrust her fingers into his hair as she pulled him down into a deep kiss.

"Finish it," she whispered.

He carefully withdrew and her eyes widened at the myriad of sensations that bombarded her. She was tender, aye, and the discomfort was there, but there was also an incredible burn that had nothing to do with pain.

"Easy now," he murmured. "Give it time, lass. You'll feel pleasure."

He pushed forward again, slowly and with such tenderness that she sighed. He seemed so determined that the experience be as pleasant as possible for her.

His fingers found her nipple and he rubbed the pad of his thumb over the peak until it stiffened and became erect. Then he caressed the other until both breasts were achingly tight.

He smiled down at her, a wicked gleam in his eyes. "You grow wet around me. The breasts you try so hard to hide bring you much pleasure. And me. They are beautiful like you and a credit to your womanhood. They are soft, as a woman should be, and pleasing to look upon. There is naught I can find fault with you, lass. God fashioned you a perfect woman. I am a lucky man, indeed."

Oh but she planned to remind him of his honeyed words the next time he turned his scowl of disapproval on her. And she'd remember each and every one of his endearments. She'd hold them close to her heart and pretend that she was his cherished love and not a bride thrust upon him for the sake of loyalty and honor.

Keeley had warned her that a man would say a lot when his cock was involved. Things he didn't necessarily mean. Now Rionna understood what Keeley had meant.

He withdrew and thrust again, this time with much more ease. He was right. She had grown damp the moment he fondled her breasts. For so long they'd been such a source of irritation but now she was discovering that they had their uses after all.

For the first time she embraced the idea that somehow she was feminine. Beautiful even. She didn't despair of appearing softer and not as fierce. It felt good to be a woman in a strong warrior's arms. Aye, it felt good indeed.

"Do I hurt you still?" he asked.

She raised her mouth to his. "Nay, warrior. You feel very, very good."

"As do you, wife."

He slid his hands underneath her buttocks and cupped her, spreading her wider and holding her closer to him. He thrust, burying himself deeper than before.

Gone was the tender warrior who'd strove not to cause her any pain. Now that he was assured of her comfort, he began planting himself inside her as if he were proving his possession, his *right* to possess her.

His teeth scraped her jaw and then moved lower to her neck. His breath blew hot over her skin, scorching a path from her ear to her shoulder.

He alternately nipped, sucked, and kissed her until she was sure she'd wear the marks for an entire fortnight. He was insatiable, as if he'd starved himself of her for too long and could no longer control his intense hunger.

She threw back her head, surrendering to his power. She offered her submission freely. He awoke a fierce longing within her. Feelings that she'd never considered. She wanted to belong to him. She wanted to be cherished by him.

She was his wife. She closed her eyes and her heart to the reason for their marriage. Just because it had begun one way didn't mean it couldn't change to something else entirely.

She wanted his love.

Aye, she demanded it.

Now that she'd had a taste of his regard and his tenderness, she knew he was capable. Aye, he was more than capable of more tender feelings. No matter what he thought, his heart wasn't completely closed to love.

It was up to her to show him.

Faster and harder he moved between her legs. Refusing to lie passively as he staked his claim, she returned each kiss and each caress with equal fervor.

He might be claiming her, but she was staking her claim as well.

This warrior was hers. He was her husband. Her lover.

Never would she let him go.

He slipped one hand between them and brushed his fingertips over her quivering flesh just as he thrust fiercely into her once more.

'Twas all that was needed for her to lose all sense of herself. The flash bewildered her. One moment she was drawn as tight as a bowstring and the next she was being flung across the star-filled sky, scattering just like the twinkling lights.

Her mind went completely and utterly blank. All she could process was the incredible pleasure that flooded her veins and slugged like thick honey through her limbs.

She couldn't draw a breath. She panted, her nostrils flaring with the effort it took to pull air into her lungs.

Above her, Caelen gave a shout and then thrust forward so hard that he collapsed onto her body, driving them both deep into the mattress.

His forehead hit the pillow beside her head and he dug his arms underneath her so that he gathered her tight against his body.

Between her thighs, he flinched and flexed as his big body shuddered helplessly above her.

His chest heaved, and she knew that he had the same difficulty in drawing breath.

With a smile, she wrapped her arms around his waist and hugged him tightly. She closed her eyes and rested her cheek in the curve of his neck as she absorbed the wondrous sensation of their bodies joined so tight that naught could separate them.

CHAPTER 12

Rionna woke to blissful warmth. She was surrounded by heat. She flexed her toes experimentally and sighed when they dug into the warm furs. Lazily her eyelids fluttered open and she saw a fire blazing in the hearth. Waking to a fire was a luxury she was unused to, and she quickly decided that it was one she could quickly grow to like.

She glanced sideways to see the space beside her bare. There was not even any sign that Caelen had lain beside her, their limbs tangled together for most of the night.

She stretched her arm over the furs where Caelen had indeed spent the night and stroked the pillow where his head had rested.

Her body felt the effects of her husband's possession. When she moved, the tenderness between her legs was more pronounced and there was a soreness in her muscles like she usually felt after a vigorous sparring session.

'Twas the truth she had no desire to move from the bed.

Aye she was sore but it was a delicious soreness. One she'd willingly suffer again and again. She closed her eyes and stretched leisurely, calling back the images of

Caelen over her, inside her, stroking deep, his mouth making sweet, sweet love to her flesh.

A sound at the door had her opening her eyes and turning to see who was about. Sarah stuck her head in and once she saw Rionna was awake, she bustled in and shut the door behind her.

"You're awake, I see."

"Observant as ever," Rionna said dryly.

Sarah clucked under her breath and rolled her eyes in Rionna's direction. "The laird thought you'd like a bath before you begin your instructions. I'm having water brought up to fill the tub."

"Tub? What tub?"

Rionna sat up, pulling the furs to her chest. She rubbed her eyes and stared around the room to see a large wooden tub situated in front of the fire. Such a thing had escaped her when she'd just awoken. When had Caelen had a tub brought in? Likely before he carried *her* into his chamber the night before.

Then something else Sarah had said registered.

"Instructions? What instructions?"

Rionna swung her feet over the edge, still clutching the furs to her naked body.

Sarah smiled. "The laird wants me and the other women to instruct you on the duties of the lady of the keep. He said 'tis obvious you have no knowledge of such, and now that you are wife to the laird 'tis time for you to take your place."

Rionna sat in the tub, water up to her ears, silently fuming. After a night of pure heaven, a night when she was sure that she and Caelen would start anew, that he would actually act as though he cared something for her, he'd gotten up from their bed and ordered her to start acting like his meek little wife.

To make matters worse, Sarah was sitting by the tub, ticking off the list of instructions from Caelen.

She was not to dress as a man. She was not to indulge in activities unbecoming a lady, and he went on to specify swordplay, fighting, or any other activity assigned to a warrior. She wasn't to bind her breasts.

That directive had Rionna turning scarlet, her cheeks so scorched that the steaming water suddenly seemed tepid. Could he have humiliated her any further?

"Now, lass, don't look like that," Sarah soothed. "'Tis not as if he told the entire keep. He pulled me aside, he did. Told me his wishes and instructed me not to say a word to anyone."

"If he had anything to say, he should have spoken to me," Rionna hissed.

Sarah snorted. "And you would have ignored him and gone about your usual practices."

Rionna bared her teeth. "What is so wrong with my usual practices?"

Sarah poured a bucket of water over Rionna's head and then shoved her underneath the water. Rionna came up sputtering and glaring at Sarah, who sat grinning with a look of satisfaction.

"'Tis the truth, I've waited a long time to get my hands on you, lass. Your father cared naught how you behaved even though he disapproved. He was a lazy man who should have taken you in hand long before you reached the age you are now. And your mother should have taught you the ways of the lady of the keep, but she was too busy keeping your father away from the other lasses. You've not had a good example to be sure, but that's all going to come to an end starting today. I'm going to mold you into the finest lady of the keep the McDonald clan has ever seen."

The determination in the older woman's eyes made Rionna's shoulders sag in resignation. There was unholy delight in Sarah's gaze. She was practically rubbing her hands in glee.

"First we're going to measure you for new gowns. The bodices of your current dresses will never fit you with those breasts out of bondage. I've already got three of the women altering one of the dresses that your mother wore. A few stitches here and there and you'll have dresses you can wear until we can outfit you in a new wardrobe."

"We haven't the funds to outfit me in a new wardrobe," Rionna said darkly.

Sarah shook her head. "You're not to worry over that. The laird is expecting all manner of supplies from his brother in the next fortnight. He told me himself that he specifically sent word that you needed warm clothing and all the trappings befitting a lady."

"'All the trappings befitting a lady,'" Rionna mimicked.

"Hush now. The water's growing cold. Your grumbling doesn't change the fact that you've a lot of learning ahead of you. 'Twill be better for all if you go about it with a good attitude."

"Oh let me sulk a bit," Rionna said. "I know you have the right of it, but 'tis the truth I have no liking for the task."

Sarah smiled and reached over to pat Rionna's cheek. "I love you like you were my own bairn. And I'm going to treat you like my bairn, which means I'll cuff you on the back of the head if you give me any sass."

Rionna grinned and then sobered. "What think you of the new laird?"

Sarah cocked her head as she gave the matter consideration.

"I think he's a gruff man, but I think he's fair. He's hard, and he likes things a certain way. It might take the clan a bit to grow accustomed to his ways, but I think we'll be a better clan for it."

"I do, too," Rionna said grudgingly. "I just want . . ."

"What do you want, lass?"

Rionna pressed her lips together, determined not to show weakness in front of Sarah. What she wanted were things a girl wanted. Dreams a girl dreamed. Not what a woman full grown with a responsibility to her clan spent her day being foolish over.

"'Tis no matter what I want," she said quietly. "'Tis what the laird wants that matters."

Caelen stood in the courtyard, arms crossed, expression stony as he surveyed the McDonald soldiers training. Gannon stood beside him and every once in awhile shook his head in dismay.

"We've not time to shape these men into a decent army," Gannon said. "We won't stand a chance against Cameron."

"Not if I have anything to say about it," Caelen said grimly. "They have the skill. They just haven't had the proper training."

"Their best warrior is a woman," Gannon said in disgust. "Rionna bested Diormid, remember?"

Caelen scowled. He didn't need a reminder of his wife's prowess with a sword. He had no intention of allowing her to get herself killed. The sooner he got her with child, the sooner she'd settle down and turn her attention to more womanly pursuits. Then he wouldn't have to worry over what trouble she got into.

"Find me the leaders," Caelen said to Gannon. "'Tis obvious they have no regard for my authority yet. I'll make my case to the most senior men and let them know I'm no threat to their leadership."

"I've been watching," Gannon murmured. "Simon McDonald wields much influence within his clan. The men listen to him and look to him for guidance. Arlen McDonald is another elder whom the younger soldiers look to for guidance. He's adept with a sword."

"Tell them I want a meeting with them in the great hall. Invite them to have the noon meal and we'll talk then. We'll have need to break the men into smaller groups for training purposes. I'll need the help of the McDonald men in positions of leadership if we are to accomplish all we need to."

"Aye, I agree. It won't be an easy task."

Caelen grinned at his commander. "You said you desired a new challenge."

Gannon shot him a disgruntled look. "When I said that, whipping an entire army into shape wasn't what I had in mind."

Caelen sighed. "Nor is it what I had in mind either. 'Tis the truth I don't even know where to begin. The task before us is overwhelming in its enormity."

Gannon laid a hand on Caelen's shoulder. "A more able taskmaster I've never met. 'Tis the truth if anyone can do it, you can."

Caelen scanned the sparring warriors and grimaced. He hoped Gannon was right. The next weeks would be grueling, and his only chance of success was in gaining the cooperation of his new clan.

So far no one had greeted him with anything but reserve and suspicion.

"Find Simon and Arlen," he ordered Gannon. "I'll be in the hall waiting."

As he strode into the keep, he glanced at the serving women scurrying to and fro, in the midst of their chores. He searched for his wife but didn't see her. But then neither did he spot Sarah, who'd promised to take Rionna under her wing and guide her with a gentle hand.

He entered the hall to find it barren. He frowned, knowing it was close to time for the noon meal. There was no activity to suggest such a thing was forthcoming. No fire burned in the hearth. No smells emanated from the kitchens. No places had been set at the table.

He didn't even know the name of someone to summon to answer his questions. In disgust, he left the hall and walked in the direction of distant voices.

When he entered the room he could only suppose was where the women did the washing, he found his wife in a state of agitation, her hands on her hips and her face red as she stared back at Sarah.

The dress she wore was fine, if a bit worn. The bodice was a little—a lot—too tight and Rionna's supple breasts pushed up and over the embroidered neckline. She looked . . . beautiful. Dainty and feminine. He was hardpressed to place her in the scruffy men's clothing, with a dirt-smeared face, shapeless bosom, and hair tightly plastered to her head.

She looked every inch the elegant mistress of the keep. She rivaled Mairin and Keeley in beauty and form.

That was until she opened her mouth and cut loose with a string of blasphemies he was certain had never crossed his sisters-in-law's mouths.

She was still cursing when she turned and saw him standing in the doorway. Her lips snapped shut and she glared at him as if peeved over his intrusion. He lifted one eyebrow when no request for pardon came forth.

Her palms dug deeper into her hips as she stared him down. Her eyes flashed, an odd mixture of amber and gold.

"Are you coming to check up on me, husband?"

His lips tightened and he pinned her with a glare of his own.

"I came to find out why no meal is being served in the great hall. It's past the time for the noon meal. The soldiers have already put in a hard day's work and will be hungry. As am I."

Rionna stared at him, her brows drawn together in puzzlement. The other women stared at him as well, as if he'd said something utterly ridiculous.

Sarah was the first to speak. She glanced at Rionna and then took a step forward. "We don't serve a meal at noon, Laird."

He frowned again. "Any particular reason why not? 'Tis important for the men to eat. Their strength must be kept up, especially now that they'll be training even harder."

Rionna cleared her throat. "What she's so delicately trying to say is that we don't have the food. We break our fast with bread and cheese, when we have it to spare, and we end the day with whatever we've been able to hunt."

"And when the hunt isn't successful?"

"We don't eat," she said simply.

He shook his head. None of this made sense. The McDonalds might not be the best trained when it came to the might of their army, but they'd always been a well-placed clan.

"Your father wagered my brother three months' worth of food from his stores."

"He didn't have it to wager," Rionna said bitterly. "He left us with nothing to eat and no coin to trade with other clans."

Caelen bit back a blaspheme of his own. "Show me your larder."

With a shrug, Rionna turned and walked down the hallway away from the great hall and past the kitchens to a small, airless chamber. He walked in and glanced around, his stomach sinking as he took in the empty shelves.

If possible, the McDonald clan was in poorer circumstances than his own clan had been before his brother married Mairin.

"This is unacceptable," he gritted out. "The clan must eat."

"We're used to surviving on little," Rionna said matter-of-factly. "'Tis our way of life for some years now."

"Was your father a complete wastrel?" he demanded.

"My father was only concerned with his own comfort and filling his own belly."

"'Tis a wonder you haven't been invaded long before now," Caelen said in disgust. "You certainly would have been an easy conquest."

Rionna's mouth tightened and her eyes narrowed in fury. "'Tis your clan you speak of with such disdain."

"Nay, 'tis not my clan I have such disdain for. 'Tis your father. 'Tis a sin for a man not to provide for his clan. Do your children go hungry as well? And what of your old and the sick?"

Rionna gave a weary sigh. "'Tis no use venting your outrage, husband. The man to whom you have need to direct your anger is not here. My clan has suffered long enough. We don't deserve your censure."

Caelen blew out his breath in disgust and turned to stalk from the room.

"Where do you go?" she called after him.

"Hunting," he bit out.

CHAPTER 13

"Change the order," Caelen said to Gannon when he found his commander in the courtyard. "Have Simon and Arlen pick their best hunters and pack the horses."

Gannon looked at him curiously but went immediately to do his laird's bidding.

A moment later, Gannon returned with a small group of warriors.

"We go hunting, McCabe?" Simon asked.

Caelen's eyes narrowed at the slight. Now wasn't the time to show any softness with his new clan. If he did, he'd lose any and all credibility. They didn't have to like him, but they damn well better respect him.

He drew his sword before the other men could blink and he sliced the blade through the air, a bare inch from the older man's neck.

Simon blinked in surprise but didn't dare move lest he cut himself.

"You will address me as Laird," Caelen said. "You may not like the fact that a McCabe has replaced a McDonald, but you'll show the respect that's due or you'll find yourself on the ground."

"You can bloody well try," Simon bit out.

Caelen had to hand it to the man. He might be older and he might be speaking from a clear disadvantage of having a sword to his throat, but he showed no fear or lack of courage.

Caelen slowly lowered the sword and then tossed it in the air toward Gannon. He smiled slow and his lip curled as he stared at Simon. "I'll do more than try, old man."

Without warning, Simon charged. A shout went up through the courtyard and the men pressed forward, eager to see the impending clash.

Simon drove his shoulder into Caelen's abdomen, knocking him back several feet. But Caelen stood his ground and didn't go down under the onslaught.

The McDonald men quickly circled Caelen and Simon and began shouting encouragement to Simon. Shouts of "Take him down" and "Show him what we think of our new laird" filled the air.

Caelen rotated, wrapping his arms around Simon's waist. The movement coupled with Simon's forward momentum unbalanced the man. Caelen picked him up and swung, slamming him into the ground as he came down on top of him.

They rolled, snow kicking up amid the flurry of arms and legs. Simon landed a punch to Caelen's jaw, knocking him back enough that he could scramble from Caelen's hold.

The two warriors stood and circled warily, feinting left and right as they waited for the other to make a move.

Caelen punched, landing a forceful blow to Simon's chin and knocking him back a few paces. Simon wiped at a trickle of blood at his mouth and then curled his lip into a snarl.

"Now to see your measure, McCabe."

He lunged forward, wrapping his beefy arms around Caelen's waist and drove them both into the snow. The impact drove the breath from Caelen. He rolled then dodged the fist that flew at his face. He wasn't quick enough to avoid the full impact, though. He tasted blood on his tongue.

He drove his knee into Simon's midsection and then flipped the man over his head to land in the snow several feet away. Caelen was quick to his feet and he stood back as Simon picked himself out of the drift.

"What is your issue?" Caelen barked. "Your laird was a waste of good, clean air. He left your clan in dire circumstances. He acted without honor. He has brought shame to all of you."

Simon spat blood onto the snow. "You are not our choice. Aye, the old man was not a good laird. He didn't deserve the mantle of leadership. But you haven't proved yourself worthy of it either. You walk onto our land, shouting orders by writ of the king who hasn't shown himself to us to make this decree."

"You treat Rionna without respect," James called from the crowd.

"Aye," several others chorused.

Simon nodded. "Rionna is a good lass who cares only for her clan. She fights alongside us. She goes without when we go without. She is loyal to her bones," Simon said. "She deserves a husband who will see her for the treasure she is."

Caelen took advantage of the older man's momentary distraction and charged. They went down again and Caelen used his momentum to flip Simon over his back.

The man landed facedown in the snow and Caelen pressed his knee into Simon's back. He gripped Simon's hair and pulled until his face was clear of the snow.

"Is that the way of things in the McDonald clan? You allow your women to do your fighting for you? Rionna is a laird's daughter. She is now wife to your new laird. Think you she should be gadding about as a man, putting herself at risk? She could be killed or grievously injured. If you want her treated as the treasure you say she is, doesn't it make more sense for her to remain inside the keep where she can be protected? How can you speak of respect when it's apparent none of you have any for her and her station?"

Caelen dropped his hold and eased back to stand over Simon.

"Women are to be protected, taken care of, and provided for. The day I need a woman to do those things for me is the day they'll put me in the ground and no longer call me a warrior."

Simon grimaced as he got to his feet and brushed the snow from his tunic. "Aye, you have the right of it. Rionna . . . she's a different lass, Laird."

Caelen grunted in satisfaction at the manner of address Simon issued. "Aye, I know it. She's a strange lass to be sure. But 'tis not too late to instruct her on the proper ways of a lass. Soon she'll carry my child and your next laird. Would you have her risking her safety and that of her child by taking up a sword and fighting as a man?"

"Nay."

The murmur went up through the crowd as each man shook his head. Not all were convinced, though. They may agree that Rionna was in need of protecting, but they weren't accepting of him as laird.

It would take time. Time that Caelen didn't have if he was going to transform this meager army into a fighting force as good as the McCabes'.

"Where do we go this day, Laird?" Simon asked.

The fact that Simon addressed Caelen as laird didn't meet with approval by many. The men scowled and shook their heads before turning away in a show of blatant disrespect.

"We go hunting," Caelen said. "Our larders are empty. Our women and young go hungry while we stand out here acting as children. We have much training to do in the coming weeks. Our men will have need of adequate sustenance in order to keep their strength up. I'm going to work you hard and without mercy. I'll make warriors of you if it kills me."

"My son James is a good shot with a bow. He's our best hunter."

"Then I'll welcome him along. Gather your best. I want you and Arlen and whomever you choose to accompany us. We leave immediately."

Simon nodded and started to turn away but then paused. He took a breath as if he debated what he wanted to say.

"Speak," Caelen ordered. "'Tis obvious you have something you want to get off your chest."

"Try to have patience with the lass. Her ways are all she's ever known. She has a good and fierce heart."

Caelen frowned. It irritated him to receive advice at every turn for how to handle his wife. Even his brother had offered his opinion on the matter after marrying another woman. But then Alaric fancied himself an expert on women.

"What the lass needs is a firm hand. She's been allowed to run wild for far too long."

A few snickers went up from the crowd. Even Simon grinned as if they all shared some secret amusement.

"Then I'll wish you luck, Laird. Something tells me you're going to need it."

CHAPTER 14

Rionna stood in the window of the guard tower and stared over the snowy landscape. It had been three days since the hunting party had departed and there was still no sign of their return.

On the first evening, one of the younger warriors had returned with a fine stag. He bore Caelen's instructions for the meat to be dressed, stored, and properly cured with a generous portion to be prepared immediately for the women and children to eat.

The rest of the party was remaining on the hunt until they killed enough game to refill the larders.

She watched the men below training to Caelen's specifications. For three days she'd held out against the temptation to join in the exercises. Instead she'd remained indoors and listened to endless instructions about the preservation of meat, how to properly stock a larder, cleaning schedules, not to mention sleep-inducing lectures on proper etiquette for ladies and how to greet and be hospitable to important guests.

As if they ever had important guests at McDonald keep.

It was apparent that her husband wasn't returning this day, and there were several hours of daylight yet. She fairly itched to be down in the courtyard where she could vent her frustration with a good sword fight.

The problem was Sarah would have no compunction about ratting her out to her husband. Which meant she'd have to sneak to the courtyard after telling Sarah that she was retiring to her chamber.

She turned, wrapping her cloak tighter around her as she began the descent from the tower. At the bottom, she was met by one of the serving women that Sarah had no doubt set to monitor her whereabouts.

"I'm going to retire to my chamber," Rionna said in a low voice.

"Are you not feeling well, my lady?"

Rionna smiled at the woman not much older than herself. "I'm fine, Beatrice. I'm just a little tired."

Beatrice smiled knowingly. "You're not sleeping well since the laird's departure. He'll be home soon, my lady, and with meat to take us through the winter."

Rionna smiled faintly as she turned toward the stairs up to the chamber she shared with Caelen. While the men were not as accepting yet of Caelen as their laird, the women of the keep suffered no such hesitancy. Whatever he'd done, he'd inspired confidence in the female members of her clan. They all accepted that he'd see them through their difficulties and restore their larders and their might.

Rionna supposed that if he did, indeed, accomplish all that, she should be well content with her marriage.

Should be.

When she entered the chamber where she'd slept alone three nights past, she marveled at the mark her husband had already left on the room. It wasn't as though he had a lot of things. Indeed, he'd packed very sparsely for his journey from his former home.

But whereas the chamber had been barren and nondescript before, it now felt masculine, as if he'd breathed his very essence into the small space.

The furs he'd brought from McCabe keep covered the bed. Luxurious, thick furs that she'd already grown accustomed to sleeping beneath at night. Even the furs covering the windows had been replaced by his own.

There was a small table with a chair by the fire that housed his scrolls and quill and ink. They roused her curiosity. She'd love to know what was contained in the scrolls, but she hadn't the ability to read. The fact that her husband was so learned surprised and intrigued her.

Caelen had many hidden depths, which she hadn't even begun to plumb. He'd certainly shut himself off from others, only allowing people to see what he so chose. It was frustrating for her because she desperately wanted to know everything there was to know about the man she'd married.

She went to the chest that housed the dresses the women had fashioned for her. She stretched her hand behind it, in the small space between it and the wall, and pulled out the tunic and trews she'd hidden there.

The material slid lovingly over her fingers. Worn but comfortable. Familiar. Anticipation tugged relentlessly at her until she hurriedly stripped the dress from her body and began pulling on the tunic.

When she was dressed, she pulled her boots from the corner where they'd rested ever since they're arrived back on McDonald land. First she pulled on her precious stockings and then the boots over them.

The stockings made the boots a bit snug, but they weren't uncomfortable. More important, her feet were warm.

She practically danced to the wall where Caelen had hung her sword. She was grateful he hadn't had it melted down for armor. 'Twas a sin to abuse so fine a weapon.

She slid her fingers over the hilt and carefully lifted it

from its perch. It felt glorious in her hand. The weight. The grooves, fashioned just so for her grasp. Light enough that she could wield it with a deft hand but heavy enough to inflict a mortal wound.

She tested the sharpness of the blade, satisfied when the hair she brushed across fell neatly into two.

Now to brave the stairwell and hope she didn't run into Sarah.

A few moments later, she burst into the courtyard and hurried through the line of men so she could position herself at the fartherest point away from the entrance to the keep. If Sarah came looking, she wanted to be well out of sight.

The mixed greeting from the men bewildered her. A few looked genuinely glad to see her and called out a greeting. Others seemed more reserved and exchanged uneasy glances. A few were more bold and stepped in front of her, though their stance wasn't in the least aggressive.

No, they looked concerned. And protective.

Hugh McDonald frowned and then swallowed uncomfortably. "Rionna, perhaps 'tis better if you remain indoors. 'Tis cold today. You shouldn't be indulging in a man's training."

Rionna's mouth gaped open as she stared back at the burly warrior. Hugh was directly responsible for most of her skill. Aye, he'd taught her almost everything she knew. He'd knocked her on her arse more times than she could count and always taunted her to get up and try again.

"He's gotten to you, hasn't he?" she demanded. "He's not been here a week and already he's turned you against me!"

Hugh put out a placating hand. "Now, Rionna. 'Tis not what's happened at all. The laird has made us see that 'tis not the best course for you to be fighting. 'Tis not a seemly pursuit for a woman."

She scowled at him and drew her sword. "How seemly would it be for a woman to put you on your arse?"

Hugh put up his hand to the others. "The man who puts sword to hers will answer to me."

Hurt squeezed her chest, turning her insides into a knot. "You'll forbid the men to spar with me?"

Hugh looked as though he'd swallowed a mace. "'Tis sorry I am, lass. Aside from the fact the laird would have my hide, I'd not have you hurt. Or any bairn you might find yourself pregnant with."

She closed her eyes and turned away. Desolation swept through her, leaving her empty and aching. Tears pricked her eyelids and her shoulders slumped in defeat.

"Give me your sword, lass," Hugh said gently. "I'll put it away."

She turned to see the rest of the men standing behind Hugh, their faces set in agreement. None would battle her now. Biting back tears, she slowly extended the sword to Hugh. He took it and then handed it back to one of the other men. She didn't wait to see what they did next. She turned and hurried out the back of the courtyard, never looking back.

Her chest felt near to bursting.

The wind blew cold over her damp cheeks. Tears she hadn't registered froze on her skin. Her sense of loss was keen. It cut deep and festered like a week-old wound.

She felt horribly betrayed. Like her life would never again be the same. The people she loved, who loved her, had been swayed by her husband's firm beliefs about a woman's place.

How she longed for the days when she'd run free and her only worry had been avoiding her father. She missed the euphoric rush of victory when she bested one of her father's men with a sword.

Out here, with her blade, her faults fell away. She didn't feel inadequate. She was just another sword in a sea of warriors. Strong and capable. Not just a woman in need of protection.

She was no good at simpering or playing coy. She didn't have the social graces necessary not to embarrass herself or her kin. 'Twas why her father had never shoved her in front of the noses of anyone of import.

She trudged down the hill toward the bubbling brook that connected the two lochs on McDonald land. 'Twas a pretty sight with ice crusted on the banks, reaching toward the middle where water still rushed over rock. Snow drifted on either side, framing the icy-cold water and blanketing the land in white.

She stopped at the water's edge and hugged her arms to her chest. She closed her eyes and breathed deep of the crisp winter air. The faint smell of smoke from the keep's chimney wafted through her nostrils, and for the first time in a long while, the smell of meat over a spit.

For how long she stared over the water she wasn't sure, but shivering with cold she had the realization that what she hated wasn't the loss of her freedom. It was the fear of the unknown.

She was acting like a petulant child whose favorite toy had been taken away. She could be part of the rebuilding of her clan. Perhaps not in the way she had the most knowledge, but everyone else was having to cope with change. She wasn't the only one who didn't like it.

If her husband wanted the perfect lady, a well-kept manor, the epitome of feminine grace, she could give him all of that even if it killed her.

She'd give him no reason to be shamed by her.

Her chin notched upward and her gaze settled across the brook. To her shock, men on horses bolted from the trees and charged toward her.

She turned and let out a yell just as the horses splashed

into the water. She ran along the shore, knowing she had no chance trying to run up the hill to the keep. She'd never outrun the horses.

She opened her mouth to yell another alarm, praying the men would hear from such a distance, but a boot slammed into her back, knocking her to the ground.

She landed in the snow with such force, it knocked the wind from her chest.

Ignoring the pain, she planted her palms down and got her feet under her once more to flee.

A hand twisted in her hair and her attacker yanked her backward and then flipped her onto her back. She stared up at a group of five men. The taste of fear was vile on her tongue. She faced them down, unwilling to show them just how terrified she was.

"What do you want?" she demanded.

The man holding her backhanded her across the face, shocking her into silence. Furious, she attacked, her fingers flying into his eyes. He howled in pain and stumbled back, giving her just a moment to make a break for it.

She didn't get far before another of the men tackled her, driving her face into the snow. It filled her nose and mouth, numbing the throbbing ache from the vicious slap a moment ago.

Again she was turned and this time the second attacker clipped her with his fist on the cheek. His hand closed around her neck, squeezing with enough force to prevent her from drawing breath.

He held her there until she went slack. The other men gathered near and then the first attacker staggered up, blood dripping from one of the scratches she'd inflicted.

"Little bitch," he spat.

He grabbed the neckline of her tunic and ripped downward until her breasts were bared. Once more she began to struggle but the man holding her neck squeezed again until she was forced to quit.

She tried to scream but no sound came out. Tears of rage blurred her vision as one of the men fondled her breasts and then tweaked one nipple.

Just before she blacked out, the hand relaxed at her throat and she sucked in deep breaths. As soon as she had enough air, she opened her mouth to scream just as her face exploded in pain again.

He administered methodical, forceful slaps to her face, alternating sides until a haze of pain enveloped her. The other hands continued their lewd groping, twisting, and pawing her like an animal.

Hot tears slipped over her battered cheeks. Never had she felt so helpless in her life. Where was her sword? How was she expected to defend herself?

She would be raped here on her own land, helpless to do anything but lay there and cry.

When she was barely conscious, her attacker leaned in close until his hot, fetid breath blew over her face.

"You're going to deliver a message to the new laird," he hissed. "Tell him no McCabe is safe from Duncan Cameron. Not Mairin McCabe or her new daughter. Nor anyone the McCabes call dear. Cameron will destroy all who ally themselves with Ewan McCabe. He won't rest until Neamh Álainn is his. You can tell him that your pretty face is a token of Duncan Cameron's esteem."

He climbed over her, kicking snow on her face as he walked back to his horse.

The sounds of horses crossing the stream filtered through her muddled mind. She tried to raise her head but pain swamped her. Her stomach revolted and nausea boiled up into her throat.

She closed her eyes and took small, steadying breaths until the nausea abated. Then she slowly rolled to her side and lay there for a long moment collecting her strength.

When she tried to get to her knees, she pitched forward. Tears of frustration bit angrily at her eyes. By all that was holy, she had to make it back to the keep even if she had to crawl.

She nearly passed out again when she pushed herself upward. She glanced up the hill and sighed wearily at the seemingly interminable distance.

And then she began to crawl.

CHAPTER 15

"My lady! My lady!"

It took all Rionna's effort to raise her head and stare ahead, though she couldn't make out who was yelling. Her right eye was nearly swollen shut and her vision was blurry out of the other one. Her ears still rung from the blows she'd received.

"Dear God, lass, what happened to you?"

"Hugh," she whispered. She made a feeble attempt to hold the tattered tunic to her breasts.

"Aye, lass, 'tis Hugh. Tell me what happened."

She licked her lips and tasted blood. "Men." Her voice was raspy, barely recognizable. Her throat was swollen from the attacker's grip. "Came across the brook."

"To arms!" Hugh roared.

Rionna pitched forward, the last of her strength gone as she listened to Hugh shout orders for the men to get to their horses.

"Rionna!"

Gentle hands touched her shoulders and carefully turned her. Then shoved the mass of hair from her swollen face.

"Oh, lass," Sarah moaned. "What has happened to you?"

"C-Cold. Help me inside."

"Nay, don't move. I'll have one of the men carry you. Does anything feel broken?"

For some reason Rionna found amusement in that. She grinned crookedly and promptly regretted moving any part of her mouth. "Just my face."

"Mangan, come carry your mistress to her chamber," Sarah ordered.

Rionna groaned when she was lifted by the burly warrior.

"'Tis sorry I am, lass," Mangan said gruffly. "I don't mean to hurt you."

"I'm fine, Mangan. Just a little bruised."

"'Tis disgraceful for a man to abuse a woman so," he growled.

"Aye, 'tis," she whispered. She shivered, remembering Caelen's reaction to her father striking her. He would be furious when he learned of the attack.

Mangan bore her inside and up the stairs, with Sarah and several serving women following along the entire way.

"Put her on the bed. Careful now!" Sarah said briskly. "Neda, fetch me warm water and rags and have hot water brought up for the lass to have a bath. She's going to catch a chill. Mangan, bring up wood for the fire. I need a brisk flame to warm her."

Rionna sank onto the bed and moaned softly. Now that she was safe and inside the keep, the battle to remain conscious was lost. The room grew dimmer and dimmer, and despite Sarah's attempt to keep her awake darkness crowded in and she let go with a weak sigh.

"'Tis a fine shot you made," Caelen said to James as he stood over the fallen stag. "Your father is right. You've a steady aim with a bow."

The younger man grinned in acknowledgment. "That

makes two. Three, counting the stag we sent back to the keep. One more and 'twill be enough meat for many weeks to come."

"Aye, perhaps on the morrow we'll down another one. 'Tis getting dark. We should seek a place to camp for the night and start a fire."

Little more than an hour later, the men sat in front of a warm fire with one leg of the stag roasting over the flames. Simon pulled a piece from the bone with his knife and tossed it toward Caelen.

Caelen took a bite and nodded in approval. "'Tis a fine piece of venison."

Simon carved pieces for the rest of the men until the bone was picked clean. Gannon hunkered down next to Caelen and leaned back against the log.

"It's been awhile since I've been on a long hunt. All I've done of late is trail after difficult women."

Caelen snorted and coughed as a piece of meat got stuck in his throat. Gannon pounded him on the back and both laughed.

"'Tis the truth I didn't envy your duty," Caelen said ruefully. "I took my turn at trailing after Mairin. 'Tis not something I want to do again. I oft wondered what bad thing you'd done to make my brothers choose you to look after their women."

Gannon shook his head. "And I've oft wondered if Cormac got himself married just to avoid the duty."

Caelen chuckled. "'Tis possible, I suppose. You have to admit Mairin ran him ragged."

Simon took a seat on the other side of Caelen as the rest of the men settled around the fire. "Tell me something, Laird. Do we stand a chance against the might of Duncan Cameron's army? Would we even be in his sights if we hadn't allied ourselves with your kin?"

Caelen's eyes narrowed at the innuendo. "Gregor approached us because he feared Cameron. This alliance was at his instigation."

"But you benefit."

"This is not intended as an insult, but the fact of the matter is, Gregor commanded a poor army. The benefit we see from this alliance is the joining of McCabe land on either side. McDonald land was all that separated Neamh Álainn from McCabe keep. But the main benefit is the other lairds who were willing to join with us once Gregor agreed to an alliance. Our strength is in our numbers and the McCabes' superior fighting force."

"You're a cocky lot," Simon said.

"There isn't a force who can match our skill," Caelen said bluntly.

"Then why do you wait to destroy Cameron?" James asked.

"Aye," one of the other men said as he sat forward. "Why wait?"

The other McDonald men who'd accompanied them on the hunt also leaned forward, taking a keen interest in the turn of the conversation.

"Because patience is required when vanquishing one's enemy," Caelen said. "We've waited many years to rid the world of Duncan Cameron. He's a dangerous, ambitious man who will stop at nothing to control all he sees. He's set his sights on our land. All of our land. We believe he has struck a bargain with Malcolm. If Malcolm leads another rebellion against David and takes the throne, Scotland will once more be split in two. Cameron's reward will be the highlands. He will in effect be king without the title while Malcolm will rule over Cumbria. No more will lairds rule over their own lands. Cameron's power would be absolute. No distinction. No legacy to hold for our children and our children's children. All would be controlled by him."

"We cannot allow this," James muttered.

"Nay, we cannot," Caelen agreed.

"And what of Gregor? Where has he gone? Where does his loyalty lie?" Simon asked.

Caelen turned his gaze on the older man. "That I do not know. He disappeared with many McDonald men. He was not content with the king's decree. We must be wary, not only of Cameron but of Gregor as well. He may well try to take back what he believes is rightfully his."

"We should have voted him out long since," Simon said grimly. "'Tis as much our fault. Aye, he was a poor laird and he did much damage to our clan, but we allowed it and we must answer to God for our sins."

"'Tis not too late to right the wrongs of the past," Caelen said. "Once we have provided food for our clan, we must turn our focus to strengthening our men. We must send a message to our enemies. We are not an easy conquest."

Simon leaned back and stared intently at Caelen. "'Tis the first time you've called it your clan, Laird."

Caelen's brows came together. "So it is. Perhaps 'tis settling well with me."

The men nodded their satisfaction. There was still wariness in their gazes, but Caelen felt as though he'd scored much needed headway with the men he now commanded. His acceptance wouldn't be overnight, but at least they weren't ignoring him outright.

Gannon put his hand on Caelen's arm and put his finger to his lips. The men immediately went quiet. Not waiting to hear for himself what had alarmed his commander, Caelen got to his feet and drew his sword.

The others followed suit, impressing Caelen with their speed and quiet. Perhaps they could be formed into skilled warriors yet.

"Laird! Laird! Laird Caelen!"

Hugh McDonald rode into the encampment, four

men right behind him. 'Twas evident the horse had been ridden hard and without rest. Hugh slid from the saddle and staggered in Caelen's direction.

Caelen resheathed his sword and grabbed the much larger man by his tunic. "What is it, Hugh? What has happened?"

"'Tis your wife, Laird."

Caelen's blood ran cold. "What mean you?"

Hugh caught his breath. "She was set upon by intruders two days past. They came across the brook between the two lochs. From the forest. They were hiding in the trees."

Caelen got into Hugh's face, his pulse pounding harshly at his temples. "Is she all right? Was she hurt? What did they do to her?"

"She was badly beaten, Laird. I know nothing more. I saw her when she crawled back to the courtyard, but I left soon after to pursue her attackers. When I lost their trail, I came directly to find you."

Caelen thrust him away, his hands shaking as he attempted to collect his thoughts.

"She is alive?"

"Aye, Laird. She was alive when I left. I do not think the injuries were serious enough to cause her death."

Caelen turned to Gannon. "You ride with me." Then he gestured at Simon. "You and the others pack the meat and return to the keep at once."

Gannon strode swiftly to ready the horses and Caelen turned back to Hugh. "Who were they?" he asked in a deadly voice.

"I know not that either, Laird. The lass barely spoke a word. I did not wait for her to relate the tale before I left in pursuit of the ones who launched the attack."

"You did right, Hugh."

Simon pushed forward, his expression serious. "Laird,

I would ride back with you and Gannon. 'Tis not safe for two men alone."

Caelen raised one eyebrow. "You seek to protect me?"

Simon paused a moment before he finally answered. "You're my laird. My duty is to watch your back at all times. I cannot do that if I am left behind."

"Very well, Simon. I'll be glad of your escort. Let us make haste so that I may see to my lady wife."

CHAPTER 16

The sun hadn't yet risen when Caelen, Gannon, and Simon rode into the courtyard. Caelen was off his horse before it had fully stopped. Sarah met him at the bottom of the steps leading into the keep.

"How is she?" he demanded.

Sarah wrung her hands, her face creased with worry. "Thank God you've come home, Laird. I don't know what to do with her. She's not left her chamber since the attack. She's not herself. She won't eat. She just sits and stares out her window."

Caelen grasped Sarah's arms, shaking her from her hysteria. "Is she well? How badly is she hurt?"

Tears shimmered in Sarah's eyes. "'Tis the truth I don't know what all was done to her. Once she regained consciousness she was so quiet. She refuses any company. She won't confide in me."

"I'll see to her," Caelen said as he brushed past Sarah. Dread gripped him as he hurried up the stairs. He realized when he reached the door to his chamber that he was afraid. It was an odd sensation and even odder to admit such. He'd watched his brothers go through hell with the women they loved, but he hadn't imagined he could feel that same fear that had gripped his brothers.

He shook his head. He'd feel concern for any woman

who'd been abused. And outrage that another man had dared to touch what was his.

He stood in the hallway, his hand raised to knock when he realized what he was doing. He dropped his hand and then opened the door.

He'd expected to find her asleep but when his gaze fell over the bed, it was empty. It didn't look as though she'd slept in it recently. He turned his head, scanning the room to find her sitting by the fire, her head cocked to the side.

His breath caught at the bruises shadowing her face. He could see only her profile, but her eye was swollen and even from across the room he could see fingerprints around her neck.

Carefully he shut the door, not wanting to awaken her. Then he crossed the room so that he could look more closely at her.

Sweet Jesu, but someone had sorely beat the lass. His hands tightened in rage as he stood over her. She looked so fragile. So delicate. How had she ever survived such brutality? Worse, just how much had been done to her?

His stomach heaved as he imagined just what could have occurred. Sarah had said she had closed herself off in her chamber ever since the attack and would confide in no one. Had she been violated?

His hand trembled as he reached out to caress her cheek. Dear God, he couldn't stand the thought of someone touching her. Of hurting her. He had to sit down on the stone hearth before his legs gave way.

She stirred when his hand left her face. Her eyelids blinked and then she squinted as if opening her right eye had caused her pain.

"Caelen," she whispered.

"Aye, lass, 'tis me. Are you well? Do you hurt still?"

She licked her lips and then raised a hand to massage her throat. The delicate movement only brought more attention to her fragility, and fury sizzled through him like a whip.

"I'm sore, but I am well. 'Tis nothing serious. Was your hunt successful?"

The formality of their conversation baffled Caelen. 'Twas as if nothing amiss had occurred during his absence and he'd come home to a polite greeting from his wife.

The shadows around her eyes troubled him, for they went deeper than the bruises. The fragility that he'd already noted was more pronounced the longer she was awake. There was something off about her, and now he realized why Sarah was so concerned.

"Rionna," he began gently. "Can you tell me what happened to you? 'Tis important I know all. Take your time. 'Tis no hurry for 'tis just you and I alone in our chamber. There is naught you can't tell me."

Her eyes flickered dispassionately as her gaze rested on him. He wanted to touch her but, God's teeth, he didn't know where he could lay hand on her that wouldn't hurt her.

"I was standing at the brook. When I looked up, I saw men on horses across the water. I knew I would never be able to run up the hill before they caught me so I ran along the bank, but they quickly caught up to me."

He slid his hand over the top of hers where it rested on her lap. He eased his fingers underneath hers and rubbed his thumb along her knuckles. Her hand was tiny in his, and he was reminded of how small and slight she was.

"One knocked me to the ground and backhanded me. I put my fingers in his eyes and scratched him."

"Good," Caelen said gruffly.

"I escaped a moment but was caught by another man."

For the first time, her voice wavered, fringed with emotion as she broke off and fixed her stare into the fire.

"'Twas naught I could do," she whispered. "He hit me. He tore my clothing. He . . . touched me," she choked out.

Caelen went completely still. He tried to swallow but couldn't manage it. "Did he rape you?"

She turned her gaze back on him, her eyes wide and startled. "Nay. He groped my breasts. He bruised me and humiliated me. He gave me a message for you."

Relief that she hadn't been molested was tempered by the fact that she'd still been sorely abused. And now it appeared as though it had all happened because someone wanted to hurt what was his.

"Tell me his message."

"He said that no McCabe is safe from Duncan Cameron. Not Mairin. Not Isabel. Not anyone who a McCabe calls dear. He said to tell you that my face is a token of Cameron's esteem."

He ground his teeth together so hard that he feared breaking them. His jaw ached as he tried valiantly to keep his rage at bay. His wife needed gentleness and understanding from him. Not a warrior bent on killing everyone in his path.

"What then, Rionna?" he asked gently.

Her eyes found his again, so dark and troubled. There was shame and pain in the golden depths. She looked . . . beaten. Not just in body, but in spirit. It was like a dagger to his gut.

"They left and I crawled up the hill to the courtyard. I don't remember much else."

His chest hurt. His stomach heaved. The idea that his proud, spirited wife was beaten so badly that she had to crawl on the ground like an animal. *Crawl.*

It was too much for him to bear.

He stood abruptly and turned away so she wouldn't see the ugly rage on his face. It took him a moment before he could breathe normally again. Then he turned back to see Rionna staring into the fire, so still and rigid.

He went back and knelt beside her, touching her chin until she turned to look at him. "Have you slept?"

She was confused by his question. Her eyes became cloudy. The fact that she couldn't answer told him that she likely hadn't slept at all beyond brief moments by the fire.

Not waiting longer for her to respond, he carefully looped his arms underneath her body and lifted her as gently as he was able. He held her close to his chest and rested his lips atop her head as he carried her to the bed.

He settled her onto the mattress and pulled the furs over her body so that she'd be warm. "I want you to rest. You have need of your sleep, Rionna. I'm here now. Nothing will hurt you."

She dutifully closed her eyes, but she was still tense. He leaned down and brushed his lips across her brow. "Sleep now, lass. I'll be here when you awaken."

At his words, she relaxed a bit and seemed to sink deeper into the bed. Some of the strain around her eyes and mouth eased and she let out a tiny sigh.

He stroked a hand over her hair until she seemed at ease and then he rose and backed from the bed. Her eyes opened and she locked her gaze with his.

"Be at ease, Rionna. I won't leave. I have need to speak with my men and to see your care. Sarah says you've refused food."

She didn't respond but the look in her eyes suggested she still had no desire to eat.

"You have to keep your strength up. I'm going to bring up some broth, something that won't hurt your mouth or jaw to chew. You'll eat it."

He expected sparks in her eyes at his command. He'd never issued one yet that hadn't elicited a scowl or outright defiance on her part. But her eyes remained dull, and she turned into her pillow, closing her eyes. He'd all but been dismissed.

Cursing under his breath, he turned to the door to find Gannon standing against the wall just outside. Gannon straightened when Caelen softly closed the door behind him.

"How is she?" Gannon asked.

"They beat the hell out of her," Caelen bit out.

"Who?"

"Cameron's men. They gave her a message to give to me. The sons of bitches brutalized her. There isn't a part of her face or neck that isn't bruised."

Anger glittered in Gannon's eyes. "Cameron has no compunction about waging war against women. But why now? Why Rionna? What is the point? Why not just attack? They obviously knew you'd gone out on the hunt."

"He wants to draw me out," Caelen said grimly. "He wants to make me angry enough that I do something foolish like charge after him in the dead of winter with inferior warriors, where if we survive the cold and starvation, we'd be easily defeated once we confront him at his holding."

"He must think you a fool," Gannon said in disgust.

"It matters naught what he thinks. What matters is what he will *know* when my sword slides through his heart."

"I think you may have to fight your brothers for that honor. He has brought much harm to Mairin and Keeley."

"And Rionna," Caelen said. "He thinks to weaken us through our women."

"'Tis not much mark of a man when he wages war against those weaker than himself."

"I want you to send word to Ewan and tell him what has happened. Tell him there are new threats against his wife and daughter and that Cameron has escalated his attacks. Then I want you to put men on an around-the-clock watch. I want someone watching all approaches to the keep at all times. I want you working with the men immediately. They're going to train and train hard. They should have plenty of motivation now if they had none before."

Gannon nodded and started down the hall.

"Tell Sarah to bring up water and broth for Rionna," he called after Gannon.

Gannon held up a hand in acknowledgment before disappearing down the stairs.

Caelen quietly reentered the chamber to check on Rionna. She hadn't moved from where he'd put her on the bed. The furs were pulled over her shoulders and her eyes were closed.

Wanting to see if she was truly sleeping, he leaned close and listened to her soft, even breathing. When she didn't stir, he drew away and went to add more wood to the fire so she'd be warm.

When the flames were blazing once more, he sank into the chair and bowed his head. He'd been so cavalier in leaving for the hunt. Food had seemed like the most important priority. He'd thought to feed his clan and *then* see to its protection. His first action and decision as laird and he'd made a huge mistake. A mistake his wife had paid dearly for.

CHAPTER 17

Rionna pressed gingerly at her still swollen eye, wincing when she touched a particularly sore spot. Caelen was below in the courtyard directing the training of the men. He'd left her after making sure she ate a good meal and instructing her to rest.

'Twas the truth, she'd had more rest over the last week than she could bear. She'd wallowed. She'd sulked. She'd dealt with her fear and her sense of failure. Now . . . Now she was just furious.

Furious with the men who'd trespassed on her lands. Furious with the cowardice of Duncan Cameron. Furious that she'd been rendered helpless against a vicious attack.

No longer could she accept her husband's decree that she become a meek, feminine version of whatever fantasy he'd built in his mind of the perfect wife. That wasn't who she was. He should have given more thought to stepping in to marry her if he wasn't prepared to accept a wife he considered wholly unsuitable.

She dressed in trews and a tunic she saved for what she viewed as special occasions. It was soft. No holes, no stains, and the hem was finely stitched.

It was overlayed in red velvet with gold stitching. It

had taken every coin she'd saved for three years, but it was the finest thing she'd ever owned.

She wiped at the dirt on her boots and rubbed a finger over the toe where the leather was so thin that a hole had nearly been worn. She had need of a new pair, but it was a luxury she couldn't contemplate, not when everyone else in her clan had shoes and boots just as worn, if not worse.

Still, she could dream of how a new pair would feel on her feet. Fur lined. She could practically feel the softness surrounding her toes.

She stood and her hand went automatically to her throat where she tested the soreness. It still hurt to swallow and her voice had a soft rasp that hadn't yet gone away. She probably looked a fright, but after so many days, she was ready to be out of her chamber.

She took to the stairs, feeling a moment's panic that she'd left the safety of her chamber. She stopped midway down, black dots swimming in front of her eyes as she panted for breath.

Such weakness infuriated her. She clenched her fist, slammed her eyes shut, her nostrils flaring as she sucked in deep breaths.

For too long she'd hidden in her chamber because the idea of going out terrified her. It was a weakness she'd never admit. The attack and the days following were a humiliation she'd live with for the rest of her life.

"My lady, you shouldn't be out of your chamber. Do you need my aid returning? Is there something you have need of? I would be happy to fetch it for you."

She glanced up to see Caelen's commander standing on the stairwell, blocking her path down. His hand gripped her arm and concern burned bright in his gaze.

She brushed off his hand with a push of her own and

nearly took a step back from the warrior before she caught herself. She forced her chin up and then leveled a calm stare at him.

"I am well and nay, I do not require anything. I'm on my way below stairs."

"Perhaps 'tis best to wait the laird. I'll summon him and tell him you'd like to leave your chamber."

She frowned. "Am I a prisoner in my own home? Am I not allowed out of my room without the laird's permission?"

"You mistake me, my lady. 'Tis my concern for your well-being that drives my statement. I'm sure the laird would want to escort you himself once he's ascertained whether you're well enough to be below stairs."

"I can ascertain for myself that I am well enough to be up and out of my chamber. Kindly remove yourself from my path so that I may continue downward."

Gannon didn't look happy with the dictate. He wavered a moment, clearly trying to decide whether he should cleave to his initial idea.

She wouldn't wait. Knowing he would do nothing to harm her, she pushed at his chest until he relented and stepped aside. He didn't allow her to pass, though. He cupped her elbow and took her hand in his, tucking it around his arm.

"At least allow me to escort you. I would not want you to fall on the stairs."

She nearly yanked her hand from his, so great was her frustration. But she was getting what she wanted and she didn't want to risk him forcing her back to her chamber and summoning Caelen, who'd likely burst a blood vessel over her apparel and the fact that she was out of bed.

When they reached the bottom, she retrieved her hand and hurried away from the warrior. She had no clear direction in mind, only that she wanted to be away from Gannon.

Fresh air was top on her list of priorities, but she couldn't go into the courtyard. Caelen was there training with the men. She opted to go through the kitchens and out the side where the distance between the keep and the stone skirt was greater and she could see the mountains in the distance.

Ignoring several of the women's surprised exclamations on her way out, Rionna breathed deep as soon as the crisp air hit her in the face.

It was heavenly. Freeing. Her throat and lungs seemed to open up and loose the horrid constriction she'd lived with for so many days.

She stepped into the snow, enjoying the loud crunch and the coldness seeping around her toes. Finally, she felt alive again. Reinvigorated.

The wind whipped at her hair and sent a shiver down her spine. She'd completely forgotten her cloak, so in a hurry had she been to get out of her chamber.

Clutching her arms around her waist for warmth, she walked along the wall of the keep, leaving small footprints in the fresh powder.

As a child, she had lain in the snow and made shapes with Keeley. They'd pretended to be snow princesses waiting for their prince to rescue them. He wore only the warmest furs and the finest clothing. His steed was unmatched in beauty and speed. He'd ride in, wrap her in his furs, and bear her away to a land where it was always warm and sunny.

Rionna laughed softly. Such imaginations she and Keeley had. Always with their heads in the clouds. The worst day in Rionna's life had been the day her father had attacked Keeley. And then Rionna's mother had cried Keeley a whore and banished her from the clan.

Keeley had been her only friend. The only other girl who'd understood Rionna's odd tendencies. Keeley had encouraged Rionna's practice with a bow. She'd applauded every time Rionna had struck the center of the target. She'd exclaimed over Rionna's skill with a knife, swearing that Rionna could hold off an entire army just by wielding a dagger.

Rionna had tried to teach Keeley those skills, warning that lasses needed to know how to protect themselves. But Keeley had laughed and said she was hopeless in such matters and that she would one day have her prince to protect her anyway.

Well, Keeley had gotten the prince, and Rionna had gotten the skills to protect herself. She wasn't sure who had come out ahead in the bargain.

She found a large bolder and eased down onto the cold surface. Her arse would freeze if she stayed long, but she wasn't quite ready for the confrontation that must be forced with her husband.

Caelen walked through the kitchens, his expression grim. Rionna shouldn't be below stairs yet. Hell, she shouldn't even be out of bed. He intended to keep her there at least another fortnight.

But what worried him more than her being out of bed was her state of mind. The attack had deeply affected her. She'd been quiet, reserved, timid even. And Rionna was not a timid lass. He feared that the attack had irrevocably changed her or damaged her in some way. And he was helpless to change it.

He stopped at the doorway leading outside, after the women in the kitchens reported that she'd not paused on her way out. As he stepped into the snow, he looked up to see her sitting in the distance, her back to him as she stared up at the mountains.

The knot he suffered so frequently since his return from the hunt clutched his throat as he watched her hair blow this way and that in the breeze.

She seemed so slight. Fragile. It was a word he kept coming back to over and over, but it aptly described her appearance.

She looked alone and vulnerable, as if she had no one in the world to protect her. No one *had* protected her when she'd needed it the most. It was something he'd have to live with for the rest of his life.

"Laird, do not be angry. What she wears is a comfort to her. She needs that right now."

Caelen turned in surprise at Sarah's words. The woman stood behind him, watching Rionna with worried eyes.

"Think you I give a damn what she wears? I'm more concerned with her well-being."

Sarah nodded approvingly and Caelen gestured her away.

He stepped softly through the snow, not wanting to frighten or disturb Rionna. He thought she resembled a doe, poised to run at the slightest sound or provocation. But as he drew closer, he could see the vacant, distant look in her eyes as she stared away from the keep.

Had the attack damaged her permanently? Would she never be right again? It was early to worry over such possibilities, but he couldn't help but wonder at how deep the scars would run.

"Rionna," he called softly.

He heard her quick intake of breath as if he had indeed startled her. She whirled around, her eyes a little wild until her gaze settled on him and then she quieted.

She went so still and continued to stare at him in a way that unsettled him. It was eerie. She studied him as if she were about to announce judgment on him and find him lacking. Perhaps 'twas his own guilt speaking volumes, but he couldn't shake the feeling that she was angry. Very, very angry.

"'Tis cold. You should be indoors where it's warm."

He slid a hand over her shoulder and squeezed, trying to bring her comfort.

To his surprise she laughed. 'Twas not a joyous sound that bubbled from her throat. It was harsh and hoarse. It sounded pained.

"You probably think I'm daft," she said.

"Nay," he said gently. "Not daft."

"You also probably think I'm a scared rabbit now, afraid to leave my chamber, afraid to venture outside for fear of being attacked again."

"Nay, lass. I think what you need is time to heal. Your courage will come."

She turned then and pinned those glowing eyes upon him until he felt unsettled by the directness of her gaze.

"I'm not afraid, Laird. 'Tis the truth I'm furious."

Anger was an appropriate response under the circumstances, and she did look furious. Sparks fair shot from her eyes and her entire body trembled. For the first time he relaxed, relief sudden and fierce. He knew how to respond to an angry Rionna. But the beaten, worn-down, fragile woman who'd occupied her body for the last week baffled and confused him.

"'Tis good you're angry," he offered sagely.

She shot to her feet and spun around, glaring at him. Her fists were formed into tight balls at her sides, and she looked like she wanted to take a swing at him.

"Even if 'tis *you* I'm furious with?"

Now *that* he wasn't prepared for. He frowned, knowing that he had to tread lightly here. The lass wasn't right yet. Her emotions were all over the place, and he didn't want to upset her further.

"'Tis sorry I am that I wasn't here to protect you, Rionna. 'Tis something I'll regret my life through. I should have better seen to your protection. 'Tis not a mistake I'll make again."

A garbled sound of rage roared from her throat. She looked as though she wanted to clench her fingers around her hair and pull.

"Nay, you shouldn't have protected me better, husband. What you should have done was allowed me to protect myself!"

"You're not making sense, lass. Calm down. Let's go inside. You should be above stairs in your chamber."

"Do you know what had just happened before those men attacked me?" she asked, ignoring his suggestion to return indoors. "I'll tell you what happened. My sword had just been taken by Hugh because he said he didn't want me to be harmed and 'twas not a womanly thing to be wielding a sword. He warned the other men that any who engaged me in swordplay would answer to him."

She advanced on Caelen and poked a finger into his chest. "If I had my sword, those men would have never gotten close to me. They wouldn't have shoved me to the snow. They wouldn't have touched me. They wouldn't have hit me."

Ah, but the lass had worked herself into a fit of rage that was impressive to behold. It shamed him that he fair quivered with lust as she bore down on him aggressively as a warrior about to deliver a death blow.

'Twas all he could do not to bear her into the snow and divest her of her tunic and those hated trews.

"If you wanted a meek lady of the manor with all the social niceties and the proper grooming and breeding to be a perfect hostess and compliment to you, then you should have thought before you stepped forward to marry in your brother's stead. He *knew* what he was getting."

She planted her hands on her hips and stepped forward again until her chest was pressed against his midsection.

"I am none of those things. I have no desire to be those things. I had set my mind to relent and to apply myself to be the perfect wife, and then the men came across the brook and overpowered me as easily as they would a child. What good am I to you or to my clan if I cannot even defend myself? How am I supposed to protect my kin? The children? The other women of the keep? Will I stand over the graves of others and murmur that I was a good wife and a gracious lady? Will that be of comfort to their families? Will they forgive that I stood by and allowed their loved one to die because my husband wanted a wife who could smile prettily and curtsy without getting her feet tangled?"

Caelen battled the smile that threatened. He bit at his bottom lip and valiantly tried to keep his amusement at bay, for if he laughed now, she might well spit him on her dagger.

'Twas the truth he should be angry at her blatant show of disrespect. He should even now be reprimanding her. But 'twas the first sign of life he'd seen in the week since her attack, and God's truth, she was glorious in her rage.

"Think you this is funny?" she demanded.

She shoved at him with all her might, surprising him with her sudden move. He went down in the snow, landing with a thud. He glared up at her as he dusted the snow from the tops of his legs.

She stood over him now, holding him captive with her fiery gaze. Then her expression became pained, and the shadows returned to her eyes.

"Let me be who I am, Caelen. I would not ask you to

change who you are. I can help you if you'd let me. Don't relegate me to the shadows, pulling me out only when 'tis convenient for you. Maybe 'tis the way of things in the world, but it doesn't have to be that way for *us*."

Caelen sighed as her impassioned plea made a direct hit to a region of his heart he'd long thought dead. "'Tis so important to you to dress as a man and wield a sword?"

She frowned and shook her head. "'Tis not the manner of dress that 'tis important. If you can show me how to successfully wield a sword in a woman's gown, I'll not gainsay you if you tell me not to wear this manner of dress again."

"You can't go about swinging a sword in a gown," Caelen muttered. "You'd trip over the hem."

For the first time she smiled, her eyes lighting up with more life than he'd seen in quite some time. "Then I have your permission to wear these garments?"

He sighed in disgust. "When have you ever sought my permission for anything, lass?"

"I can be accommodating," she defended.

He rolled his eyes. "When it suits your purposes, aye." Then he narrowed his gaze to stare intently at her. "There are conditions, Rionna. Henceforth, my commander will accompany you everywhere. And I mean everywhere. You'll go nowhere unescorted. I'll not have happen again what happened in my absence. If I have need of Gannon to accompany me, then Hugh will take over as your escort."

She nodded her acceptance.

"Second, you'll train with me and only with me. You are to spar with no other man. If you want to learn, you'll be trained by the best, and I won't be easy on you because you're my wife."

She grinned cheekily. "I would expect no less, husband."

"You'll not take to binding your breasts."

At that she raised an eyebrow and looked suspiciously at him.

He grinned lazily up at her. "'Tis not just for my pleasure. 'Tis nonsense. I may let you dress as a man, but you'll not try to look like one."

"Anything else, husband?" she asked as she tapped her foot in the snow.

"Aye, help me up."

With a roll of her eyes, she reached down to give him her hand. The lass would never learn. He grasped her wrist and with a quick yank, tossed her into the snow beside him.

She rose up, snow covering her face, blinking at him as if she had no idea why he'd done such. He merely smiled back. "Revenge, lass. Revenge."

With a disgusted look she launched herself at him, rolling them both into the snow. He gave a laugh and then came astride her. With a free hand, he balled some of the snow and held it menacingly over his shoulder.

"You wouldn't dare," she said.

He let fly and laughed again as she blinked away the snow from her face. It slid over her cheeks, revealing her look of shock. Then her eyes flashed with the light of battle.

Worried that her mistress and the laird had been out in the cold for so long, Sarah hurried to the doorway. When she opened the door, she was shocked to see the laird atop Rionna in the snow.

How could he have so little care when she was so fragile from her attack? The man had gone mad. It was on the tip of her tongue to issue a sharp reprimand to her laird when she heard Rionna's laughter ring out through the cold air.

Rionna rolled atop the laird and began stuffing snow in his face. The laird fought back and snow flew fast and furious.

A wide smile formed on Sarah's face and she quietly retreated back indoors, closing the door behind her to give them privacy.

CHAPTER 18

For the first time since the attack, Rionna came down to the hall for the evening meal. She could feel the stares of the men and women alike and it was all she could do not to cover the bruises and hie herself back up to her chamber.

But she'd spent enough time hiding. She wouldn't do so any longer.

Caelen looked up in surprise and then stood as she neared the table. The other warriors did the same and then Caelen motioned for Simon to vacate the seat so that Rionna could sit next to Caelen.

"I would have made sure you had your meal in our chamber," Caelen said in a low voice when he retook his seat.

She smiled. "'Tis sweet of you to attend me so, but 'tis time I came out of hiding. The bruises make me look hideous, but 'tis nothing wrong with the rest of me."

He tipped her chin upward and turned her face this way and that in the light, a pensive expression on his face. He didn't offer false compliments or tell her she really didn't look hideous. Strangely she found that comforting.

"The bruising is fading. In a few days' time, 'twill be completely gone."

His fingers rubbed over the faint fingerprints at her neck, and his nostrils flared before he pulled his hand away and resumed eating his meal.

At the meal's end, Rionna stood to excuse herself. The meal had been quiet, as if the men feared upsetting her in some way. It would take time to convince them she wasn't going to fall apart at the least provocation. 'Twas her fault they'd gained that impression with the way she'd acted, but how could she explain in words how helpless and angry she'd felt at the hands of her attackers?

'Twas not something the men would understand. She much preferred to move ahead and not dwell on past events. In time they'd forget as well.

Caelen stayed her with his hand and then nodded toward Gannon. "I'll go up with you," he said to Rionna, surprising her.

Caelen made a point of relaxing with the men after the evening meal. 'Twas his way of building camaraderie after a long day's training. He listened to their ideas, indulged in ribald jests, most of which made Rionna's eyes roll, and talked about the day's events. He and Gannon both made attempts to reach out to the McDonald warriors, a fact Rionna appreciated even if the men still hadn't fully accepted or embraced Caelen as laird.

But tonight he excused himself, his fingers still wrapped gently around Rionna's wrist. Then he guided her toward the stairs and they went up to their chamber.

"'Twasn't necessary for you to come up with me," Rionna said when he shut the door behind him.

"Aye, I know it. 'Twas my choice. Perhaps I preferred to converse with my wife instead of the men tonight."

She turned and rested her gaze on his face, searching his eyes for some sign of his intent. "Have you something specific in mind?"

"Perhaps. Make ready for bed, wife. You look tired. I'll add more wood to the fire, and we'll retire early this night."

Puzzled by his odd mood, she did as he bade and began to undress. She reached for her nightdress when he made a sound of disapproval. She looked up to see him bending over the hearth, wood in hand and shaking his head at her.

"Nay?"

"I would feel your skin next to mine."

'Twas not an unreasonable request, but tonight it made her feel shy and a little uncertain, and it angered her that she would feel this way.

As if sensing her uncertainty, Caelen rose from the hearth and crossed the room. Gently he took the night-dress from her grasp and laid it over the chair by the fire.

"I'll not make any demands of you, Rionna. I would do nothing to frighten you. But I've missed the feel of you next to me and your warmth and scent on my skin. I would have that tonight if it causes you no upset."

She put her hand on his chest and stared up at him, her heart going soft at the tenderness in his voice. "You do not frighten me, Caelen. 'Tis the truth I feel safest when I'm near to you."

He laid his hand over hers and then pulled it to his mouth. He kissed the inside of her palm and left it against his lips for a moment before lowering it once more.

"Come to bed. 'Tis cold tonight and the wind howls through the furs at the window."

Rionna climbed underneath the furs and watched as Caelen disrobed in the glow of the fire. When he turned to the bed, she pulled back the furs, an invitation.

As soon as he got into bed, she snuggled close, sighing as his warmth enveloped her.

Caelen chuckled against her hair. "You sound near to purring, wife."

"Mmm. You feel good, husband."

He laid the flat of his palm over her back and stroked up and down, his even breathing sounding close to her ear.

"I've been thinking on things," he said.

She frowned against his neck. A conversation never ended well that started with such words. She pulled away and his hand stilled on the small of her back.

"What matters have you been thinking on?"

"Tell me why you dress as you do and why you've put so much practice in with a sword."

Her eyes widened. Of all the subjects she thought he might broach, this wasn't one of them.

"'Tis plain to see you've devoted a lot of time to the practice of warfare. You have to admit 'tis an odd undertaking for a lass. Your father wasn't approving. I saw his reaction when you bested the McCabe warrior when you were visiting McCabe keep."

When she remained quiet, he stroked over her back again, his touch light and soothing.

"And now, when you were attacked and sorely beaten, a traumatic event for anyone, much less a lass as slight as you are, I thought it had made you afraid, but you were angry because you'd been stripped of the ability to defend yourself."

"Aye," she whispered. "It made me feel helpless. I hated it."

"What has made you so fierce in your determination to protect yourself, Rionna? 'Tis not something a lass usually thinks upon. 'Tis up to her kin, her father, brother, or husband to watch over her and protect her from harm, and yet you ask no one to do these things for you."

She closed her eyes as shame crowded in. Caelen knew

of her father's disgraceful actions, but saying her fears aloud only made it worse.

"Rionna?"

He pulled away and tipped her chin up so that he could look into her eyes. The candles he'd left burning provided just enough light that she could see his grim expression and the determination in his eyes to uncover her secrets.

She sighed and looked away. "You know what kind of man my father was. And that when my father tried to force himself on Keeley, my mother made her an outcast. She was my *cousin*. And Keeley wasn't the only young lass my father targeted. I knew of his evil from a very young age and I always feared . . ."

She sucked in a deep breath and looked back at Caelen. "All I could think was what if he turned his attention to me? If he could do such a thing to his niece, what would it matter if I was his daughter?

"I grew breasts at a young age. I had a pleasing shape that I knew men liked to look at. So I began to hide my attributes and make myself look more like a lad than a woman. And I learned to wield a sword because I swore if my father ever tried to force himself on me, I would be able to protect myself."

Anger and disgust simmered in Caelen's eyes. He touched her cheek, stroking his finger from her jawline to her temple and back down again.

"You were right to do so," he admitted. "His obsession with Keeley never ended. Even years later. He would have raped her just weeks past if I hadn't intervened when he dragged her into a chamber at McCabe keep."

"His desires are unnatural, and he cares not who he hurts. He thinks only of himself and his pleasure. I would kill him for what he did to Keeley alone."

"If he ever touches you again, whether in anger or with lust, I'll feed his carcass to the vultures."

"'Tis when you're not near that I worry," she said quietly.

"Aye, I know it, lass, and as much as it pains me to admit, you have a solid argument for why I should allow you to continue with your training. 'Tis the truth I gifted Mairin with a dagger so she would have means to protect herself. It only stands to reason I'd afford my wife the same opportunity and the skills to do so."

"Thank you," she said softly. "It means much that you support me in this."

"Don't thank me yet," he warned. "I'll not be easy on you just because you're a lass. If you are to protect yourself, then you'll have to learn to best a man twice your size and with twice your strength."

She nodded but he continued on.

"I'm a brutal taskmaster and I'll work you long and hard until you're ready to cry mercy. I'll expect the same from you that I expect from my men."

"Aye, I understand," she said. "Now hush and let me thank you properly, husband."

His eyebrow went up. "Define *properly.*"

She smiled and wrapped her arms around his strong body. "I don't think you'll issue any complaints."

CHAPTER 19

"Get up and try it again, Rionna."

Rionna staggered to her feet and rubbed her poor abused bottom. Her arm felt near to falling off. She'd long since lost feeling in her hand. She was so weary that her eyes crossed, and still, her husband pressed on.

There was no impatience in his command. He had to be the most patient man she'd ever come across. Even Hugh, when he'd instructed her, had often thrown up his hands and stomped away, grumbling about the impossibility of teaching a lass to fight.

But she'd shown him. Just like she'd shown all her father's men who'd mocked her early efforts. And she'd show her husband, who seemed determined to see how many times he could knock her on her butt.

The tip of her sword nearly dragged on the ground as she stepped forward to face Caelen again. But she was careful to prevent the blade from doing so. Caelen had already taught her a lesson about abusing her weapon.

"God's teeth, lass, you're making me daft," Gannon grumbled. "Pivot this time. You weigh naught. Should be easy for a lass your size to be quicker than a man of the laird's size. Use that quickness to your advantage."

Sucking in painful breaths, Rionna circled warily around her husband, looking for any movement.

"Stop. Just stop a moment, Caelen."

Caelen sighed and lowered his sword as Gannon strode forward.

"A word, my lady?"

Not trusting that this wasn't a trick devised by Caelen to distract her, she backed slowly away, holding her sword toward Caelen the whole time. Her husband grinned.

"She's learning, Gannon. Don't be overharsh."

"I just want this done with so we can go eat," Gannon muttered.

He drew Rionna to the side. "You're acting as though this is an exercise with set rules and parameters. Battle is anything but, lass. You circle Caelen waiting for him to make the first move and then you react. As a result you're always on the defensive and he always has the advantage. This time, you initiate the action. Go after him and use your quickness. You've not his strength. 'Tis foolhardy to try and stand your ground against a man who is three times your size. Think of other ways to compensate and be quick about it. I'm starving."

Rionna grinned. "I'll try my best not to further inconvenience you, Gannon."

"He'll stay here all night. Don't think he won't, lass. He'll either get the result he wants or he'll completely wear you down. Whichever comes first. My suggestion is to give him the result he wants so we can all go indoors where it's warmer."

"You're turning into an old woman."

"You best hope he never allows me to spar with you. I'll show you old woman. And I won't be as merciful as he's being."

She raised an eyebrow. "Who says he's being merciful? My arse would disagree that he's shown any mercy."

"You're not bleeding. That's merciful."

Rionna shrugged and turned back to face Caelen who stood waiting, no sign of fatigue or annoyance in his eyes. He looked as though he were on a casual outing. Nothing ruffled him. She wondered if he'd ever been caught off guard in his life.

Remembering Gannon's advice, she began to circle, just as she'd done every time before. There was truth in Gannon's words. She was predictable by the sheer fact that she performed the same ritual every time and waited for Caelen to strike.

Digging deep to find the last of her flagging strength, she raised her sword, let out a yell to rival any warrior, and charged.

Caelen grinned then let out a *whoop* of his own as their swords met. The clash could be heard all over the courtyard. Invigorated, Rionna thrust, parried, and kept driving him back, using her quickness and the fact that she swung a much lighter sword keep him from launching a counterattack.

Aye, he was on the defensive now. Just where she wanted him until he provided an opening.

Despite the frigid air, sweat poured from her brow. Her jaw ached from her clenched teeth and her eyes were narrowed in intense concentration.

Caelen swung his sword but she turned and thrust out her blade to block. The force drove her to one knee and before she could recover, with a flick of his wrist, he knocked the sword from her hand.

"Better, wife. But not good enough."

Deciding she'd had enough of that smug superiority, she ducked low and launched herself at him. She lined up her shoulder and hit him right below the waist.

He let out a string of curses that blistered her ears. Then he slipped to his knees, his hand cupping his cods. His sword fell from his other hand and landed in the snow.

Rionna stumbled back, retrieved her sword, and then put the tip to his neck. "Do you yield?"

"Hell yes, I yield or you'll likely slice off what's left of my cods."

The strain in his voice and the pain creasing his forehead might have ordinarily concerned her, but then she remembered the hours of hell he'd just put her through and all sympathy disappeared.

Gannon stepped forward, wheezing with laughter. Caelen sent him a dark scowl.

"Shut the hell up, Gannon."

Gannon let out another guffaw and then pounded Rionna on the back, nearly knocking her to the ground. "And that, my lady, is how you fell a warrior."

"Did you tell her to rearrange my balls?" Caelen demanded.

"Nay. I only told her to go on the offensive. I'd say she thinks well on her feet."

"Sweet Jesu," Caelen said as he struggled to his feet. "I was rather fond of that portion of my anatomy, wife."

Rionna grinned cheekily and then leaned close to Caelen so Gannon wouldn't overhear. "So was I. I do hope there's no permanent damage."

"Disrespectful baggage," Caelen complained. "'Tis a situation I'll remedy later."

Then he touched her cheek where one fading bruise still smudged her skin. "Do your injuries still pain you? Did you overreach today with your training?"

"Nay," she whispered. "'Tis naught but a twinge now and then. 'Tis been a fortnight and I can see near to perfect from my eye again."

"Laird! A messenger approaches the gates!"

Caelen shoved her against Gannon and picked up his sword from the snow. "Take her inside at once and alert the rest of the men."

Knowing this wasn't the time to protest, Rionna allowed Gannon to hustle her inside the keep. He relinquished her in the hall next to the fire and then he shouted orders that were echoed throughout the keep.

"My lady, what is about?" Sarah asked as she hurried into the hall.

"I know not, Sarah. A messenger approaches our gate. We'll know when the laird tells us what is happening."

"Sit then and let me bring you hot broth. You tremble with cold and your clothing is wet through. Warm yourself by the fire before you catch your death of cold."

Rionna looked down at her bedraggled clothing and shook her head ruefully. She'd put in a hard day's work. She hadn't even registered the dampness spreading over her clothing, but now that Sarah had mentioned it, Rionna could feel the chill wrought by the wet material clinging to her body.

She moved closer to the fire and stretched out her hands as the keep buzzed with activity around her. She sighed as some of the heat thawed her fingertips and warmth traveled up her arms.

She turned when she heard her husband's footsteps. How quickly she'd become attuned to him. She knew even with her back turned that he'd entered the room.

"Is aught amiss?" she asked.

"Nay. 'Twas a McCabe man bearing a message from my brother. He is to arrive soon and requested shelter. He travels to Neamh Álainn with Mairin, Crispen, and Isabel."

"In this weather?"

It shocked Rionna that Ewan would chance traveling in such conditions when Isabel was so young.

"He fears waiting longer. I sent him word of your attack and the message they delivered. He wants them safely ensconced at Neamh Álainn where he can avail himself of the contingent of soldiers who have guarded the holding since Alexander's death."

"I would excuse myself to see to their arrival," Rionna murmured.

Caelen nodded then turned to Gannon. The two men strode from the hall, deep in conversation. Rionna took a deep breath and tried to recall the few lessons that Sarah had imparted. She instructed the women to ready food and drink. Thank God, Caelen had been successful in his hunt. Now they wouldn't shame Caelen in front of his kin by setting an inferior table.

She set several of the women to cleaning the hall. The fire was built up and the furs shoved aside to usher in cleaner, sweet-smelling air.

Content that the women knew their tasks and would perform them quickly, Rionna hurried up the stairs to her chamber to change her clothing.

She wet cloths in the washbasin and wiped the sweat and dirt from her face and body. She shivered as chill bumps dotted her damp flesh and she hurried to pull on a gown from her wardrobe. It was the first opportunity she'd had to wear one of the dresses Sarah and the other women had altered for her and she was well satisfied with the result.

Caelen would find no fault with her appearance. She looked every bit the lady of the keep. He had made concessions—important concessions—for her, and she felt compelled to do the same for him.

She sat by the fire and brushed out her hair until it

sparkled and shone like liquid gold. Then she plaited the long tresses and used a leather tie to secure the end.

Satisfied that she looked presentable, she rose and hurried back down to oversee the preparations.

The hall was busy as the tables and floors were hurriedly cleaned. Just airing the room out had made a remarkable difference.

"Venison stew is being warmed and we have several loaves of bread leftover from the noon meal. We even have a bit of cheese left that I put back for just such an occasion," Sarah told Rionna.

"And ale? Have we a sufficient amount for our guests? Have one of the men melt some snow for fresh water."

Sarah nodded and hurried away once more.

An hour later, Caelen strode back into the hall and searched out Rionna. His eyes widened and the glint of approval warmed her to her toes.

"They're riding to our gate now. Gannon and I will go out to greet them. You stay inside where it's warm."

She smiled up at him and then nodded.

Caelen sniffed the air appreciatively and then glanced around the hall. Then he leaned in and brushed his mouth over her temple. "Thank you for making my brother and his wife welcome."

An odd flutter began in her belly and worked its way up to her throat as he walked away.

"Warm some cider in case Lady McCabe would like a hot drink by the fire," Rionna said to Sarah. "And have ale ready to pour for the men."

Rionna paced back and forth as she waited for Caelen to return with his guests. She'd never suffered such unease when she and her father had traveled to McCabe land. But she hadn't cared about impressing them. Such was not the case now. They were coming to her keep, her home, and how they viewed her reflected on Caelen, and it was suddenly all important to her not to shame her husband.

She wanted him to be proud of her, to look upon her with favor and not find fault.

Several long moments later, the door burst open and Ewan McCabe hurried inside with Mairin and his son, Crispen, tucked against his side. Rionna rushed forward to take Mairin's arm.

"Come by the fire before you unwrap the babe," Rionna urged. "I have cider waiting."

Ewan took Crispen with him to the table where the men had already gathered, as Rionna ushered Mairin toward the hearth.

Mairin gifted her with a sweet smile. "'Tis good of you to offer, Rionna. 'Tis the truth I'm cold to my bones."

She and Mairin stopped in front of the fire and Mairin began unwrapping the heavy furs from around her. Nestled against her bosom was baby Isabel, sound asleep, looking remarkably unperturbed by all the goings on.

Rionna was transfixed by the babe. She was a beautiful lass, with a head full of black hair just like her parents. Tiny, delicate features and a bow-shaped mouth.

Mairin reached out to gently touch Rionna's eye. Startled, Rionna drew away and stared at the other woman.

"'Tis sorry I am you were drawn into our fight," Mairin said in a low voice. "Caelen said you were badly beaten."

Rionna pressed her lips together in a frown. "Nay, 'tis my fight as well. I'm married to a McCabe."

Mairin smiled. "Caelen is lucky to have one as fierce

as you. I worried so about him leaving our clan to become laird here, but I think my worry is misplaced. You'll keep him safe."

"Aye, I will. I'll not let harm come to him, if I can help it."

Mairin squeezed Rionna's hand and then let out a weary sigh that spurred Rionna to action. "Please do sit," she urged Mairin.

Mairin nodded gratefully. "Isabel will be wanting her meal soon. We've traveled since yesterday morn. Ewan was afraid to stop."

Rionna waved to one of the men standing nearby and bid him to add wood to the fire. Then she sent one of the women for cider.

"The meal will soon be served," she told Mairin.

"Don't think me ungrateful, but 'tis the truth I'd prefer to sit by the fire. I'm too tired to go to the table and 'twill be more comfortable here holding Isabel."

"I'll sit with you and hold the babe while you eat," Rionna replied. "The men can have the table so they can discuss matters. 'Tis likely they'll be at it all night. You and I can escape upstairs and they'll never notice."

Mairin chuckled. "Aye, I think you're right. Thank you, Rionna. You're sweet to look after me so."

Rionna's cheeks warmed at the other woman's praise. She glanced over at Caelen, expecting to find him deep in conversation with his brother, but to her surprise, she found him watching her and Mairin, a most peculiar expression on his face.

She smiled hesitantly. He nodded in her direction, but his gaze continued to linger as she looked away.

"You must tell me how marriage is suiting you, Rionna. I must confess you look quite well. And . . . happy. You have a glow about you that was absent before. You've always been a beautiful lass, but now you outshine the sun."

Flustered by Mairin's words, Rionna ducked her head and then reached clumsily for Isabel when Sarah arrived with cider and a trencher for Mairin.

The babe squawked in protest but then nuzzled against Rionna's breast when Rionna held her close. Mairin chuckled. "She's not a picky child. Any breast will do. 'Tis amusing to watch Ewan's face when she roots against his chest."

Rionna laughed softly and touched her fingertip to Isabel's tiny palm. Isabel promptly curled her fingers tight around Rionna's finger and waved it about as her unfocused gaze found Rionna.

"She's just beautiful, Mairin." Rionna sighed.

"I thank you. She is a true treasure. Ewan and I delight in her every day."

It was hard to hold Isabel and not imagine holding her own babe in her arms one day. A son or daughter with Caelen's green eyes. Aye, that would be perfect.

Mayhap she was already breeding.

The thought sent a jolt through her veins, shocking in its discovery.

Could she be carrying his child already? It had been some weeks since they'd arrived here on McDonald land. Even now, a child could be growing in her womb.

She slid her hand from Isabel's bottom to her flat belly and splayed out her fingers. 'Twas a marvel she hadn't considered it until now.

Oh, she knew children were inevitable if God chose to bestow such a gift on them. But she hadn't considered that it could happen so soon, even though Caelen had all but guaranteed she'd deliver a child within a year of their marriage.

She'd thought his prideful statement to be a natural boast of a newly married man.

She caught her bottom lip between her teeth and nibbled as she contemplated the possibilities. She knew it was her duty to provide heirs for Caelen. 'Twas a duty she owed her clan as well, to provide them with the next laird.

But 'twas God's truth, she wasn't sure she was up to the task quite yet.

It wouldn't cause her distress if 'twas a little while longer before her womb bore fruit.

CHAPTER 20

Rionna was fair to falling over by the time Caelen sought their chamber. She'd sat by the fire yawning for the past hour, waiting for him to come to bed.

When he opened the door and stepped inside, he looked surprised to see her. Then a faint frown drew his brows together.

"You shouldn't have waited up for me. 'Tis late and you have need of your rest."

It would have been a thoughtful statement if he hadn't accentuated it with that frown.

Ignoring his gruffness, she rose and went to help him undress. He went still as she unlaced the leather ties of his trews. So still that she wasn't sure he was even breathing.

When her fingers brushed his firm belly, he flinched. She was sorely tempted to run her palm up his midriff to his chest, but she was going to properly attend him first.

She guided him toward the chair she'd vacated by the fire and urged him down. He watched through half-lidded eyes as she tugged at his tunic and then pulled it over his head, baring his broad, hair-roughened chest.

She sucked in her breath. The man was beautiful. Never had she seen his equal. She fingered a puckered scar across his right shoulder and slid her hand lower to a much older, nearly flat scar on his left flank. She frowned as she studied it. 'Twas a knife wound.

"Someone stabbed you from behind," she mused as she knelt to give it a closer look.

He stiffened, his muscles coiling and going rigid. His profile was set in stone as he stared into the fire.

"Aye."

She waited but he offered nothing more.

"Who did this?"

"No one of import."

She leaned forward and kissed the scar. He reacted in surprise, turning, his arm raised so he didn't elbow her in the head. Then he lowered his hand to her hair and stroked his fingers through the strands.

He ran his fingers over her jaw and then cupped her chin, tilting it so that she looked up at him. A teasing glint twinkled in his green eyes.

"I barely recognize the woman before me. She's acting almost like a wife. What has happened to my fierce warrior? I came in to a fine table. The lady of the keep directed the welcoming of my kin and she played hostess to my brother's wife. And if that wasn't enough, she awaited me in my chamber to attend me with a gentle hand and a soft mouth?"

She scowled up at him. "'Tis true what they say of men."

He raised an eyebrow. "Oh?"

"Aye. They never know when to keep their mouths shut."

He chuckled and rubbed his thumb over her bottom lip and then lowered his mouth to hers until they touched in a most gentle fashion.

"I was proud of you this day, Rionna. You speak of having none of the social graces of a lady and yet you performed as a laird's wife would be expected."

"I would not shame you in front of your kin," she whispered.

He kissed her again and then drew away to pull at his boots. When he was done, he sat there, laces undone at his waist, shirtless, his flesh gleaming in the firelight. He was a feast for her eyes and she was determined that on this night she'd have him.

Her gaze skittered downward to the bulge at the apex of his thighs. With only a little encouragement, he would be free of his trews.

"I've been thinking."

Caelen regarded her lazily, the spark of amusement back in his gaze. "'Tis a universal truth that when a lass says she's been thinking, a man ought to be wary."

She moved between his legs and ran her hand up his thigh to cup him intimately. "I was thinking that since I did harm to a portion of your anatomy you favored that I could make it up to you. But if you're wary. . . ."

He caught his breath. "Nay. Not wary. Not wary at all." Then he reached down to cup her chin again, his thumb brushing over the spot where her bruising was fading. "Are you sure 'tis something you wish to do, lass?"

Her heart clenched at the concern in his voice. He'd treated her with the utmost care since her attack. He'd only touched her to offer comfort or to ensure himself that she was all right. It was almost as if he'd worried that he would frighten her or remind her in some way of the men who had hurt her.

"'Tis my wish that you allow me to have my way this night."

"Your way? 'Tis the truth I'll grant such a wish every night if you desire it."

She reached inside his clothing and caressed the long, rigid length of him. His breath hissed out in the silence. He gripped her shoulders with both hands and then abruptly stood. In a moment's time he'd torn the offending material from his body and tossed it across the room.

Her gaze slid up his body, illuminated by flame, so exquisitely rendered. The body of a warrior, not a lad. Heavily muscled. Scarred. Rough.

At his groin, his manhood extended from the dark whorl of hair, thick and heavy.

"'Tis a sight destined to seduce a man," Caelen rasped as he stared down at her kneeling at his feet.

She smiled. "You like a woman at your feet?"

"I'm not a stupid man. Admitting such would be akin to cutting off my cods."

She shifted and rose up, her hands skimming along the outsides of his thighs. "But you like it."

He groaned when she cupped his sac and massaged the weight in her hand.

"Aye, I like it. I like it very much. 'Tis no sweeter sight than you between my legs on your knees ready to pleasure me."

Tentatively she circled his length with her other hand and lightly caressed. 'Twas the truth that she'd begun this seduction, but she had no idea how to go through with it. Keeley hadn't been overly detailed with the how. Just what to do in the beginning.

Caelen was a man who valued control. He liked the sight of her on her knees enough. 'Twas clear he liked a submissive wife. 'Twas entirely possible that the best seduction she could give him would be to allow him to conduct it. And then she wouldn't have to admit just how ignorant she was of such matters.

"Instruct me, husband," she said in a husky, sweet voice she hoped was pleasing. "Show me what you like for your lass to do."

The flicker in his eyes should have alarmed her. 'Twas a fierce, animalistic light that sent a shiver down her spine. His fingers tangled in her hair and he pulled back just enough that her head tilted back and her neck arched forward as she stared up at him.

"I want you naked so I may look upon you and know that every inch of your beauty is mine."

"May I rise then so that I may do your bidding, husband?"

She watched desire smolder like coals in his eyes and realized that the coy game she played pleased her husband very much. The intricacies of a man's mind never ceased to fascinate her.

Not awaiting his answer—'twas needless after all— she slowly got to her feet and then backed away a pace so that the warmth from the fire flickered over her skin.

Hiding her smile, she turned until her back was presented to him and then she began untying the sash at her waist. She glanced over her shoulder to find him watching her with avid fascination.

"I have need of your help, husband."

His hands shook against her nape as he unfastened her dress. When he'd undone enough that she could step from the folds of the material, she let it fall to the floor so that she stood in only her undergown.

Turning so that she faced him once more, she reached up and threaded her fingers underneath the straps over her shoulders. Then she hesitated before pulling ever so slowly until they eased over her shoulders and down her arms.

The neckline caught at her breasts but with a gentle tug, it slid over her nipples and fell into a pool at her feet.

"Now shall I attend you, husband?"

"Oh aye, wife. Aye, indeed."

She slid to her knees in front of him, her hands gliding down the sides of his legs. She memorized every swell, the bulge of his muscles, the uneven puckers of scars, new and old.

Then she tilted her head back and stared up at him. "Show me what pleases you."

"God's teeth, but you're beautiful, lass. Your eyes shine like a thousand sunsets. And your mouth, so perfectly formed. I cannot wait another moment to feel such sweetness around my flesh."

He grasped his straining erection with one hand and cupped her nape with his other before guiding himself toward her mouth. Such intimacy shocked her, though it shouldn't. After all, he'd loved her thoroughly with his own lips and tongue until she'd been senseless with pleasure.

The idea that she could make him just as insensible thrilled her. She licked over her lips in a nervous gesture just as the tip of his cock brushed against her mouth.

"Open for me, lass. Take me inside your heat."

His husky drawl drifted over her, bringing her body alive with the images his request invoked. She was alternately nervous and excited. And restless. She wanted to rub her body against his and purr her satisfaction like a cat being stroked.

She parted her lips and tentatively took him on her tongue. His fingers rubbed impatiently at her nape and then threaded upward into her hair.

Growing bolder and more confident in his reaction, she slid her lips farther up the base, taking more of him into her mouth. 'Twas a sensation like she'd never imagined. She shook from head to toe, her body tight and aching with need.

Letting her instincts guide her, she began to suck lightly, using her tongue to further torment him. His taste was wholly masculine and a hint of musk danced through her nostrils.

The sound that came from his throat was one of agony. His hand tightened in her hair and he moved his other hand from his cock and cupped her face as he slid deeper into her mouth.

"I've never known such fire and sweetness," he said behind clenched teeth. "You are a temptress, wife. 'Tis the truth you kneel at my feet, but 'tis I who am for all practical purposes at yours."

His words brought her feminine power roaring to life. She'd always considered that embracing her womanhood somehow made her weak, but 'twas the truth, she'd never felt more powerful than at this moment.

Here was this man, a fierce warrior, and he was completely and utterly at her mercy. She held his pleasure, his pain, his satisfaction in her very hands.

She curled her fingers around the base of his manhood and followed the path of her mouth, up and down, exerting pressure as she served him with her lips and tongue.

He dragged both hands over her head, clenching and unclenching as if he were in unspeakable agony. His face was drawn into harsh lines and his head thrown back, eyes closed as he thrust his hips forward.

She sucked to the tip and pulled his erection away before leaning in to press her lips and tongue to the plump vein on the underside. She licked a sensual trail from base to tip before sucking the head back into her mouth.

Warm liquid seeped onto her tongue as his harsh groan split the air.

"You're going to be the death of me, wife. Cease this torture, for I cannot take any more."

"I know not what you speak of, husband," she said innocently. "'Tis for you to show me the way of things."

He reached down, grasped her arms, and dragged her up his body. He found her mouth in a heated, impatient rush. Breathless. Raw. Bone-melting and shiver-inducing.

She wrapped her arms around his neck and returned his kiss with a fervor equal to his own.

He turned and carried her to the bed, his mouth never leaving hers. "'Tis what I like most about you, lass. You give no quarter in loving. You're so passionate and wild in your responses."

She landed with a thump and he came down over her, his body pressing urgently to hers.

"And here I thought 'twas my submissive side you liked so well," she teased.

"'Tis the entire package. You can be so devilishly coy and yet so sweetly innocent that you make me daft with wanting."

He kissed her neck, sucking wetly at her pulse before nibbling a path to her ear.

"You're an unselfish lass. Willing to do much to please me. I've never had a woman willing to put my pleasure before hers."

She thumped him on the chest and scowled. "Now 'tis not the time to speak of other women. Even if I compare more favorably."

He chuckled and lowered his mouth to her breast. 'Twas her turn to groan as he sucked at one nipple. He teased it over and over, sucking and nipping, alternating until she writhed beneath him and begged him to cease his torment.

"I've considered the next way you may please me, wife."

She regarded him suspiciously.

He toyed with her breasts, touching the plump swells and then tracing lines around her nipples.

"You have beautiful breasts. So very beautiful. I wager they're the most perfect breasts I've ever seen."

"Again with the comparisons," she growled. "'Twould seem you're destined to bring harm to that portion of your anatomy you love so."

He grinned and then rolled, bringing her atop him.

She sprawled rather indelicately across his body, her hair spilling over his chest.

"I am trying to pay homage to your beauty."

"Perhaps you could just say I am beautiful and that my breasts are incomparable and that my face is worthy of a bard's poem. No need to bring other women into it."

"You are beautiful. Your breasts are incomparable. Truly, truly incomparable . . ."

She thumped him on the chest and broke into laughter. "Enough. Now tell me this way you mentioned to please you."

"'Tis a simple enough thing," he murmured as he curled his fingers around her hips. He lifted and positioned her so that his erection was tucked against her opening. Her eyes went wide as she caught on to his intention. "You simply ease down . . . here . . ." he breathed as he slid inside her. "And then you ride me."

She braced her palms on his shoulders, her entire body rigid as she adjusted to the unfamiliar position.

"Surely such a thing is not done," she whispered as she stared down into his eyes that were cloudy with pleasure.

"I care not if such a thing is not done. 'Tis done here."

"Some might consider me a wanton for indulging in such activities," she said primly.

He groaned and closed his eyes when she clenched down on his cock. "I care not what others think. Only what I think. And what I think is that you astride me is the most desirable thing I've ever encountered in my life."

"Oh very good," she murmured as she leaned forward. "See? You didn't ruin it by saying that me astride you was better than the other women you've had astride you."

His body shook with laughter and he wrapped his

arms around her to pull her down to his chest. "'Tis an easy omission since you're the only lass to ever have me between her knees thus."

"Then I must make the experience a memorable one."

"Aye, indeed. By all means."

"I mean to have you insensible," she warned as she took his mouth with hers. She kissed him, tangling her tongue wetly with his.

"Lass, if you make me any more insensible, I'll be a blithering idiot."

Mimicking his earlier attentions, she grazed his neck with her teeth and kissed her way up to his ear. He went even more rigid inside her, stretching her until she was unbearably tight around him. Such delicious friction. She moved the tiniest bit and they both let out sighs as she tugged relentlessly at his length.

His arms felt so strong around her. She felt safe. Protected. Cherished even. 'Twas a wondrous sensation. One she didn't want to end.

Astride her warrior, she didn't feel small and insignificant. The look in his eyes, the tight coiling of his body told her that he enjoyed her wanton seduction. And in this moment, 'twas all she desired. To please him and make him want her more than he'd ever wanted another woman.

If she had her way, he'd never even consider another female. Forgotten would be the one he used to love, the one who had betrayed him. Rionna would prove to Caelen that she was fierce and loyal and that she'd never waver.

He would love her. It was a vow she made herself.

She would give him every reason to love her. She would fight beside him to make their clan strong, but she'd also be a proper wife, as proper a wife as she knew how to be in the privacy of their chambers. She'd even temper her demeanor outside the bedroom, if 'twas a more submissive wife he wanted.

"How close are you to your woman's pleasure, wife?"

"'Tis not important," she whispered against his mouth. "'Tis your pleasure that is important this night."

"Your pleasure *is* my pleasure," he murmured back.

Oh, but the man knew exactly how to pierce a woman's heart.

"Then 'tis not long I think. 'Tis the truth each time I move I feel as though I'm going to tumble down a steep mountain."

"Then let go, lass, because I already have one foot over that peak."

She fused her mouth to his as his arms tightened around her. She rocked forward and then back, moaning into his mouth as bliss flooded her veins, warm and whispering to her of deeper, darker pleasures to be had.

He gripped her hips, and his fingers dug into her buttocks. She was sure she'd wear his marks tomorrow, and it only heightened her excitement.

He took over, pulling her downward as he bucked upward into her body. Hot and slick. The sharp slap of flesh meeting flesh echoed through the chamber. Their low sighs and moans rose erotically and danced in time with the flames from the fire.

He slammed her back down and held her tightly, so tightly she felt stretched in places he'd never reached before. His large hand splayed over the swell of her behind and he squeezed and caressed, his touch firm and possessive.

Unable to keep still, she bucked and writhed over him, squirming, undulating until she knew not what she did.

When she finally regained awareness, she was sprawled limply over her husband's chest, her hair covering her face as he ran one hand idly up and down her back in a soothing, caressing motion.

They were still tightly joined. Indeed, he was still hard within her, even though the sticky feel between them told her that he'd found his release as well.

He kissed the top of her head and gently smoothed the hair from her face. "I find I like this submissive side of you, wife. 'Tis pleasing when you obey my every command."

She snorted at the amusement in his voice, but she was too sated and tired to move a muscle.

"And you make a fine pillow, husband. I plan to sleep here tonight."

His hold tightened around her and his cock pulsed once again deep inside her.

"'Tis a good thing, because I have no plans for you to move."

CHAPTER 21

Rionna woke to hands at her hips and a rigid cock sliding deep into her sheath. She gasped and came more fully awake, blinking as pleasure sizzled through her body.

She was belly down on the bed, face turned sideways with her legs over the side. Her behind was perched high in the air, held up by his firm grip.

Caelen stood behind her, mounted over her, tucked deep inside her body. He uttered not a single word as he pushed into her again and again.

His silent intensity only spurred her excitement to greater heights. He was firm, unyielding. The thoughtful, careful lover of before had been replaced by a fierce warrior intent on slaking his own desire.

Her release, when it came, shocked her. It happened so fast, and was so sharp, it took her breath away, leaving her panting and sagging against the bed.

Still, he hauled her up higher, supporting her as he continued to drive into her, over and over. Pleasure stirred within her once more, rising and tightening her body all over again.

He leaned over her until she could feel the ripple of each and every muscle. Tension whipped through his body and bled into hers. Then he let go of her hips and planted his hands on either side of her shoulders. She fell forward and he came with her, still thrusting deeply.

A shudder rolled through him and then he stilled, deep inside her. He pulsed and warmth flooded her, easing his passage. She went slick around him and uttered a soft moan as he strained against her.

Then he raised himself just enough that he pressed a gentle kiss to the center of her back.

"Sleep now," he whispered. "'Tis too early for you to rise yet."

He eased out of her and returned a moment later with a damp cloth and cleansed her. When he was done, he positioned her properly in the bed and tucked the heavy furs around her.

She listened as he dressed in the dark. He added more logs to the fire and stoked it until the flames burned brightly. Then he quietly left the chamber, leaving her to sleep once more.

She snuggled deeper into the warmth, her body still tingling from his masterful possession. This time when she drifted back to sleep, a smile curved her lips.

"You're up late this morn, Caelen," Ewan said when Caelen entered the hall.

Caelen eyed his brother, who sat by the fire breaking his fast. "I was detained."

Ewan smothered a grin and nodded. "Aye, 'tis interesting how that happens when a man is married, is it not?"

"Shut the hell up," Caelen growled.

Ewan sobered when Caelen took his seat and motioned for his goblet to be filled. "I'll not tarry long, Caelen. I want to reach Neamh Álainn as soon as possible. Cameron would use this opportunity to attack us as we travel. We departed McCabe land in the middle of the night and traveled straight through without stopping. I plan to do the same tonight."

"Is there anything I can do?"

Ewan shook his head. "Nay, you have much to do here. How goes it thus far? How does Rionna fair after her attack?"

Caelen frowned. "The lass was badly beaten. 'Twas a coward's attack meant to anger me into foolhardy action. Cameron seeks to lure me to him. He has no desire to launch an attack in winter. He remains behind the walls of his keep, warm and sated with food while he has hired mercenaries to do his cowardly deeds for him."

"Have you any luck in training the McDonald soldiers?"

Caelen sighed. "They work hard and are diligent in their efforts. 'Tis not that they aren't worthy soldiers. They've just not had proper training until now. 'Tis hard to correct years' worth of inefficiency in a few week's time."

Ewan clapped his hand on his brother's shoulder. "If anyone can do it, you can. I have every faith in your ability to fashion your men into a formidable army of warriors."

"How does Alaric fare?"

"He's taken over the duties of laird as if he were born to the position. The clan is in good hands. He will be a good laird and Keeley will be a credit to him."

"'Tis good that he is happy," Caelen murmured.

Ewan glanced sharply at his younger brother. "And you, Caelen? Are you well satisfied with your marriage and your position as laird?"

Caelen thought for a moment. He hadn't stopped to

analyze whether or not he was well content with his new wife and clan. There had been too much to tend to. Was he happy? Before, his happiness hadn't come into the picture. It mattered not whether he was happy. It only mattered that the alliance would be kept and that he would be able to aid his brother in the fight against Duncan Cameron.

Happy?

He frowned.

"'Twas not a trick question I was putting to you," Ewan said dryly.

"It matters not if I'm happy. What matters is that we have the might to destroy Cameron. I have more reason than ever to want his blood."

"Aye, you do," Ewan agreed. "We all do. He's brought much harm to our clans. To our wives."

"He killed our father."

Ewan sighed. "You cannot still blame yourself for that, Caelen."

"'Tis not a martyr I make of myself. I was young and foolish and we all paid the price. The signs were there for me to see but I purposely blinded myself to them. Our clan paid the price. We lost our father and you lost your wife. Crispen lost his mother."

"I have never blamed you," Ewan said in a low voice. "Not once. If Elsepeth hadn't done the deed, Cameron would have found another way."

Impatient with recounting the past, Caelen waved his hand dismissively. He didn't like to dwell on just how young and stupid he'd been. Elsepeth had found an easy mark in him. She'd turned his head, seduced him, and kept him under her spell. He would have done anything for her.

He'd loved her.

He still winced when he made that admission, but he

made it freely to remind himself of his past sins. It was a mistake he wouldn't make again. Dealing with a woman required a clear head, one unclouded by emotions.

"Are you up for a little exercise, or has marriage and fatherhood made you soft?" Caelen challenged.

Ewan's eyes glittered. "Are you prepared to be humiliated in front of your men?"

Caelen snorted. "You can certainly try, old man."

Rionna stretched languidly and smiled even before she opened her eyes. 'Twas a wonderful morning. Her feet were toasty warm and she had no desire to get up from bed.

Then she opened her eyes and blinked sleepily as she gave another lazy stretch. She turned on her side and her gaze rested on a pair of leather boots on the floor next to the bed.

She blinked more rapidly and sat up, clutching the covers to her breasts.

New boots. Not just newly fashioned, but fur-lined.

And beside them, was a neatly folded fur-lined cloak with a hood.

Her feet hit the floor and she dove toward the treasures. She grabbed one boot and turned it over and over, inspecting the fine stitching and craftsmanship. Then she plunged her hand inside and sighed at the luxurious feel of the warm fur.

With a delighted squeal, she clutched the boots and the cloak to her chest and danced around the room.

She stopped in front of the fire and buried her face in the soft fur. What a wonderful, wonderful thing for Caelen to do. How had he laid hands on such fine things?

Not able to wait a minute longer to try them on, she hurriedly donned her gown and then sat on the bed as she pulled her boots on.

She closed her eyes and sighed idiotically as her heel slid into the boot. She stood and paced about the chamber, testing the feel and the size. They fit her perfectly. Not too big and not even a pinch too small.

She ran to the window and threw aside the fur then stuck her head out. Snowflakes drifted lazily from the sky and collected on the ground below. 'Twas a perfect day to try out her new treasures.

With a grin, she spun around, donned the cloak, and hurried out of her chamber.

'Twas remiss of her to not even check the hall to see if her guests were in attendance, but she didn't care. Caelen would be outdoors with the men, as he was every day, and he was the one she wanted to see.

Her boots crunched over the snow but no dampness seeped into her toes nor did any hint of cold grip her feet.

Caelen stood with his brother and 'twas obvious the two were set to spar. She was too excited to consider whether 'twas appropriate for her to interrupt.

"Caelen!" she called as she approached.

As soon as he turned in the direction of her voice, she launched herself at him. So surprised was he that he stumbled back even as he caught her against him and they both tumbled into the snow.

"God's teeth, woman, whatever is the matter? Is someone hurt?"

She sat astride him, grinning so big that her cheeks hurt. She leaned down, framed his face in her hands, and proceeded to pepper his face with kisses. Then she fused her lips to his in a hot, lusty kiss that certainly had her toes curling in her new boots.

"Thank you," she said huskily. "I love them. 'Tis the best gift anyone has ever given me."

There were sounds of amusement on all sides of them,

but she ignored the men as they gathered. She pushed herself off Caelen, who looked dazed and befuddled by what had just transpired.

She gifted the men with an equally dazzling smile and then she performed a perfect curtsy in Ewan's direction.

"I'll leave you to your duties," she said.

She chanced one more look at Caelen, who still lay sprawled in the snow, a look of complete bemusement on his face, and then she turned and all but skipped back toward the keep.

Caelen blinked and stared after his wife as she hurried through the snow. Then he glanced around at the men gathered and scowled at their looks of amusement.

Ewan stood to the side, contorting his mouth so he didn't laugh aloud, and then he extended a hand down to Caelen.

"I take it Rionna liked her gifts."

Caelen grasped Ewan's hand and hauled himself out of the snow.

"For God's sake, the woman has no self-control," he muttered.

Ewan laughed softly and then clapped Caelen on the shoulder. "I'd say you just scored some points with the lass. I'm sure we'd all understand if you chose to excuse yourself for a time."

Laughter rose from the assembled warriors and Caelen scowled even harder. Then he punched Ewan directly in the gut, satisfied when his brother let out a pained grunt.

"What the hell was that for?" Ewan demanded.

"Payment for the time you did the same to me when I needled you about your wife."

Ewan laughed as he rubbed his belly. "I believe you made mention of me missing my cods. Strange that you seem to suffer the same affliction when it comes to a certain, golden-haired lass."

Caelen went to hit him again but Ewan dodged this time and both men went down in the snow. The men pressed forward and shouts rose as they urged the two brothers on. Wagers were quickly placed and the snow began to fly.

CHAPTER 22

Crispen threw his arms around Rionna's waist, surprising her with his exuberance. He was a sweet child but a typical boisterous lad. She kissed the top of his head and he bounced away to pounce on his Uncle Caelen.

"Farewell, Rionna, and thank you for your hospitality," Mairin said as she hugged Rionna.

Rionna kissed her cheek and then pulled aside one of the small blankets that encapsulated Isabel and nuzzled the baby's soft cheek. Oh but babies smelled so sweet. It filled her with longing for her own babe, and then she shook her head at the insensible urge.

"Safe journey, Mairin. I'll pray for you and Isabel."

Mairin smiled and then went to say her farewell to Caelen, while Ewan waited by the horses. Rionna watched in amusement as Caelen softened into a pile of mush as he stared down at Ewan's tiny daughter.

There was something powerful about a warrior brought to his knees by a babe. Rionna stifled her laughter as Caelen uttered something nonsensical to Isabel. He followed it with a promise to cut off the heads of all men who'd pursue her in the future.

Rionna and Mairin exchanged eye rolls. At least he hadn't suggested another part of the male anatomy.

Ewan and his men mounted and then Caelen lifted Mairin and Isabel up onto Ewan's horse. Ewan wrapped his arms securely around his wife and child and then gave the order to ride.

They filed out of the courtyard, over the wooden drawbridge, and into the moonless night.

Caelen returned to her a moment later. "'Tis late. We should retire now."

She nodded and allowed him to take her arm as he escorted her inside. He paused at the bottom of the stair to discuss the next day's events with Gannon while Rionna proceeded up the stairs.

She had plans for her husband this evening. Daring plans that no lady should ever entertain, which delighted her even more.

Once inside her chamber, she quickly added logs to the fire and straightened the furs on the bed. Soon she heard her husband's heavy step on the stairs and then right outside the door.

She turned, hiding her smile, so that her back was presented when Caelen stepped inside the chamber.

"Rionna, there is something we should discuss," he began sternly.

"Hmm, can you help me with my dress?"

She turned in time to see him frown. But he crossed the room and began to unfasten the buttons of her gown.

"Now what is it you'd like to discuss, husband?"

He cleared his throat. "There are certain things that should not be done in front of others."

She lowered the sleeves of her gown and turned, holding the bodice barely over her nipples. She stared innocently up at him as she allowed one side to slip, baring the tip of her breast.

"Like what?"

His gaze tracked downward and he sucked in his

breath. It took him a moment before he continued. "Displays of affection should be contained to our private chamber."

She turned away again and let the gown fall, stepping from it and reaching for her sleeping gown. She tossed her head, allowing her hair to skim along her buttocks, and then she arched as if stretching before tossing aside the gown, seeming to change her mind about donning it.

"Such displays are never appropriate in front of my men," Caelen continued in a strangled voice.

Rionna turned once more and stepped forward to loosen the ties of his trews. "Aye, husband, I'm sure you're right. No show of affection in front of others. 'Tis unseemly."

She reached inside and cupped his heavy sac, squeezing gently.

"'Tis not just . . . What on earth are you about, wife?"

She stroked up and down and then withdrew her hand. "I'm undressing you. 'Tis my duty, is it not?"

"Well, aye, 'tis sometimes. But right now 'tis important we have this discussion."

"Oh, I agree. Do continue. Where were you? Ah yes, you said 'tis not just . . . 'Tis just not what?"

He frowned and shook his head as her hand grazed over his chest and then began pulling at his tunic.

"'Tis not just unseemly. 'Tis a matter of respect. The men's respect for me. I cannot command their respect if I'm being tumbled to the ground by my wife."

He had mustered another grim scowl, but she tugged at his trews and freed his cock into her greedy grasp.

"Am I allowed to tumble you to the ground in the privacy of our chamber?"

His brows drew together in confusion. "What?"

She hooked her leg behind his knee and gave him a mighty shove. He stumbled back against the bed and went down on his back.

She climbed atop him and stared triumphantly down at him. "Now what is it you were saying, husband? I am ever obedient and am awaiting your instructions."

He tucked his hands behind his head. "I wasn't saying a damn thing. Not a thing. Carry on, wife."

She smiled in satisfaction. "'Tis what I thought you said." She lowered her mouth to his as she reached down to grasp his cock to fit it to her opening.

As he sank deep into her welcoming body, he sucked in his breath and then murmured against her mouth, "You have my permission to tumble me anywhere and as often as you like."

CHAPTER 23

Rionna viewed the courtyard with an unhappy grimace as Caelen lit into a group of the warriors. The McDonald men weren't happy with Caelen's dressing down. Many of them glared defiantly at their new laird while others cast sullen glances in his direction and then openly defied him by turning away.

Simon and Hugh did their best to back their laird, but even they weren't successful in rallying the men from their anger.

'Twas hard to hear that they were deemed inferior. 'Twas even harder to hear that they weren't putting in enough work and they fought like women.

That last line drew Rionna's ire, considering she fought better than most of the men. There was no need to insult women when drawing attention to the men's inadequacies.

For a week now, since Caelen's brother's departure, Caelen had worked the men from dawn well into the night. The warriors had grown increasingly more vocal in their displeasure and more defiant with each day. Rionna worried that if things continued on their present course, Caelen would have a full-scale rebellion on his hands.

She shivered and pulled away from the window. She

didn't want Caelen to know she was observing. He had very distinct ideas on how he handled the men and he didn't brook any interference. 'Twas the truth she wanted to step in and soothe the warriors. Remind them of what they fought for. And Caelen likely knew how tempted she was because he headed her off by warning her that he'd tolerate no intervention on her part.

She trudged back to the great hall and stood by the fire, smothering the yawn that overtook her. She was weary to her bones and it was God's truth she hadn't done much this day.

Malaise had gripped her for days and at first she'd worried she was taking ill, but she suffered no malady other than fatigue. 'Twas the truth her husband interfered with her sleep with his insatiable demands. Demands she met with many of her own.

She woke every single morning before dawn to him deep inside her, possessing her with ruthless determination. Always he left her with a gentle kiss after taking her roughly, and then he'd leave her to sleep when he departed the chamber.

They began the night with loving and they ended it thus.

She yawned again and wondered if she shouldn't take to her bed a little earlier this night in preparation for the vigorous bout of loving she knew they'd indulge in. How Caelen met the daily demands of training and survived on so little sleep she'd never know.

She stuck out her hands to the fire to ward off the chill that had set in deep and stared into the flames as her eyes grew heavier and heavier. 'Twas unlike her to be so listless.

She shook herself out of her fog when Gannon strode into the hall.

"My lady, Caelen is ready for your lesson. He says if you're wanting to practice, you're to hasten. He's only set aside an hour's time for you today while the men are breaking."

Rionna frowned. "Does he never plan to take a break?"

Gannon looked at her oddly as if 'twas a ridiculous question, and she supposed it was. Caelen was inhuman in his stamina.

"Let me fetch my sword," she said.

"I'll fetch it for you, my lady. You go to Caelen."

Rionna murmured her thanks and then hurried toward the door. She stepped into the snow and grimaced. Caelen would lecture her about forgetting her cloak but 'twas much easier to spar without it.

He waited for her on the outer perimeter of the training area where they practiced every day. Rionna had never been tempted to beg off, but today she'd give most anything to crawl into her bed and stay there the rest of the afternoon.

She refused to say a single word to Caelen. She'd fought too hard to get him to agree to let her continue practicing with the sword. She'd give him no reason to forbid her from it again.

"Where is your sword?" he asked impatiently.

His mood was black. He'd be unrelenting today. She wanted to groan but bit her lip.

"Gannon is fetching it."

Caelen cast an impatient glance over his shoulder and then turned back to her.

"We'll practice hand to hand until he arrives. If you lose your sword in battle, you must rely on your wits and your hand-to-hand skills to remain alive."

She looked warily at the glint in his eye. He was spoiling for a fight today, but she didn't want to give him one. He'd crush her like a bug.

She nearly wilted in relief when Gannon strode up and

handed her the sword. Caelen looked faintly disappointed.

"Don't disappoint me today," Gannon muttered before he retreated.

"I'll try my best," Rionna said with heavy sarcasm.

As soon as her hand curled around the hilt, she let out a yell and charged. Surprise glinted in Caelen's eyes a mere second before blistering satisfaction set in.

He met her attack and she was jarred to her toes when she blocked his forceful swing. Her teeth threatened to vibrate right out of her head.

For several minutes they fought furiously, but her strength quickly flagged. Every movement was like slogging through mud and her arms grew heavier with each passing second.

She was forced back when he advanced, circling his sword around his head and cutting in a downward slash. She blocked and then took another step back as her sword dipped precariously.

The tip swung down and dug into the earth. Her vision blurred and she gripped the hilt with both hands and hung on to keep from falling. Caelen's look of surprise and then worry faded in and out of her sight as blackness crept in.

She sank to her knees, still gripping the sword, and then pitched sideways, hitting the snow as she lost consciousness.

Caelen reached her at the same time as Gannon. Both men went to their knees, and Caelen reached underneath her to pick her up before the dampness seeped into her clothing.

His heart thundered, pounding against his chest like a mace. Had he injured her? Had he in some way hit her with his sword? Surely he would have realized it.

He'd lost his concentration at a time when he could least afford it. He was sparring with his wife, not a warrior of equal size and strength. He'd been thinking of his difficulties with the men and how to remedy it, instead of taking care and ensuring that no harm came to his wife.

He gathered her close, holding her tightly to his chest, as he ran through the snow toward the entrance to the keep. He ignored the startled shouts around him and bounded up the stairs, Gannon hot on his heels.

He burst into his chamber and carefully laid Rionna on the bed. Then he began a thorough examination from head to toe, looking for any sign of injury. What he found baffled him.

There wasn't a single mark on the lass. No blood. No bruises. No reason whatsoever for her to have lost consciousness.

It appeared that she had simply fainted. Was she ill?

"Send for Sarah," Caelen ordered Gannon. "And tell her to hurry."

When Gannon had gone, Caelen touched Rionna's pale cheek and cursed under his breath. He should have never allowed this foolishness.

"Rionna. Rionna, lass, wake up."

She didn't stir and he became even more worried. What if she were gravely ill? She was a stubborn lass. It would be just like her not to say anything.

He looked up in relief when he heard a noise in the hall. Sarah hurried in, followed by Neda, who served as their healer.

"What happened, Laird?" Neda asked.

Caelen stood so that the women could crowd in around Rionna to examine her. "I don't know," he admitted. "We were sparring and she fainted. I can find no sign of injury."

Sarah made a shooing gesture in Caelen's direction. "Wait in the hall, Laird. Give us some breathing room.

We'll see to the lass. I suspect 'tis not a serious matter. She's been tired of late."

Caelen frowned and reluctantly allowed Gannon to herd him outside the chamber. He hadn't noticed that Rionna had been tired. Guilt crowded his mind. He woke her early each morn with his demands and kept her up late into the night. He hadn't considered the toll on her. She'd become a need he couldn't explain.

He woke beside her, needing her, wanting her so badly that 'twas no longer desire that motivated him. It was a bone-deep need to possess her, to imprint her on his skin.

And at the end of the day, he was eager and impatient to retire to their bedchamber where they took turns being the aggressor. His favorite times were when she climbed astride him, as determined to have him as he was her.

He was possessive, aye, but so was she. He'd decided he liked it very much.

"What can be keeping them?" Caelen bit out as he paced back and forth in front of the door.

"It's only been a few moments," Gannon said. "I'm sure the lass is fine. She might have a touch of upset. Perhaps 'twas something she ate."

"Sarah said she'd been tired of late. Why didn't I notice this?"

"You've been busy training the men. It doesn't leave a lot of room to notice much else. She's a sturdy lass. I've no doubt she'll be up and kicking your arse again in short order."

Caelen scowled and shook his head but before he could give voice to the fact that he had no intention of accommodating her swordplay any longer, the door opened and Sarah poked her head out.

"I'd like a word with you, Laird. Out here since the lass is awake now."

"Is she all right?" Caelen demanded. "I would see for myself."

Sarah held up a hand. "Now don't go getting yourself worked up. The lass is fine. Nothing a little rest won't cure. I'm guessing you didn't know she was carrying."

Caelen gave her a blank look. "Carrying what?"

She rolled her eyes. "A babe. She's pregnant she is."

Caelen stood there processing what Sarah had just related but he couldn't quite grasp it. Fury tightened his muscles and he shook his head at his wife's daring. Sarah obviously thought it an odd reaction to the news, but at the moment he didn't much care beyond the thought that he was going to blister his wife's ears just as soon as she'd sufficiently recovered from her current weakness.

He turned to Gannon and pointed at the door. "She is not to leave this room for the remainder of the day, nor is she to rise from her bed. See to it."

He turned and stalked down the hallway. He had a sudden need to shed some blood. Whose wasn't of consequence. He'd had enough of the McDonald men and their unseemly reluctance to put in the work required to shape them into a decent fighting force.

'Twas a shame when their mistress was more of a man than they were.

Chapter 24

"Normally I wouldn't ever encourage gainsaying your husband, but the men think he has done something to harm you, lass, and 'tis the truth they're not happy over the prospect. If you don't make an appearance, the laird is likely going to have an unruly mob on his hands."

Rionna glanced up at Sarah and then pointedly over to where Gannon stood, arms crossed over his chest, as he listened to the conversation.

Sarah cast a look of exasperation in Gannon's direction.

"You said he didn't take the news of the babe well," Rionna said, bringing Sarah back to the matter at hand.

"Now I didn't say that," Sarah began.

"But he didn't," Rionna persisted.

"I don't rightly know what his reaction was. He ordered his man to make sure you didn't rise from bed or leave the chamber and then he stomped down the hall."

"And you find nothing unusual about such a reaction to siring a child?" Rionna asked sarcastically.

"Give the man time. 'Twas obvious was news he was unprepared for."

"I wasn't any more prepared," Rionna muttered.

Sarah shook her head and muttered under her breath. She stood, shaking her head, and threw her arms up in agitation. "The two of you are dense. Why it should surprise either of you to find you are with child is a mystery to me. It's not as if you haven't worked hard enough at it."

"I wasn't ready," Rionna said defensively.

"And you think a babe waits until his parents are ready?" Sarah made a rude noise and continued shaking her head. "You have months yet to become ready. You'll get used to the idea quick enough. Be happy you haven't suffered from sickness. It would seem fatigue is your only symptom thus far."

Rionna wrinkled her nose. "'Tis likely now that I know I am carrying that I'll promptly be sick tomorrow morning."

Sarah laughed. "You might at that, lass. The mind plays interesting tricks."

Rionna laid a hand over her still-flat belly and felt a tremor of uncertainty roll through her. She glanced up at Sarah. "What if I'm not a fit mother?"

Sarah's gaze softened and she sat on the bed next to Rionna. Then she glared up at Gannon and motioned him to go away. Gannon frowned but took his leave, though he made it clear he was standing guard outside the door.

Then Sarah turned back to Rionna and took her hand. "You'll be a wonderful mother, lass. You're fiercely loyal and protective of your people and those in need of protection. How could you be any less with your own bairn? You worry overmuch. After you've had time to grow used to the idea, you'll find that all will be well."

Rionna heaved out a sigh. "I hope you're right. So far my husband doesn't seem thrilled with the idea of fatherhood, and yet he seemed eager enough to plant his seed. He boasted that I'd deliver an heir within a year of our marriage. I guess he knew what he was about."

"The laird has a lot on his mind. His responsibilities

are great right now. He'll come around. 'Tis likely a shock to him at the moment. You watch. He'll be boasting and spreading tales of his virility before you know it."

"He just seemed so . . . angry," Rionna said softly.

Sarah shrugged. "He'll get over the shock of it soon enough. Now about the men . . ."

"Aye, I should reassure them that I am well and that Caelen hasn't murdered me. He's had enough trouble with them of late." Rionna sighed unhappily. "I know not what is going on with my clan, Sarah. Only a few have given Caelen their loyalty and support. I know not what they wait for or why they hold back. Surely they cannot have been more content under my father's rule."

Sarah patted Rionna on the hand. "Some men just don't like change. They don't like anything that isn't their idea. Having a new laird forced on them—an outsider to our clan—'tis a hard thing for many of them to swallow. And 'tis pride that gets in their way, for the laird is pointing out their shortcomings and 'tis a humiliation to them."

"Help me up and into a gown. 'Twill ease my husband's mood if he sees me in womanly apparel. Perhaps he'll not bellow at me too loudly for gainsaying his order to remain abed."

"I wouldn't count on it," Sarah said wryly. "'Tis enough if you soothe the men's worry that he's dispatched you and is even now having his man bury you."

Rionna rolled her eyes at the amusement in Sarah's voice and threw her legs over the side of the bed. A few moments later, she was attired in a gown of amber cloth with gold-colored threads. 'Twas the first time she'd worn the gown since Sarah had sewn it for her. She'd wanted to save it for a special occasion. Avoiding her husband's ire seemed good enough.

"You look beautiful, lass. Already, carrying the babe has given you a softer glow about you."

Rionna paused on her way to the door and turned with a sigh. "Gannon."

Sarah frowned as if just remembering Caelen's commander herself. Then she shrugged. "'Tis unlikely he'll lay a hand on you. Oh he'll bluster and try to bar your way, but between the two of us we should be able to make him back down."

Rionna didn't have Sarah's confidence that Gannon wouldn't physically subdue her.

"Perhaps 'twould be better if you called Gannon inside. I'll stand behind the door and when he comes in, I'll hurry out behind him."

Sarah chuckled. "You've a devious mind, lass. 'Twill work if I inject enough panic into my cry. Take your position, but remember to be quick. He won't like our trickery."

Rionna gathered her skirts in her grip and then hastened to stand behind the door. Sarah positioned herself across the room and then cried Gannon's name.

Immediately the door burst open and Gannon ran inside the room. Not taking even a moment to see his reaction, Rionna grasped the door, darted around it, and ran down the stairs. His bellow of outrage followed her all the way down.

Urged on by the heavy tread of his footsteps on the stairs, she ran for the door leading out into the courtyard. She nearly slipped in the snow, righted herself, and ran toward her husband, whose back was to her.

But the men saw her. They lowered their swords in the midst of one of Caelen's instructions and stared curiously as she skidded to a stop just beyond Caelen's right elbow.

They glanced between her and Caelen, their expressions wary, and when he turned so that she could see his face, she knew why.

His expression was so coldly furious that she took a step back, her heart leaping into her throat. Gannon strode up behind her and suddenly she was pinned by two extremely angry warriors.

"You were not to allow her from her chamber," Caelen snapped at Gannon.

"'Twas not his fault," Rionna said softly. "Sarah and I tricked him."

"You have a deft hand at trickery, wife, wouldn't you say?"

His tone took her aback. Her mouth fell open at his accusation. She couldn't be sure exactly what he accused her of, but whatever it was, it wasn't good.

Her chin went up a notch. "I merely wanted to assure the men that I was well."

He gestured widely, his hand sweeping over the assembled warriors. "As they can see, you are hale and hearty, no thanks to your foolishness. Now if that is all, we've training to finish."

Her chest clutched at his dismissive, caustic tone. "My foolishness? What is it you speak of, husband?"

He took a step forward and stared down at her, his face so cold that she shivered. "I will speak to you later, when I am not so gripped by anger. Until then, return to our chamber and do not leave it. Are we understood?"

Her mouth fell open. She gaped incredulously at him. What on earth could she have done to anger him so?

She was sorely tempted to knee him in the cods and leave him writhing on the ground in agony. She pressed her lips into a thin line and sent him a stare that would wither a flower in full bloom.

She turned and when Gannon would have taken her

arm, she jerked away and gave him an equally icy stare. Over her lifeless body would she obey her husband's dictate to wait in their chamber for him to take her apart for some imagined slight.

She stomped inside and went in search of Sarah. Caelen should be filled with joy. He was going to be a father. It had been his wish for his seed to bear fruit with all haste so as to further seal his leadership over his new clan.

Now the McCabes and the McDonalds would be joined by blood. Caelen had everything he wanted. Why then did he look upon her as though she'd handed him the worst betrayal?

"You cannot avoid the laird forever," Sarah warned.

Rionna shot her a glare. "'Tis not avoiding as much as it is me not obeying his almighty dictate. He can go to the devil. And to think I wore a dress for him." She looked down in disgust at the beautiful amber gown that had a fair number of wrinkles in it now.

Sarah chuckled and resumed her knitting. The two women sat in Sarah's cottage as the fire blazed in the hearth. 'Twas past the hour of the evening meal but Rionna had eaten—at Sarah's insistence—in the quiet of Sarah's cottage.

"You can't miss meals now, lass," she'd cautioned Rionna. "'Tis likely what made you faint. You didn't break your fast and then you overexerted yourself."

Rionna had given in to Sarah's prodding and eaten a bowl of stew but she couldn't even remember the taste. The only thing firmly entrenched in her memory was her husband's furious expression. And his coldness to her. She had no explanation for it. One moment they were sparring, and aye, he'd been in a black mood because of the men, but surely that couldn't be blamed for the horrible way he'd reacted to her pregnancy. Was he really so angry because she was carrying? It made no sense. Not when her bearing an heir was of such import to the alliance between the McCabes and the McDonalds. Her babe could go a long way in mending the animosity the McDonald men currently bore Caelen.

"I admit, I'll never understand the mind of a man," Rionna said with a sigh.

Sarah *tsk*ed under her breath. "'Tis good you learn that now, lass. 'Tis a foolhardy endeavor to even attempt such. The mind of a man changes on a daily basis and a woman is never sure which way it bends from one moment to the next. 'Tis why 'tis best to allow them to think they are the master of their domain and go quietly behind them and do things the way you like."

Rionna laughed. "You are a wise woman, Sarah."

"Having outlived two husbands already, I've gained more wisdom about men than a woman needs to know." She shrugged. "'Tis not hard once you've learned they're mostly bluster and gruff. If you can look beyond that and ignore their bite, they're not hard to live with. You give them a little petting, stroke their pride a bit, and follow it with a kiss here and there, and they're well content."

"Aye, I used to think you were right," Rionna said as she stared into the flames. "But my husband . . . 'tis disloyal of me to discuss him so, but he drives me daft. One moment he is as tender as a man can be and the next he's as cold as the winter's snow."

Sarah smiled. "Because he's not yet decided what he thinks of you, lass. You've got him so flustered that he doesn't know if he's coming or going. He'll figure it out eventually."

"How typical that I must wait on him to make his mind up before we can be at peace," Rionna grumbled.

"'Tis hard to soothe a savage beast when you're here and he's there," Sarah pointed out.

"'Tis cold and I'm not venturing out," Rionna grumbled.

"The problem is you're both as stubborn as an old mule. Neither of you will give an inch. 'Tis no way to make a success of a marriage."

"If I make a practice of yielding so easily, then I'll always be yielding and he'll never bend."

"Aye, that's true as well."

"Then what am I supposed to do?" Rionna asked in exasperation.

Sarah chuckled. "If I knew that, no one would ever be discontent, now would they? I think 'tis something you'll have to muddle through on your own."

"Maybe," Rionna said grudgingly. "But 'tis nothing I'll discover tonight. I'm tired."

"And grumpy."

"With good reason."

"Go to sleep, lass. Your husband will be looking for you soon enough and you'll not be getting to sleep then."

"I'll not hide from him," Rionna vowed.

Sarah raised an eyebrow. "Oh? And what exactly do you call what you're doing?"

"I'm defying his order."

"And hiding while you do it," Sarah said in amusement.

"Nay, I'll not hide from him. 'Tis high time I discovered why it is he's angry."

Rionna stood, her fingers curling into fists.

"You be careful on the walk back, lass. 'Tis snowy and icy out tonight. The good Lord doesn't seem to be able to decide if he wants it to rain or snow."

"I'll be careful, Sarah. Thank you for your company.

And your counsel. 'Tis good sometimes to have some-one to listen."

Sarah smiled. "Aye, lass, it is. Go now and make peace with the laird. 'Tis celebrating the two of you should be doing now."

Rionna said her farewells and hurried through the snow back to the keep. By the time she made it to the steps she was shivering, as a mixture of snow and rain drizzled down her neck.

She went inside, stomping her boots free of the ice and snow, and walked into the great hall to warm herself by the fire before going in search of her husband.

She didn't have to look far.

He was sitting at the table with Gannon and many of the McDonald warriors. When he saw her, he rose, his eyes narrowed and his lips set into a fine line. He crossed his arms over his chest and stared her down. The man hadn't even realized she hadn't obeyed his command to retire to their chamber. Had he planned to starve her to death?

Ignoring his less-than-pleased look, she marched over to the fire and stuck out her hands to warm them, pre-senting her back to the laird.

The more she gave thought to the matter, the more furious she became. She'd done nothing to gain his ire. And if he wasn't happy about the babe, 'twas his own fault. He certainly hadn't done anything to prevent her becoming with child.

When she was sufficiently warmed, she turned with-out looking in her husband's direction and walked calmly toward the stairs.

"You sorely try my patience, wife," Caelen called out.

She halted at that and slowly turned until she pinned him with a glare that hid none of her own mounting ire.

The men stared between their laird and Rionna with ill-disguised curiosity. It didn't suit Rionna to have it out with Caelen in such a public fashion, but she was just furious enough not to care.

"And you try mine, husband. Perhaps when you've figured out what it is that I've done to displease you, you can let me know. Until then, I'm going to bed. 'Tis been a most eventful day."

CHAPTER 25

Rionna was shaking by the time she reached her chamber. It had taken all her courage to calmly walk out of the hall with Caelen's face a storm cloud of anger. 'Twas wrong of her to show such disrespect in front of the men, but 'twas just as wrong for him to air his grievance with her in front of others.

She had no desire to remain in this chamber, or wait his convenience, stewing all the while she waited for him to make an appearance. But neither would she give the impression that she was hiding by retreating to her former chamber.

But 'twas God's truth all she really wanted was to be alone so she could sleep in peace. She was so weary and tense that she wanted to melt into her bed and remain there an entire day. And her head was beginning to throb.

She paced back and forth in front of the fire until she realized that he was going to make her wait. With an irritated sigh, she undressed and put her gown carefully away so that it wouldn't be ruined. 'Twas a beautiful gown and perhaps one day she'd have a chance to wear it when it could be appreciated.

She was chilled in just her nightdress so she donned

her cloak and curled into the chair by the fire. A bath would feel next to heaven, but 'twas late and she had no desire to be caught in the tub when her husband decided to make his appearance.

As warmth invaded her limbs, her eyelids grew heavier and heavier. By the time she heard Caelen's footsteps outside the door, she was so drowsy that she couldn't muster any outrage that he'd taken so long to retire.

The door quietly opened and shut much the same. She didn't turn to greet him, opting to remain exactly where she was.

For several long moments, silence loomed in the chamber. Then finally his footsteps sounded again, closer this time, before he came to stand just behind her.

"I have battled my anger all day today and yet I find I'm as angry now as I was before."

At that, Rionna turned in her chair, clutching her cloak tightly around her.

"And what sin have I committed, husband? Are you so displeased at the thought of becoming a father? Did I misunderstand your boasts that I would deliver within a year of our marriage?"

His brows drew together and he stared at her in obvious consternation. "Think you I'm upset that you are pregnant with my child?"

She stood, her cloak swirling around her legs. "You've done nothing to make me think otherwise! From the moment you discovered that I was pregnant, you've been coldly furious. I've done nothing to gain your ire and yet you've cut me to ribbons with your gaze at every turn."

"Nothing? God's teeth, woman, but you are a test of my endurance. You don't tell me that you are with child. At what point were you going to confide in me? When I held the point of my sword to your swollen belly? Or maybe when 'twas time for you to push the babe into the world?"

Her mouth fell open as she understood his meaning. "You think I purposely kept secret my condition? You think I would put our babe at risk?"

"You were participating in activities no pregnant woman should ever be doing," he said through clenched teeth. "You had to know I would have never allowed it."

"So you think so little of me that you think I would resort to subterfuge so that I could continue to indulge in training, never mind that I was pregnant with the next laird of my clan."

"Why did you not tell me then?" he demanded.

Tears of disappointment and frustration burned her eyelids. His opinion of her hurt. Did he truly believe she'd be so selfish and foolhardy as to put her child at risk?

"I did not know!" she said fiercely. "I did not know until I awakened and Sarah told me. I would have told you. It would have given me great joy to do so."

Caelen looked shocked for a moment, as though he'd given such a possibility no thought. "Jesu," he muttered. Then he ran a ragged hand through his hair and turned swiftly away. His hand fell to his side, curled into a tight fist. "When I think of what could have happened, what almost *did* happen. When you fell, I thought I had hurt you. I could have harmed our child. I could have harmed *you*."

Realization was quick to dawn on Rionna. Her anger and hurt melted away and her heart throbbed a little harder. She crossed the distance between her and her husband and laid her hand on his arm.

"You were afraid," she said softly.

He jerked around, his eyes blazing. "Afraid? I was bloody terrified! I carried you to our chamber sure that I would find some grievous wound. I looked for blood or a bruise, something to suggest that I had harmed you."

She wrapped her arms around his waist and leaned her head against his chest. For the longest time he stood rigid in her arms, not returning her embrace. Then slowly, he circled her shoulders and crushed her to him.

He rested his cheek on the top of her head and held her so tightly that she could scarcely breathe. He trembled against her, and it awed her that this fierce warrior had been afraid. For her. That he shook with it. It shamed her that she'd thought even for a moment that he didn't want their child, even if it was a logical conclusion at the time.

Now she wanted confirmation. She wanted to hear it from his own lips that he was joyous over her pregnancy.

"So you're happy about the babe?"

Her question was muffled by his chest, but he went still and then slowly drew her away so that he looked down into her eyes.

"Happy? I think happy is too mundane a word. There are many words that accurately describe my reaction. Wonder. Aye, wonder. 'Tis not something I've contemplated until recently, and even then I spoke as a man boasting to be boasting. It didn't really settle with me that I would become a father until Sarah bore the news to me in the hallway. The image hit me with force enough to stagger me. I had to quit the keep and go out alone lest I completely unman myself in front of others."

His fingers touched her cheek and grazed along her jaw.

"Fear. I was immediately filled with such fear like I've never felt. Fear that I wouldn't be able to protect our child from men like Duncan Cameron. That if we had a daughter she would be as Mairin had been for most of her life. Always hiding, always living in fear of discovery. Wary of being used by a man for what she could bring through the birth of a child."

She reached up to palm his cheek and he turned into her hand, brushing a kiss across her flesh.

"And joy, Rionna. 'Tis God's truth I experienced a burst of joy that is indescribable. I imagined a daughter with your beauty and strength and a son with your spirit and stubbornness."

She laughed. "And you, husband? What think you that our children will inherit from you?"

"I care not as long as they are healthy and that you deliver them free of complication."

She hugged him again. "I'm sorry I worried you. 'Tis the truth I didn't know I was with child, I swear it. I would have taken more care in our training."

He clutched her shoulders and pulled her away from him, his expression one of utmost seriousness. "You'll not lay hands on a sword again. 'Tis done with, this foolish idea of yours."

"But, Caelen, now that we know, we can fashion our sparring so that no harm is done to our child. 'Tis important I am able to protect myself and our child."

"I will protect what is mine," he said fiercely. "I will take no chances with your health or that of our child."

"But—"

He held up a hand. "'Tis not up for debate. 'Tis my final word on the matter."

She sighed but couldn't bring herself to be irritated when she could still see the worry shadowed in his eyes.

"Now come here, wife. I have need to hold you."

She smiled and went into his arms. He kissed her hungrily, framing her face and holding her in place as he ravaged her mouth.

He slid his hands down her body, coming to stop at her waist. Then he placed his palm over the flat of her belly through the folds of her cloak. Suddenly impatient, he pulled at the material until she was free of the garment and standing only in her nightdress. Then his hand returned to her stomach and he held it there as he stared into her eyes.

"My son or daughter," he said hoarsely. "I'd not thought I'd ever have children."

"Do you like the thought now?" she asked with a smile.

"Oh aye," he said softly. "I find I like the idea very much. I owe you an apology, Rionna."

She put her finger to his lips and then followed it with a kiss. "It's been an eventful day for both of us. Perhaps 'twould be best if we go to bed and start fresh on the morrow."

"You've a very generous spirit, wife."

"There is something I want in return," she said as she slid one hand down to cup him intimately.

His eyes gleamed with quick understanding. "Oh? And what is that?"

She continued to caress him through the material of his trews. "A good husband would be mindful of his wife in her present condition. She needs lots of care and attention."

"Does she now?"

"Oh aye, she does," Rionna whispered. "Lots of tender, loving handling by her husband."

"I think I can accommodate her."

He bent and picked her up and walked to the bed where he lowered her onto the straw mattress.

"In fact, I think I should give her lots of extra loving."

"Oh, I do, too," Rionna breathed.

He stood back and stripped off his clothing, and then he leaned over her and worked the gown over her head until she was naked and breathless beneath him.

For a long moment he simply stood over her and stared down at her body. Then he cupped both hands over her belly before kneeling on the floor in front of her. He parted his hands and then pressed a kiss to her stomach, so soft and tender that her heart felt near to bursting.

She smoothed her hands over his hair and then dug her fingers into his scalp, holding him against the very heart of her.

"You hold our future in your womb, lass," Caelen murmured against her belly. "'Tis what binds our two clans and makes them one."

"'Tis an important obligation you give our child."

He kissed her again and then kissed a path down to the juncture of her legs. With gentle fingers, he parted her flesh and pressed his tongue to the sensitive flesh at her core.

She moaned softly and writhed beneath his mouth as he loved her with his lips and tongue. He was exceedingly patient, never tiring as he brought her wave after wave of pleasure.

He pushed her to the brink only to let up and let the tide slowly recede. Then he'd work her back up again, each time more intense than the last.

He left her panting for breath and so tense that her muscles ached. She begged for him to stop and then for him never to stop. Her hoarse pleas rose, each one making less sense than the last.

Then his mouth left her and he fitted his cock to her opening and slid deep in one forceful lunge. His body blanketed hers, warming her to the bone. Never had she felt quite so safe, like nothing could ever hurt her.

He was inside her, not just physically, but in her heart and soul. He was all she could think of, all she could see and hear. He'd spoken of her carrying their future, but he was her future. He was all she wanted. All she needed.

There was no sign of her rough, possessive lover this night. The man who'd so ruthlessly taken her so many nights past had been replaced by a gentle warrior who treated her as though she were infinitely fragile, a priceless treasure to be cherished above all else.

He held her to him and stroked back and forth, gliding effortlessly through her damp heat. Through it all, his mouth never left her flesh. He kissed her lips, her cheeks, her eyelids, and then he nuzzled down to her ear and below to her neck.

Never had she been so thoroughly worshipped by a man, not even by her husband till now. He'd loved her, aye. He'd loved her as well as a man could ever love a wife, but there was a marked difference this night.

Tonight . . .'twas as if he loved her with his heart instead of just his body. Tonight, she loved him not just with her body, but with her very soul.

When she cried out with her release, he held her against him, not taking his own until he'd seen to her pleasure. Then and only then did he thrust deep and empty himself into her depths.

Afterward, she snuggled into his arms and laid her head on his shoulder. He was hard and sticky between her thighs, but she cared not. She didn't want to separate herself from him for the time it would take to cleanse them both.

She held him close until his breathing became deep and even. He was wholly relaxed against her, limp and sated and so very warm.

She sighed and stroked a hand over his shoulder, knowing he was already asleep.

"I love you, husband. 'Tis the truth I never expected to give you my heart. I know not if it's even what you want from me, but 'tis yours all the same. Someday . . . Someday I'll have yours in return," she whispered against his skin.

She closed her eyes and settled against him, fatigue

sliding over her skin like a blanket. Within moments she, too, slept.

Caelen lay in the dark, his arms tight around Rionna as she slept. Her words echoed in his ears, playing over and over again until he knew they were no trick of his hearing.

His wife loved him. He knew not what to make of this development. He'd loved before and it had come to no good and yet he knew that love existed. He'd seen it between his brothers and their wives. He knew his brothers loved their women with a ferocity uncommon to most marriages.

Love required sacrifice. It required trust and faith. It required making yourself completely vulnerable to the one you loved.

The thought sent a knot deep into his belly.

The last time he'd offered a woman his complete trust and faith, she'd destroyed his clan.

CHAPTER 26

When Rionna woke the next morning, it was early still and the only light in the chamber came from the hearth and one lone candle on the wooden desk that housed Caelen's personal belongings. He sat in silence, quill in hand as he scratched ink onto one of his scrolls.

She watched, fascinated by the image he presented. His brow was creased in concentration and every once in awhile he dipped the quill back into the inkwell and then went back to his writings.

'Twas the first time she'd seen him using the scrolls, but now she wondered if he did so every morn before she woke. So many times she'd awakened to him sliding deep into her body, but perhaps he tended to personal matters first.

She lay still, waiting for him to come to her, and took the opportunity to study her husband in secret.

He was such a handsome man. He had a ruggedness that appealed to every one of her feminine instincts. Strong. Scarred, not perfect. Perhaps that would be a strike against him with another woman, but not Rionna. Her warrior's heart embraced each mark as a badge of honor.

There was a slight ridge on his nose that suggested it had been broken in the past. But his face was otherwise unblemished, chiseled by strong cheekbones and a firm jaw. His pale green eyes mesmerized her. They were an odd shade shared by his two brothers, and Rionna imagined her own babe with the same green eyes.

A lass with her father's dark hair and beautiful eyes. Rionna would need all of her fighting skills to keep the warriors from her daughter's doorstep.

She held her breath when Caelen put away his quill and carefully rolled the scroll closed. He stood and walked quietly over to the bed. Her entire body tingled in anticipation of his possession.

But instead of grasping her hips and pulling her to the edge of the bed, he leaned down and brushed his lips across her forehead, letting them linger just a moment before he backed away and silently left the room.

She stared after him, mystified and . . . disappointed. Her entire body was on edge. A pulsing ache had begun deep at her center and now her husband was gone and she was lying, staring at the ceiling.

She let out a sigh and turned on her side to stare into the fire. Her gaze skirted over the writing table and the scrolls lying neatly to the side. What was it that Caelen wrote when he was alone with his thoughts?

Caelen stood before the assembled clan, Rionna at his side. He addressed them from the balcony that jutted over the courtyard. Men, women, and children had gathered to hear the laird's announcement and when he declared that Rionna was with child, the response was cheers from some and silence from others.

Simon and Arlen stepped forward, their swords thrust high in the air, but even their stamp of approval didn't sway many of the warriors.

Hugh stepped up beside Simon and Arlen and glanced back at his kin before turning and looking up where Caelen stood with Rionna.

"Will the bairn be a McDonald or a McCabe?"

Caelen frowned. "A McCabe of course."

Scowls spread through the assembled clansmen and grumbles rose. Many turned their backs and walked away.

Rionna slid her hand into Caelen's. He could feel her tremble. He squeezed to reassure her.

"I'll not tolerate disrespect toward my wife," he said tightly.

"'Tis not Rionna we disrespect," one hollered up before also turning away.

Caelen's nostrils flared as he viewed the dismay on Rionna's face. He'd had enough of his new clan and their animosity. 'Twas as if they wanted to be conquered and destroyed. He'd never been so sorely tempted to take his wife and return to McCabe lands and let the lot of them rot.

It was time to take a much harder line. He'd coddled them too long. They'd either come around or they'd leave.

Some of the joy had dimmed from Rionna's eyes as she watched her clan turn their backs on her. She stared for a long moment before Caelen gently guided her back inside the keep.

As soon as they walked in, Rionna tugged her hand from Caelen's and tossed up her hands in disgust. "How can they be so foolish? If Cameron marches on us tomorrow, we wouldn't have a chance. Our only hope is to hide behind a larger, stronger clan and allow them to do our fighting for us. 'Tis shameful. Never once have I been ashamed to call myself a McDonald, but today I weep over the disgrace."

Caelen touched her shoulder in an effort to offer comfort. She didn't need to be so distressed. Surely it couldn't be good for the baby.

It was hard to stand there and offer support when he was so furious he could barely see straight.

She wrung her hands and paced back and forth on the landing above the stairs. "Maybe I should address them. I know you are against it, but perhaps I can make them see reason."

Caelen held up his hand and waited for her to go quiet. "'Tis not your place to command these men, Rionna. I am their laird and we will not be a clan until they accept that. I cannot make them embrace their duty."

"I would not blame you if you took your leave of this place and returned to your family," she whispered. "Surely the McCabes can make a more honorable alliance than with my clan."

He pulled her into his arms and rested his chin atop her head. "We have time. Ewan will not make war when the winter is so harsh around us. I'll not quit my duty. 'Tis not just a matter of your clan and mine now. This is my son or daughter's future and I'll not walk away from that."

"What will you do then?"

He pulled her away. "I want you to remain indoors. 'Tis cold today and a storm is brewing to the north."

"And you?" she persisted.

"I have matters to attend to with the men."

Rionna looked fearful, but he wouldn't back down. Not even for her. 'Twas past time for him to beat some sense into his clansmen. Talking had done no good. Neither had explaining their inadequacies. 'Twas time to show them.

Leaving Rionna inside the keep, he strode out to the courtyard. "Assemble the men," he said to Gannon. "I want every one accounted for. If one refuses, use whatever force necessary. Spare them no humiliation. 'Tis time to stop this senseless coddling."

Gannon's mouth twisted into a savage smile of satisfaction. "'Tis about bloody time." He drew his sword and stalked away, shouting the order to assemble once again.

Caelen stood in the middle of the courtyard as the men gathered round, their expressions rife with speculation. He stared them down, his gaze stony and unyielding.

When Gannon gestured to him that the last man had assembled, Caelen drew his sword and leveled the point toward the crowd and turned so they were all included in his gesture.

"'Tis time to make a choice. If you are with me and accept me as your laird, you will step forward, make your pledge, and swear your allegiance. If you are nay accepting of me as your laird, then step forward with your challenge. If you are able to best me in battle, I'll leave McDonald land and never return."

A series of guffaws and sounds of disbelief spread through the crowd.

"You intend to challenge us all?"

The jeer came from the crowd.

Caelen's lip curled into a snarl. "I intend to show you that one McCabe warrior is worth a hundred of you."

"I'll take that challenge," Jamie McDonald said as he stepped forward.

He was a cocky lad, still afflicted by a brush of youth. He hadn't yet proved himself a man, and Caelen shook his head.

"You're starting easy on me, I see."

Jamie's face flushed a dull red, and before Caelen could draw his sword the boy ran at him with a yell. Caelen dodged the clumsy charge, drew his sword, and brought his fist down on the boy's head as he stumbled past. The lad went sprawling, his sword flying several feet in the other direction.

Caelen shook his head in disgust. "No restraint. My wife wields a sword a hundred times better."

Jamie picked himself up, his face a tight knot of fury at the insult.

"Hard to fight without a sword," Gannon drawled. He bent to retrieve the weapon and then tossed it to the side. "Stand aside, lad. You've been bested already."

As the afternoon wore on, the swords piled higher, with Gannon tossing aside one after another. As Caelen dispatched the men, they were directed to sit to the side and watch as the next clansmen took up the charge.

'Twas obvious the more skilled warriors waited until last, when Caelen was tiring. It took him longer than he had liked to dispatch Oren McDonald, and the man actually managed to stagger Caelen before Caelen sent his sword flying toward the discard pile.

When the next McDonald stepped forward, Caelen issued a silent groan. 'Twas Seamus McDonald, and he was a mountain of a man. Heavily muscled with legs and arms like tree trunks, a chest as broad as a boulder, and no neck to speak of.

He wasn't terribly adept with a sword, but he could smash a man with his bare hands.

Sensing Caelen's dismay, the McDonalds who were sitting surged to their feet and let out raucous cheers as Seamus and Caelen circled each other.

Seamus thrust first and Caelen blocked it. The clash of steel rang out over the courtyard and more cheers went up.

On the perimeter, the women had gathered as well as the older men who no longer acted as soldiers. The children were even present and a chant of "Seamus! Seamus! Seamus!" went up on all sides.

Except one.

Amidst the noise and chanting came a clear call of "Caelen! Caelen! Caelen!"

His wife had pushed her way through the crowd and stood just on the outside of the fighting circle. To his eternal surprise she wore no man's garb nor did she wield a sword. She was adorned in her wedding finery and her hair was upswept into an elegant knot, with tendrils escaping on all sides.

She was so damn beautiful she took his breath away.

Right before Seamus plowed into him, taking his breath away, and not in the metaphorical sense.

The two men hit the ground and rolled. Caelen was at a decided disadvantage the moment his sword was knocked from his hand. Seamus was larger by half and he hadn't had to fight every other McDonald warrior already.

Seamus landed a beefy fist to the side of Caelen's face and Caelen's vision blurred. Colorful spots appeared before his eyes and he shook his head to clear his rattled brain.

Caelen punched and then followed with another forceful punch with his left hand. He'd always been equally adept with either hand, not favoring one over the other as so many men did, but Seamus wasn't fazed by either blow.

It soon became obvious after the third time Caelen picked himself up off the ground that direct methods weren't going to work. Seamus was inhuman. He wasn't fast. He lacked finesse, but what he possessed was brute strength and an ability to withstand any blow delivered. Caelen needed fifty more where he came from, and then maybe they'd stand a chance against Cameron.

Caelen wiped the blood from his mouth and circled Seamus, looking for his opportunity. Quickness would be a decided advantage if Caelen weren't ready to fall over from exhaustion. The fight with the other McDonalds had taken its toll. While he'd dispatched each of them easily enough, no man could take on an entire army and come out victorious. But he was determined to give it his best try. Everything rode on this victory. The McDonalds hadn't played fair by holding back their best man until Caelen was worn down and near defeat, but a wager was a wager and if Caelen lost, he'd be forced to step aside as laird and return home a failure.

He sucked in a deep breath. Failure wasn't an option he would entertain.

He glanced at Rionna and saw the fire in her eyes. She urged him on with her gaze, infusing much needed strength into his muscles.

Drawing on reserves he didn't think he had and bolstered by Rionna's absolute faith that he'd win the day, he quickened his step and danced around Seamus until the larger man was looking left and right to keep pace with Caelen's movements.

As soon as Seamus presented his back, Caelen leaped. He wrapped his arms around Seamus's neck and held on with all his strength.

Seamus let out a roar to rival a wild beast and began to shake to and fro. When he didn't loosen Caelen's hold, he turned and ran toward the walls of the keep, Caelen holding on the entire way. At the last moment, Seamus turned and bashed Caelen into the wall.

Caelen grunted in pain but didn't give even an inch. He dug his forearm into the front of Seamus's throat and squeezed tighter until he felt the man begin to tremble and fight to draw breath.

Seamus threw himself into the wall again, trying to shake Caelen loose. But Caelen sensed victory now and strength flooded his veins.

Seamus grabbed at Caelen's arms and tried to pry them loose. He staggered back toward the circle and then went down on one knee.

"Do you yield?" Caelen rasped out.

"Nay!" Seamus roared.

Caelen jerked his arm and tightened his hold.

Seamus went down to both knees and hunched over, Caelen still atop his back like a burr. Then Seamus simply pitched forward and landed with a thump on the ground.

Caelen pried his arms from beneath the fallen man and stood, dusting the snow from his tunic. The McDonald warriors stared with open mouths at Seamus, who was soundly unconscious on the ground. Then they lifted their gazes to Caelen, who regarded them with arms crossed over his chest.

"Now I'll ask again. Who is with me?"

There was a long silence before one stepped forward.

"I am, Laird."

Another moved from the crowd.

"And me, Laird."

"Aye, I'm with you."

Suddenly the entire crowd rumbled with agreement. The cries of "Aye!" echoed across the courtyard until the sound nearly deafened him.

Gannon came to stand beside Caelen, his grin wide as he clapped Caelen on the shoulder. But Caelen turned, looking for his wife in the madness.

She stood to the side, her smile as bright as the sun. She held up a fist and then pointed directly at Caelen. He motioned her over, suddenly eager to have her near.

She came at once, her skirts swinging as she made her way through the crowd. The men were solicitous of her, stepping out of her way. Some even offered their hand as she picked her way across the snow. Still others called for her to have caution now that she carried a babe.

She stopped in front of Caelen, her smile still wide and beautiful. Then she lifted her finger to wipe the blood trickling from the corner of his mouth.

"You bleed, husband."

He pulled her to him, slid his hand behind her neck, and pressed his bloody mouth to hers. Around them, a roar went up and finally, *finally*, the McDonalds decided they had something to celebrate.

CHAPTER 27

"The men improve," Sarah said as she and Rionna watched from the balcony above the courtyard.

"Aye, they do. They have dedication now. 'Tis good, for the time to fight draws near."

She rubbed the slight swell of her belly as she spoke. Battle was inevitable, but it troubled her still. She worried for Caelen, for her clan, for Caelen's family. She worried for the future of her babe.

"You're frowning, lass. Are you feeling poorly? Perhaps you should lie down a spell and rest."

Rionna shook her head. Caelen worried endlessly and fussed over her night and day. He'd undertaken the task of ensuring that she rested and never lifted a finger so as not to overexert herself. Unfortunately, his obsession had bled over to Sarah as well.

"Tell me, Sarah, did you rest endlessly when you were pregnant with your bairns?"

Sarah frowned. "There was work to be done, lass. Of course I didn't lay around."

Then as if realizing what she'd said, she scowled and leveled a stare at Rionna.

"I was not pregnant with the next laird nor was I a slight lass like yourself. Your husband worries. You should accommodate his request that you be at ease during your confinement."

"Confinement is right," Rionna muttered. "'Tis most ridiculous. You are right about one thing. There is work to be done and we need all the hands we can manage and yet I'm pushed aside and told to rest. It makes no sense. I am healthy. I haven't even been ill, not one day. The tiredness left me after my third month."

"The laird is a determined man. It won't be me who goes against his decree. The whole clan knows of his wishes for you, lass, so it's not just me who'll be reminding you of your duty."

"If I don't have something to do soon, I'll go daft. I cannot stay inside the keep day after day moving from one chair to the next. I'll grow fat and lazy and then what will happen? Caelen will set me aside for a prettier, fitter wife."

Sarah laughed. "Come now, lass, you won't be pregnant forever."

Caelen paused in his training and looked up as if knowing he'd find Rionna there watching. A slight smile lifted his lips and he nodded his acknowledgment to her. It gave her a ridiculous thrill every time he looked her way. Even though she despaired of the fact that he was oversolicitous, at the same time, she took great joy in the fact that he was so mindful of her well-being.

He may not admit that he had any soft feelings for her, but 'twas obvious he hadn't hardened his heart to her.

"Soon you'll give me the words I want, husband," she whispered fiercely.

"What's that you say, lass?" Sarah asked.

"'Tis nothing. I was but talking to myself."

"Come away. 'Tis starting to snow."

Rionna allowed Sarah to pull her back inside the keep and the two women walked down to the great hall so Rionna could warm herself by the fire.

Despite Rionna's earlier misgivings about learning the managing of the keep, after Caelen's insistence that she remain inside, she had decided she needed something to occupy her time, so many a day had been spent by the fire as Sarah went over Rionna's duties as mistress.

As Rionna stood by the fire, her mind wandered, as it often did when she was left alone with her thoughts. One of her duties as mistress was to ensure the comfort of her husband and to see to his care as surely as he did to hers.

Of late, he'd fussed endlessly over her. He pampered her and coddled her until she was positive she was going to be thoroughly spoiled by the process of bearing a child. Perhaps 'twas his aim in order to gain her agreement to have more in the future.

She smiled at the thought. He wouldn't have to do much convincing.

Still, it only seemed fair that she reciprocate.

Deciding that an evening of pampering was in order for her husband, she had one of the large tubs delivered to her chamber and directed the women to be on standby with buckets of hot water when her husband retired to their chamber.

She laid out the plain soaps that had no scent and made sure she had clean bathing cloths. She bade Gannon to carry up wood since Caelen would suffer apoplexy if she were to do it herself. Then she laid a fire in the hearth and called for a flagon of ale and the evening meal to be served in their chamber.

Satisfied with her effort, she surveyed her handiwork and then went below stairs to await her husband's arrival from the courtyard.

She fidgeted and paced while she waited. Finally, an hour later, the men began to filter into the hall, all ready for the evening meal. As soon as Caelen made his appearance, she hastened to greet him.

"I've arranged our meal to be served in our chamber," she said in a low voice. "Come above stairs so that I may attend you."

He gave her a puzzled look but allowed her to lead him toward the stairs. They were nearly run over by the women scurrying out of the chamber, buckets in hand, as they went below to fetch more hot water.

"What are you about, wife?" he asked when she sat him by the fire.

She pulled at his boots as he regarded her with lazy amusement.

"I've arranged for a hot bath followed by a hot meal. 'Twill soothe your aches and warm you through."

He lifted one eyebrow as she tugged one boot free of his foot. "What is the occasion?"

She smiled and began work on the other boot. "'Tis no special occasion."

A knock sounded and Rionna gave the call to enter. Four women came in bearing more water and added it to the already steaming tub. As the women left, Rionna trailed her fingers over the surface.

"I think 'tis ready."

When Caelen would have begun undressing himself, she put her hand on his arm to stop him. Then she began pulling his clothing down until he was nude before her. She took his hand and guided him toward the tub. He stepped over the side and groaned softly as he sank into the hot water.

She let him sit there a moment with his eyes closed before she collected the washing cloth and soap and knelt by the tub. He opened his eyes to look at her as she pressed the cloth to his chest and began to wash.

"I am unsure of what I've done to deserve such attention, but you'll not hear a single complaint cross my lips."

"You have been working tirelessly without rest for

weeks now," she said softly. "You've insisted on my resting, but not your own. You indulge me and pamper me and yet no one does the same for you."

He laughed. "I'm a warrior, Rionna. No one pampers warriors."

"This wife does," she defended. "An evening where you are waited on hand and foot will do you good."

She began washing his back in lazy, sensual strokes. His muscles rippled underneath her touch and his breath caught and expelled in a jerky rush.

"I think you may just be right about that. I rather like the idea of my wife serving me in the privacy of our chamber. It opens up a lot of colorful possibilities."

She leaned over and silenced him with a kiss. She dipped her hand into the water and trailed her fingers down his belly to his cock. Gently she rubbed up and down over his hardness.

"I must be sure to clean everywhere," she murmured.

"Oh aye, you mustn't miss a single spot," he murmured back as he nibbled at her lips.

She leaned back and then went to collect the heavy pitcher from the washbasin. After directing him to scoot forward in the tub, she began to wash his hair.

She loved running her fingers through the long strands. She soaped and rinsed and dug her fingers through the thick pelt, massaging and stroking as she sought to give him comfort.

"Your hands are magic, lass," he murmured. "'Tis the truth I've never had so much pleasure from something so simple as a washing of the hair."

"If you stand by the fire, I'll dry you," she said as she rocked back on her heels.

"You'll not have to ask me twice if I want another opportunity for your hands on my body."

He stood, and water ran down his back, over his firm buttocks, and down his legs. He stepped from the tub and then turned to face her, his back to the fire. Her gaze was riveted to his body. Were she ninety, she'd never grow tired of looking at this man. He fascinated her. He appealed to her feminine senses in a way a man had never before appealed to her.

"If you continue looking at me so, you'll find yourself on your back with me between your thighs," he said gruffly.

She grinned then and stepped forward to began wiping the moisture from his body. She rose up on tiptoe to gather the strands of his hair and squeeze excess water away. When his hair no longer dripped, she began to rub down the rest of his body.

'Twas the truth she had every intention of pampering her husband this night, but she was so enjoying the experience herself that she felt guilty over the pleasure it brought her.

With his chest and arms now dry, she dropped to her knees to rub his hips, thighs, and lower legs. For now she avoided his groin, wanting to draw out that particular form of torture.

Then she rose up on her knees so that her mouth was mere inches from his swollen cock. "Tell me husband, will you be too weak to partake of your evening meal if I pleasure you now?"

His eyes glittered at her mischievous teasing. He slid his fingers through her hair and pulled her roughly forward until the tip of his erection rested against her bottom lip.

"I'll manage somehow."

Knowing what the image of her on her knees while he stood over her would do to him, she slid her mouth over his hardness and took him deep.

"Ah, lass," he moaned. "Your mouth is the sweetest pleasure I've ever known."

His fingers curled into her hair and then he loosened

his hold as if worried he'd hurt her with his urgency. Then he tightened his grip again when she swallowed against the head.

This time she'd not draw out his pleasure. She intended it to be quick and sharp, a precursor of what was to come.

She curled her hand around the base of his shaft and stroked down as she sucked down to the tip. Then she tightened her fingers and stroked back up as she swallowed him whole once more.

Over and over she took him hard and fast until he went up on tiptoe, straining to go deeper. He tried to pull away when 'twas obvious he was about to gain his release, but she resisted and took him to the back of her throat, holding him captive there until with a harsh shout he poured himself into her mouth.

She continued to slide her tongue and lips over his length until finally he framed her face in his hands and pulled gently from her grasp. He reached down to help her to her feet and pulled her close when she stumbled. After a moment she pulled away and offered him his trews.

"Come to the bed so that I may brush your hair," she said as he reclothed himself. "Our food will be here soon and then you can eat."

She perched on the edge of the bed, and he sat on the floor between her knees while she brushed the tangles from his hair. After awhile she put aside the brush and pulled her fingers through the strands, enjoying the feel against her skin.

He reached up and caught one of her hands and brought it around to his mouth. He kissed her palm and then turned it over to press a kiss to each of her knuckles.

"What prompted this display of affection, wife?"

"Well, you did advise me that such displays were not appropriate in front of the men," she said primly.

He gave a shout of laughter. "I'd hope not, lass. Not that I don't love the sight of you with your lips wrapped around my cock, but 'twould incite a riot among my men. 'Tis best if we keep such matters private."

She grinned and leaned forward to hug him. She kissed his temple and then released him when a knock sounded at the door. "That will be Sarah with our evening meal. Don't move. I'll return in a moment."

She made Sarah wait in the hall and returned a few times to bear in the food. When she had everything, she dismissed Sarah and closed the door.

First she poured Caelen a goblet of ale and handed it to him. He watched her all the while she prepared a plate. His gaze was intense and possessive, like he'd love nothing more than to strip her down and take her there on the floor.

'Twas the truth, she'd love nothing more as well, but there was food to be had and her husband was likely starving.

She curled up beside him on the floor, shivering softly. Her clothing was slightly damp from attending to Caelen's bath. Her husband frowned and put his hand out to touch the sleeves of her gown.

"You're cold. And wet."

"Aye, 'tis not of import."

"You're shivering."

"The fire will warm me soon enough."

He took the plate from her and set it on the bed. Then he got to his feet and pulled her up beside him. In a reversal of roles for the evening, he divested her of her gown and then removed her underdress, leaving her naked to his avid gaze.

"Your skin glows so warmly in the light of the fire,"

he murmured. "I think 'tis the way I'd like you to remain for the evening."

He settled back on the floor but instead of allowing her to sit beside him as she had before, he pulled her down so that she straddled his lap.

"'Tis too cold on the floor. You'll sit here on me so you'll not be cold."

He touched the tiny swell of her belly and then laid his palm over it. "How is our child this day?"

"I've not felt him move yet, but I think 'twill be soon. I'm small and Sarah says I'll feel him move sooner because of it."

"I hope not too small," Caelen said with a frown. "'Tis God's truth you don't look big enough to push out a child."

"You worry too much. I'll be fine."

She reached beyond him for the plate of meat, cheese, and bread. She set it on the floor next to them and picked up a piece of the meat.

She offered it to him from her hand. His mouth brushed over her fingers as he ate the offering.

"'Tis the sweetest meal I've ever eaten," he said in a husky voice. "Offered from the hand of a naked goddess while she sits astride me. 'Tis heaven I've gone to."

It was tempting to lean forward and kiss him long and hard, but she'd kept him from his meal long enough. Alternating between the meat, cheese, and bread, she broke off smaller pieces and fed him with her fingers.

He made it difficult because all the while she tended his meal, he stroked his hands over her skin. He caressed her shoulders, her back, and then he moved around to cup her ample breasts, thumbing each nipple in turn until she was fidgeting all over his lap.

"I should warn you that when this seduction of yours is at its end, I'll not last long. I mean to have you lass, but I'm so eager, I'll spill my seed at the first thrust."

She laughed. "Tonight is about your pleasure, husband. I am yours to do with as you like."

"Then free me of my trews right here so I can rest deep inside you. I'm thinking of making it a rule that when you sit on my lap, you must rest atop my cock."

She pulled impatiently at his trews, for his words licked like fire over her body and she was as eager as he was to have him inside her.

She arched up as soon as he sprang free. He gripped her hips and guided her into place and then sank deep. They both made inarticulate sounds of pleasure. When she would have moved, he anchored her tight against him so that no space separated them.

"Right there, lass. Don't move. Now feed me the rest of my meal."

Each time she moved to pick up a piece of bread or cheese from the plate, she clenched tighter around him and he swelled even larger until she was impossibly stretched.

"You clutch me like a velvet fist," he breathed.

He ran his hands up her arms and gripped her just below the shoulders. She dropped the last piece of bread when he fused his mouth to hers as if he hadn't just eaten his fill and was starving. For her.

The flats of his palms glided down her arms and then over her hips, where they came to rest. His fingers dug into her buttocks and he lifted her as he arched upward.

"'Tis too good," he gritted out. "I can't make it last."

He thrust hard and she was filled by his warmth. He held her tightly to his groin as he pulsed inside her sheath. Then his hands left her hips and he pulled her against his chest, his hands stroking up and down her spine.

For several long moments he continued his gentle caresses as he softened inside her. Impossibly, he wrapped one arm around her and put his other hand to the floor to push himself upward.

He slipped from her body as he stood, but he continued to hold her as he turned toward the bed, the tub and the food forgotten.

He laid her down and crawled into bed beside her, pulling her against his body. They sprawled there on the mattress, limbs tangled, arms thrown possessively over each other. He kissed her forehead and sighed in contentment. She savored the sound of a well-pleasured man and smiled her satisfaction.

"I am unsure what warranted such affection from my wife, but do tell me so that I may do it again in the future," he said lightly.

She squeezed him and kissed the hollow of his neck. Then she toyed idly with his hair, suddenly possessed to want to know more of her husband.

"What is it you write in your scrolls?"

He drew away, seemingly surprised by the question. He looked faintly . . . embarrassed, and she wondered if she hadn't been better served to not spoil the intimate moment between them.

"My thoughts," he finally said. "It helps me make better sense of them when I write them down."

"So it's like an accounting of your day?"

"In a manner of speaking. I find I express myself better with written words. I haven't an eloquent tongue and I don't like to speak overmuch."

"Nay. Surely you jest," she teased.

He smacked her playfully on the arse. "'Tis something I've done since I learned to read and write when I was a young lad. My father was a learned man and he taught his sons. He thought it an important skill. He oft said that intelligence served a warrior better than a sword."

"He sounded like a wise man."

"He was," Caelen said quietly. "He was a great laird, beloved by his clan."

Rionna looked into her husband's eyes and knew that

demons from his past gnawed at him this night. She sorely regretted making him think of his father, for 'twas impossible to separate his death and Elsepeth's betrayal. But at the same time, she wanted to know more and perhaps ease her husband's burden.

"Tell me of Elsepeth," she urged.

Caelen stiffened and his expression darkened. "'Tis nothing to speak of."

"I would disagree. She's made you hard. She's taken something that should be rightfully mine."

Caelen looked at her in confusion. "What is it you speak of?"

She touched his cheek. "Your heart. You cannot ever give it fully to me because she still occupies it."

"Nay," he swiftly denied.

"Aye," she argued. "You hardened the part of your heart that you offered to her. When she betrayed you, you locked that part away, never to open it again. She's trapped there. She has what is rightfully mine and I want it, husband. I'm no longer content to wait."

He looked incredulously at her. "You make unreasonable demands, wife."

Rionna huffed impatiently. "'Tis unreasonable to want the whole of my husband's heart? Would you accept that part of my heart belonged to another man and you could never touch it?"

He scowled at that. "You're making too much of it, Rionna. Elsepeth is part of my past. You are my future. The two have nothing to do with each other."

"Then tell me of her," Rionna challenged. "If she poses no threat, then 'tis nothing to speak of her."

Caelen sighed and ran his hand through his hair in frustration. He rolled to his back and stared up at the ceiling. Rionna remained still, waiting as he grappled with his irritation.

"I was a fool."

Rionna didn't respond as she watched the emotion play out over her husband's face. She didn't believe for a minute he still harbored tender feelings for Elsepeth, but his past was still very much alive in his heart and mind. 'Twas like a poison he'd yet to purge from his system.

She could still see the naked pain in his eyes and his regret at all that had transpired so many years ago.

"She was a few years older than I and she had more experience. I was but a young lad and she was my first . . . She was my first lover. I fancied myself in love with her. I had our future all mapped out. I intended to marry her, though I had nothing in the way to offer a wife. I was the third son of a laird. We weren't a poor clan then but we were never rich either. 'Twas my intention to go to her cousin, Duncan Cameron, and ask for her hand in marriage."

Rionna grimaced, for even though she knew the tale, or the crux of it, the inevitable path still made her cringe.

"My father sent me, Ewan, and Alaric to barter with a neighboring clan. While we were gone, Elsepeth drugged the men and opened the gates so Cameron's soldiers could sneak into the keep in the dead of night. 'Twas a bloodbath. Our clan was sorely outnumbered and 'twas the truth we were not as well trained then as we are now. We didn't stand a chance.

"When my brothers and I returned, we found our father dead. Ewan's young wife had been raped and her throat cut. Only his son survived because he was hidden by women in the keep.

"The remaining members of our clan told me of Elsepeth's involvement, but my shame doesn't end there."

Rionna's brows drew together. "What happened then?"

"I didn't believe them," he said in disgust. "I was presented solid evidence that my head knew had to be true but my heart told me she couldn't have possibly betrayed me. I searched her out, determined to hear her explanation from her own lips. I was sure there had been some mistake."

Rionna winced and blew out her breath. This part of the story she hadn't heard before.

"When I confronted her, she laughed. She didn't try to make up a lie. She laughed to my face and when I turned away, she drew a knife and plunged it into my back."

"The scar above your side," Rionna whispered.

"Aye. 'Tis not a mark I wear with pride. 'Tis a reminder of how I allowed a woman I cared for to destroy my clan."

"Where is she now?"

"I don't know. I care not. One day she'll pay for her sins, just as I'll pay for mine."

"You don't think you've made good on your mistakes?" Rionna asked. "Your clan is rebuilt, your people thrive, you've made an alliance that will save many from Cameron's ruthless ambition."

"Nothing I do will ever give me and my brothers back our father," he said simply. "I learned a valuable lesson that day. One I'll never turn my back on. I allowed my heart to discount evidence that my mind knew was sound. I'll never second-guess what stares me in the face again."

Rionna frowned and slid her hand over his chest as she snuggled into his side. He sounded so . . . cold. Not at all the warm, gruff warrior that she'd grown to love with all her heart.

For the first time she wondered if Elsepeth had damaged a part of him that Rionna had no hope of repairing.

Caelen closed his hand over hers and squeezed as they lay in silence. She thought on all he'd said and the more she thought on it, the more one thing didn't make sense.

"Caelen?"

"Aye."

"Why did Cameron attack? What was his purpose? He didn't take over your land. He left it in ruins and returned to his own lands."

Caelen's chest heaved as he breathed deep. "I don't know that. I've never known. 'Twas as if he was sending a message, but 'tis one I've never understood the meaning of. We were a clan at peace. We warred with no one. My father was not a man who condoned raiding or fighting for the sake of fighting. It sickens me that he met the end he met when he never brought harm to anyone."

Rionna rose up on one elbow so that she could stare down at her husband. It suddenly seemed all important that she say what it was that burned on her tongue.

"I'm not Elsepeth, Caelen. I need you to know that. I'll not ever betray you."

He stared at her a long moment before pulling her down for a kiss. "Aye, I know it, Rionna."

CHAPTER 28

May saw no break in the weather. Indeed, it was as if winter was making up for the mildness of January by stubbornly clinging on to spring.

Their food stores were depleted and the men hadn't been able to hunt in an entire fortnight because of the heavy, blowing snow.

Everyone was forced indoors, hovering near the fires to keep warm. Caelen stewed with impatience, waiting a break in the weather and waiting for word from Ewan.

At the end of the third week of the month, the break finally came. A messenger arrived bearing news from Ewan that all was well at Neamh Álainn and that plans were underway to go into battle. Ewan was even now sending word to all the other lairds. The king had delivered to Ewan a contingent of soldiers, all loyal to the crown.

Much time had been lost due to the prolonged snows and bitter cold. Now Ewan was impatient to go to war, and he directed Caelen to make ready and await Ewan's summons.

Despite the fact that she knew this day was coming, Rionna was disturbed by the news. She had no desire to send her husband or her clan to war, but she bit her lip and kept her misgivings to herself. She wouldn't burden her husband when his mind was already looking ahead to the coming battle.

He was restless, and as the days wore on he became tense and silent. Finally, when they were distributing the last of the venison, Caelen rounded up his hunting party and declared that they'd hunt as much meat as possible in the short time before they rode off to war.

Caelen's restlessness had carried over to the men, and a hunt was just the thing to quiet their minds before battle.

Caelen stood in the hall, Rionna on his right side and Gannon to his left. Rionna had twined her fingers with his and held on, drawing comfort from his touch.

"You'll stay behind and watch over the keep," Caelen said to Gannon. "I don't expect word from Ewan for some days yet, but if you receive a message, send someone for me immediately. We won't venture far on our hunt. Watch over Rionna well for me."

Gannon nodded. "Of course I will, Laird. May your hunt be successful and you return with a full bounty."

Gannon strode away, leaving Caelen alone with Rionna. She turned into his embrace before he could say anything else and she hugged him fiercely, uncaring of who looked on. 'Twas one time her husband would have to suffer displays of affection outside of their chamber.

To her surprise, he kissed her lingeringly and stroked his fingers over her cheeks as he pulled away.

"I can see the worry in your eyes, wife. 'Tis not good for you or our babe. All will be well. This day has been coming for many years. 'Tis the truth I am fair itching to get on with it."

"Aye, I know it," she said quietly. "Go on your hunt and clear your mind before you ride off to do battle with Cameron. I have every faith that you and your brothers will prove victorious."

His eyes glinted with satisfaction at her words. He

leaned down to kiss her again and then turned to walk from the hall to where the hunting party waited in the courtyard.

Rionna watched him go and sighed. The next weeks would be a test of her fortitude. She loathed the idea that Caelen and her clansmen would be miles away on a battlefield while she remained behind at the keep, ignorant of the goings-on. She wouldn't even know the outcome until after it had already been decided.

A day later, Jamie rode back into the courtyard, bearing meat from the hunt. He dismounted and greeted Gannon while Rionna stood impatiently at the steps to the keep.

After speaking a moment with Gannon, Jamie strode toward Rionna.

"The laird bade me to bring this message to you, my lady. He says the hunt is successful and to expect him home by nightfall tomorrow."

Rionna smiled. "'Tis good news you bear, Jamie. Come inside and get warm. Have something to eat while the others unpack your horse."

With no word forthcoming from Ewan, Rionna could look forward to at least a few more days of her husband being at home before he was called away to war. The news gladdened her heart and lifted some of the headache that had plagued her since his departure.

The afternoon was spent preserving the venison, but Rionna quickly discovered one unpleasant aspect of her condition. She hadn't been plagued with any sickness thus far. Indeed, other than fatigue at the beginning, she'd enjoyed an unremarkable pregnancy so far. But as soon as she got close to the carcass of the stag, the smell of blood and raw meat made her stomach heave violently.

She humiliated herself by retching into the snow, and

try as she might she couldn't rid herself of the odor that now seemed permanently implanted in her nostrils.

Gannon gently led her away from where the women were working and took her through the snow to the far side of the courtyard where she could look upon the loch in the distance and breathe crisp, clean-smelling air.

"'Tis humiliating," Rionna muttered.

Gannon smiled. "Nay, 'tis not an uncommon event for a woman in your condition. I think Lady McCabe retched from the time she discovered her pregnancy to the time she delivered. Cormac and I were forever fetching things for her to be sick in."

A shout from the gate distracted her from her still quivering stomach. She and Gannon both turned in time to see Simon ride into the courtyard, his face bloody, his horse lathered as though he'd ridden the animal relentlessly.

When the horse came to a stop, Simon slid from the saddle and landed in the snow.

Fear hit Rionna square in the chest and she was running before Gannon could stop her. She reached Simon first and dropped to her knees next to the older man. Gannon got there a second later and helped her turn him onto his back.

He was barely conscious, and blood seeped onto the snow, staining it scarlet. There was a deep gash in the side of his neck. His shoulder was cut so deep that it had nearly severed his arm from the socket.

He blinked through swollen eyes and his lips parted as he tried to speak.

"Nay," Rionna whispered, tears biting at her eyelids. "Don't speak, Simon. Remain still until we can stop the bleeding."

"Nay, my lady," he rasped out. "I must tell you this. 'Tis important. We were ambushed. An arrow struck the laird from behind. They waited until we passed and then attacked us from the rear."

"Oh God," Rionna choked out. "Caelen? Is he alive? Where is he? Where are the others?"

"Arlen is dead," Simon whispered.

"Father!" Jamie cried as he ran up. He dropped to his knees and gathered his father's head in his lap. "What has happened?"

"Shh, lad," Gannon said grimly. "He's telling us of it now."

Simon licked his lips and moaned softly. "He fell from his horse but he was alive. They took him."

"Who?" Rionna demanded. "Who did this to you?"

Simon fixed her with his stare, his eyes brighter for just a moment as anger flared in their depths. "Your father, lass. 'Twas your father and the men who sided with him. They take him to Duncan Cameron."

CHAPTER 29

"If you think I'm going to allow you to leave this keep, you're daft," Gannon said bluntly as Rionna paced back and forth in the great hall.

Rionna gripped the scroll bearing the seal of Ewan McCabe and the king, the message that had arrived barely an hour after Simon rode in badly injured, bearing the news of Caelen's capture.

She turned urgently to Gannon, knowing she must convince Caelen's commander or all would be lost. "Think, Gannon. Think on this and you'll know I'm right. We cannot wait. Cameron will kill Caelen. If he doesn't, my father will. Caelen isn't being used as a pawn against Ewan McCabe. 'Tis my father's doing and his bargain with the devil, Duncan Cameron. He spoke of this before but I thought him daft. After my wedding, he approached me to entreat me to join with him in a way to rid our clan of Caelen. He was furious that he was being forced to give over his leadership. 'Tis the truth that now I don't think he ever had any intention of handing over the title of laird to Alaric when he first suggested the alliance. His plan was to marry me to Alaric McCabe and make Alaric laird upon the birth of my first child. But why wait? 'Twas an agreement that never made sense to me, given my father's reluctance to hand over leadership of the clan. I think he intended to make sure Alaric was never laird. I think he would have murdered him after I was with child. He could have made it look like an accident and then Ewan would never have broken the alliance if I was to bear Alaric's child. He wouldn't have been able to prove that my father was the cause of Alaric's death."

"'Tis a complicated plot you speak of," Gannon said with a frown.

"I know it sounds hysterical, that I've made it all up because of my worry for Caelen, but it makes sense, Gannon. If you think on it, *it makes sense.*"

"Aye, it does," Gannon admitted.

"We cannot wait until Ewan is ready to wage war with Cameron. I need you to travel with all haste to Neamh Álainn and tell Ewan of my plan. I know not what this scroll contains. I cannot break the seal and have someone examine the contents, for it ruins my plan. But whatever instructions it contains, Ewan must do differently if we are to have the element of surprise."

Gannon shook his head vehemently. "I will not leave you, my lady. Caelen would gut me and feed my innards to the wolves if I allowed you to go through with this plan of yours."

A sound of rage blew past her lips. She was so furious and so unbelievably terrified that she could barely hold it together. She wanted to curl into a tight ball and pretend none of this had ever happened. But Caelen's life depended on her being able to save him, and save him she would if she had to battle her way through every one of her clansmen to do it.

"Will you just let him die while you wait for his brothers to gather their warriors and attack Cameron? Think you that Caelen will even still be alive? *Think,* Gannon. My father and his men bear an injured man with them. Caelen will slow their travel back to Cameron's lands. If I leave now and ride straight through, I can arrive on their heels, before they've had time to determine Caelen's fate."

Gannon thrust his hand into his hair and turned away. "What you ask me to do, my lady, is impossible. How can I abandon you while I run to Ewan for help? How can I face Caelen if something happens to you and his bairn? You underestimate Caelen's strength. It matters not if he took an arrow to the back. He *will* survive. He has much to live for."

Rionna tugged at Gannon's arm until he faced her again. "My clansmen will follow but only I will gain entrance to Cameron's domain. 'Tis important he thinks I came alone. Everything rides upon my ability to make him think what it is I want him to think. I must buy time for Ewan to arrive. I'll not ask your permission to do this, Gannon. What I ask for is your help. I need you to go to Ewan. If I send one of my men, after what has occurred, Ewan will think it a trick. He'll believe *you*. You were his most trusted man, a man he sent into service to his brother so that Caelen would have someone he trusted close by. Don't betray that trust, Gannon. I and my babe are counting on you to help us save my husband."

"You don't play fair, my lady," Gannon said in disgust.

"'Tis nothing fair when it comes to the life of my husband," she said fiercely. "I love him and I won't let him go to his death if there is anything I can do to prevent it. I'll take on my father and Duncan Cameron and his entire army if 'tis what it will take."

Gannon's expression softened and he touched her arm in a gesture of comfort. "Caelen is a fortunate man, my lady. 'Tis not often a man has a wife so fierce that she would risk her life to save his."

"Then you'll do it? You'll leave at once for Neamh Álainn?"

Gannon sighed. "Aye, I'll do it."

Rionna threw her arms around him and hugged him, much to his dismay. He disentangled himself from her grasp and scowled.

"'Tis my hope you'll defend me as fiercely as you do Caelen, because when he discovers what I've allowed you to do, he'll take off my head."

"Go now," she said. "I'll gather the men in the courtyard to tell them what must be done."

Rionna stared nervously at the assembled warriors, their grim faces outlined by the blaze of torches. Gannon had already ridden out and Sarah was preparing Rionna's bag so that she would be ready to depart as soon as the men were apprised of the situation.

"Will Simon live?"

She didn't register who called out the question. She was still numb and her thoughts were occupied with the task before her.

"I know not," she said honestly. "He is being cared for. If God wills it, he'll live this day and long into the future."

"Who did this thing, my lady?"

She drew in a deep breath. "'Twas my father, your former laird. He has allied himself with Duncan Cameron and seeks to destroy my husband so that he may regain leadership of this clan."

She held her breath as she waited their response. It was entirely possible that they'd embrace the idea of her father returning as laird. Caelen had gained their respect, aye, but Rionna couldn't be assured that given the opportunity, they wouldn't turn away.

"What is to be done?" Seamus demanded as he stepped forward, his beefy arms crossing his chest as he glared his displeasure. "Surely we aren't going to let such an insult to our laird pass."

It took all of Rionna's restraint not to throw her arms around the huge warrior and pepper his face with teary kisses.

"We ride to Duncan Cameron's land," she said when she could speak without her throat knotting up. "Gannon has ridden to Neamh Álainn to apprise Ewan McCabe of the situation. When we near Cameron land, you will all fall back and await my command to attack."

Murmurs rose from the men and Seamus stepped forward. "What then will you be doing, my lady?"

"I'm going in to save my husband," she said in a tone that brooked no argument. She may not be laird of this clan, but in this moment, she'd take down any man who tried to prevent her from going after Caelen.

"It's going to require the biggest deception of my life. 'Tis possible my husband may despise me before it's over, but if I'm successful, he'll be alive and 'tis all that matters. The question I pose to you, is whether you'll stand with me and risk your lives to save our laird."

Seamus cleared his throat and then turned to stare over the assembled men. Then he slowly looked back at Rionna. "I'm with you, my lady."

One by one, the men stepped forward and declared their willingness to back Rionna in her plan.

"Then we must go now and ride hard," Rionna said. "I must arrive before 'tis too late."

CHAPTER 30

Caelen barely held back the curse as he hit the ground. Pain speared through his shoulder, spreading agonizing flame until he had to close his eyes and grit his teeth to remain silent.

His hands were tied behind his back, making the wound in his shoulder all the more painful. Gregor McDonald had torn the arrow from Caelen's shoulder without care and Caelen had steadily bled on the rough journey to Duncan Cameron's keep.

"I've brought you Caelen McCabe, Laird Cameron," Gregor called.

Caelen opened his eyes to see Cameron standing a short distance away. Hatred was bitter in Caelen's mouth. That the man was so close and yet Caelen was helpless to do anything but lie there made bile rise in his throat. If he could manage the feat, he'd spit in Cameron's eye.

"So you have," Cameron said.

He walked over to where Caelen lay on the ground and kicked at his wounded shoulder. Caelen grimaced but stared up at Cameron, allowing the full breadth of his hatred to show.

"You'd like to kill me, wouldn't you, Caelen?" Cameron taunted in a low voice. "You hate me more than even your brothers do. 'Twas your foolishness that brought low your clan. My cousin is bonny, is she not? I haven't seen her in some time. She's likely spreading her legs for some other poor besotted fool."

Caelen continued to stare at Cameron until Cameron fidgeted uncomfortably and then booted Caelen in the shoulder again.

"I wonder if given a choice between saving his brother's life or protecting his lovely wife and daughter, which would Ewan choose? Surely not the brother who once cost him everything. Tell me, Caelen, how would it make you feel to know you destroyed all your brother holds dear a second time?"

Cameron knelt beside Caelen's head, wrapped his hand in Caelen's hair, and yanked upward so their faces were just inches apart.

"He won't have to choose, because I plan to have both. You're of no consequence to me. I'll not blink an eye over your death, and then I'll destroy your clan and the king you're so loyal to."

As he stared into Cameron's eyes, the question that Rionna had posed floated back into his mind.

"Why?" he asked. "Why did you do it? If you're going to kill me anyway, then tell me why you destroyed my clan eight years ago. We were no threat to you."

Cameron rose and took a step back, a hatred that mirrored Caelen's own reflected in his gaze.

"You'd never heard of me until that day, had you?" He shook his head. "How like your father to have never mentioned me or my father. You aren't the only one with reason to hate, Caelen. Your father took what was mine. I returned the favor."

"You're daft," Caelen said hoarsely. "My father was a

peaceful man. He wouldn't wage war against anyone. Not unless provoked."

Cameron pressed his boot to Caelen's throat, pinning him to the ground. "Oh aye, he was a peaceful man. Do you want to know why? He made a vow after my father's death. His guilt was too much for him to bear. He swore on my father's grave never to pick up arms again. I know. I was there. I heard his vow. I heard his apology to my mother. He patted me on the head as he walked away. Patted me on the head as if that would bring me a measure of comfort when my father was in the ground. If I'd had a sword, your father would have died that day and bled to death atop my father's grave. I would have seen to it."

"You lie," Caelen ground out. "My father never spoke of you or your father."

"Your father was a coward. He fought alongside my father and when my father was felled from his horse, he left him to die there. He turned his back on the man he called friend, and he ran from the battlefield. And do you know, just before your father drew his last breath, I reminded him of that boy he patted on the head at my father's grave. Do you know what his last words were, Caelen?"

Caelen swallowed against the rage knotting his throat. His blood pumped so furiously through his veins that he feared exploding.

Cameron leaned down again so that he was close to Caelen's ear. "He said he was sorry again. And then he begged me to spare his grandson's life."

"And so you murdered and raped the boy's mother instead," Caelen snarled.

"If I could have found the brattling, I would have spitted him on my sword. My only regret is that you and your brothers were not there the day I attacked. It would have brought me great satisfaction to have destroyed every last McCabe."

"I'll see you in hell for what you've done," Caelen vowed.

Cameron straightened and motioned toward his men. "Take him to the dungeon. I cannot bear to look upon his face a moment longer. Killing him now is too good a fate. I want him to suffer as my father suffered when he slowly bled to death on that battle-field."

Three of Cameron's men yanked Caelen to his feet and dragged him toward the small entryway with the steps leading into the darkness below. A fourth man bore a torch down into the cold, damp corridor.

At the end of it, a yawning hole opened in the floor, and without warning Caelen was shoved down. He pitched forward into the blackness and was suspended momentarily in the air before landing on the stone floor below. His injured shoulder took the brunt of the fall and he cried out as agony tore down his back and arm, numbing his hand.

He sucked in deep breaths as he battled uncon-sciousness. He tasted blood and realized he'd bitten his lip.

As he lay there shivering, pain his only companion in the darkness, he closed his eyes and conjured an image of Rionna's smiling face. He imagined he was home, in the privacy of their chamber, as she thought up some new way to drive him mad with lust.

He imagined tracing the swell of her belly and talking with her long into the night of their hopes and dreams for their child.

"Protect her well, Ewan," he whispered. "For I have failed her. And you."

* * *

Rionna was near collapse when she ordered her clan to surround Duncan Cameron's holding and remain in hiding until she gave the order to attack. If God was with them, Ewan McCabe would arrive with reinforcements before her clan was forced to take action. But if not, she and every one of the McDonald warriors would go down fighting.

She prayed for strength. She prayed for God's guidance for what she was about to do. She had to be convincing or she and Caelen would both die.

Gathering the reins of her tired horse, she started forward, her heart pounding as she broke from the cover of the forest, and rode down toward the gate of Cameron's fortress.

'Twas an imposing sight of stone, wood, and metal. The walls were tall and she only prayed that her men could scale them rapidly enough to avoid detection.

Her plan had to work. If God truly sided with the righteous, her clan would win the day and she would return home with her husband.

Still, she prayed, for perhaps God needed convincing on the matter.

When she reached the gate, the watchman called down to her. Rionna surveyed the top of the wall and found at least three crossbows aimed in her direction.

She pushed down the hood of her cloak and then called up. "I am Rionna McDonald and I wish to see my father, Gregor McDonald."

There was a long wait and then Duncan Cameron appeared at the top of the wall, her father beside him.

"Tell me, Rionna, have you come to beg for your husband's life?" Cameron called down.

She fixed him with a haughty stare and twisted her

lips in scorn. "I've come to see if what my men have told me is true. And if 'tis true, and my father has felled the McCabe warrior, I want to claim the right to kill him if the task is not already done."

Cameron arched his eyebrow in surprise and Rionna held her breath until she nearly swayed from the horse. Oh God, let him still be alive. They couldn't have arrived with Caelen too awfully long ago. She and her men had ridden without stop and they'd picked up a fresh trail halfway here and followed it until they reached the keep.

"Open the gate," Cameron shouted.

A few moments later, the wood creaked and groaned and the heavy gate began to swing open. She remained atop her horse and waited for permission to enter.

Soon enough, Cameron and her father appeared at the entryway and one of Cameron's men came forward to assist her from her horse. When her feet hit the ground, her knees nearly buckled, but by sheer force of will she remained standing and allowed her horse to be led away.

"'Tis an interesting tale you spin, mistress," Cameron said as he stared at her. "You have my attention."

Rionna looked at her father, wondering if he was too cowed by Cameron to offer words of his own. He stared back, his expression flat, and his eyes glittered with suspicion.

"Is he dead yet?" she demanded.

Finally Cameron shook his head and she went weak with relief. "Nay, not yet. He's only just arrived. Tell me, how did you come so quickly?"

"When my men bore me the tale of what occurred, I refused to believe my good fortune until I laid eyes on him myself. If 'tis true that my father captured Caelen McCabe, then 'tis my thanks I must offer."

"What is this nonsense, daughter?" Gregor finally demanded.

Cameron held up his hand. "'Tis only one way to solve this riddle. Come, my lady. 'Tis cold and you've traveled a great distance."

Rionna slid her hand through Cameron's outstretched arm and smiled gratefully up at him. "My thanks, Laird Cameron. 'Tis the truth I'm weary, but my relief was so great, I would not stop until I begged sanctuary at your door."

"Sanctuary? My dear lady, what would make you cry sanctuary?" he asked, as he guided her through the courtyard and up the steps to the keep.

A warm blast of air hit her as did the stench. Her nose curled and it took everything she had to keep her stomach from rebelling.

The tunic she wore disguised the swell of her belly and she wasn't far gone enough for her condition to be evident. The last thing she wanted was to reveal that she was carrying Caelen's child.

"Aye, sanctuary. Think you that I would be safe from Ewan McCabe once it was learned a McDonald took his brother?"

"Why do you want to kill your husband?" Cameron asked bluntly.

He gestured for her to sit in one of the chairs in front of the fire, and it was with great relief she did so. She wasn't sure how much longer she could remain standing.

"Does it matter?" she asked in a level voice.

"I find it hard to believe you left the protection of your clan in the dead of winter so that you could be the one to kill a man who is for all practical purposes already a dead man."

"I hate him," Rionna spat. "I hate all of the McCabes.

They have run roughshod over my clan. 'Tis the truth, I had no great love for the leadership of my father, but at least he was a McDonald. I have been humiliated by the McCabes at every turn. If you won't allow me to do the killing, I would at least like to witness it. And I would seek your protection until this matter with the McCabes is done."

"You are an odd woman, Rionna McDonald. Or should I say McCabe?"

Rionna bolted to her feet, drew her sword, and leveled it at Cameron in a show of bravado she hoped impressed him or further convinced him she was just daft enough to want her husband dead. She was so desperate at this point, she was grasping for straws and she well knew it.

"I'll not be called by that name," she hissed.

He pushed aside the blade of her sword as if it were nothing more than a pesky fly. "And I'll not have a female brandishing her sword at me in my own home."

He motioned her back to her seat and then turned to glance at Gregor McDonald, who stood on Rionna's other side.

"You have me curious, Rionna. What did Caelen McCabe do to draw your ire?"

She glanced at her father, knowing that it was here that he would be convinced and he would lend credibility to her tale, no matter how absurd it sounded to Cameron.

"He insisted I act and dress as a female. He took my sword from me and forbade me to pick it back up. He mocked and humiliated me at every turn. He . . . He sorely abused me."

Cameron chuckled and then glanced at her father. "What manner of woman did you raise, Gregor?"

"She thinks herself a lad," Gregor said in disgust. "Nothing I ever did made her act and dress as she should. I washed my hands of her years ago. 'Tis the truth he probably bedded her and this is the source of his 'abuse.'"

Cameron's gaze swept lingeringly over her body in a manner that made her grateful she'd bound her breasts. He looked for sign that she was indeed womanly, but in her current manner of dress, she looked lean and shapeless, just as a young lad would.

She shivered at the lust in his eyes. In spite of, or perhaps because of, her eccentricities, Cameron looked upon her like he'd like nothing more than to tumble her to the ground for a quick rut. Or perhaps 'twas because he coveted what Caelen had already had. Trying to discern the mind of a man was impossible.

But he turned instead and waved an arrogant hand to one of his men. "Bring Caelen McCabe up from the dungeon. His wife seeks a reunion."

The knot in her belly grew and fear nearly paralyzed her. She would have to act quick in order to convince Cameron and her father that all she'd said was true. It hurt her to do what she must. It would be the hardest thing she'd ever do, but she had to convince Caelen that she loathed the very sight of him and wanted his death.

All the while she waited, she steeled herself for the sight of her husband. She knew he was injured. He might be near death even now. She couldn't react, not as a horrified wife.

Rionna wanted to weep. She was beyond exhausted and she was more afraid than she'd ever been in her life.

When they shoved Caelen into the hall, he fell to his knees and she could see his hands were secured behind his back. Before he could look up, she was on her feet.

She stalked across the room but just as she reached him, he lifted his gaze to her.

Shock registered in his eyes and he parted his mouth as if about to speak. So she did the only thing she knew to silence him.

She reared back and slapped him as hard as she could across one cheek.

CHAPTER 31

Caelen's neck snapped back and he barely managed to stay on his knees. He whipped his head back around to stare at his wife. His *wife*. She stood before him, her eyes spitting fury, while Cameron and Gregor stood behind her looking faintly amused.

"Are you mad?" he demanded. "What are you doing?"

"I'm here to see you die," she hissed. "If God is willing and with Laird Cameron's permission, I aim to do the killing myself. 'Twould give me great pleasure to rid myself of you, Caelen McCabe."

He heard her words. He saw the very real anger in her eyes. But he couldn't make sense of any of it. Dread crept into his chest until it pained him more than the arrow wound in his back.

It couldn't be happening again. He couldn't countenance history repeating itself in such a bizarre manner.

Duncan Cameron came up behind Rionna and slid a hand over her shoulder. "Your wife is here to see you, Caelen. Isn't that thoughtful of her? She says she wants to be your executioner. What think you of that?"

Before Caelen could muster a response—what could he possibly say to that?—Cameron turned Rionna, pulled her into his arms, and kissed her savagely.

Cold rage seared over Caelen's body. He could no longer feel the pain of his wound. All he felt was overwhelming fury. His mind was muddled enough that he still couldn't comprehend the whole of it, but what stared him in the face was betrayal.

Again.

Rionna yanked away from Cameron, slapped him soundly across the face as she'd done to Caelen, and then went for her sword. Cameron grabbed her arm and hauled her up close.

"I've already been abused by one man. I'll not suffer it at the hands of another," Rionna spat.

Caelen's brows went up. "Abuse? Is that what you call it, *wife*?"

Rionna glanced at Caelen, her beautiful, deceitful eyes flashing scornfully. She looked back to Cameron and pulled at her arm. Then she stilled and stared intently into Cameron's eyes. "You doubt me. 'Twas a test. You doubt that I'm here because I seek the death of the McCabe warrior."

She wrested her arms from his grip and reached into the folds of her cloak to draw out a scroll. Even from where he knelt, Caelen could see two seals. One was his brother's. The other belonged to the king.

"I brought this. Know you what this is, Laird Cameron? 'Tis a call to arms from Ewan McCabe. In it are likely detailed battle plans. All you need to know of the coming war. Would I give this to you if 'twas all a trick?"

"Nay!" Caelen roared.

He lunged forward but was restrained on both sides by two of Cameron's men. He twisted and fought against their strength, but with his hands bound, he could do nothing.

Cameron took the scroll from her hand and turned it over, examining the seals. Without a word, he broke the wax and unrolled the parchment. It took him several minutes to read the contents and when he was done, he carefully rolled it back and then leveled a stare at Caelen.

"It would seem that your wife and clan no longer want you, McCabe."

Caelen's nostrils flared and his lip curled as he stared coldly at the woman standing before him. "I have no wife or clan save the McCabes."

"I have no desire to look upon him any longer. Return him from whatever hole you dragged him from," Rionna said in an equally cold voice.

"Well 'tis the matter of his death we need to speak on," Cameron drawled. "'Twould seem war is imminent if this message from Ewan McCabe and the king is to be believed. I did hope they'd be more original in their planning, but 'twould appear they favor the straightforward method. I'll give you a day, my lady. He dies in the morn, and then I must make my own plans in accordance with Ewan McCabe's."

Rionna drew her sword and walked slowly toward Caelen. He refused to meet her gaze, refused to acknowledge her at all. His mind was such a mass of rage and confusion that he couldn't even process what played out before him.

When she reached him, she pressed the point of her blade to his neck, forcing him to look up or have his neck severed.

"I could kill you now," she said in a voice devoid of emotion. She wore no expression, no indication of what she was thinking. She could be discussing something as mundane as the weather. Her demeanor chilled him to the bone, for 'twas a side of his wife he'd never seen. "But 'twould be too quick."

"Why?" he demanded hoarsely. "You betray not only me but also those you called friend. You betray Mairin, who has only been kind to you, and her child, who is innocent. You would send those who have been loyal to you to their deaths, and for what? So a man without honor can reclaim leadership of a clan that was once his?"

She lowered the sword to his groin. "Be silent or I'll remove your cods and feed them to the hounds."

She turned then as if she could no longer bear to look upon him. To his everlasting shame, he wanted to call after her. He closed his eyes, for it would seem some lessons were never learned.

"Burn him at the stake at first light," she said calmly. "'Tis a fitting end for one such as he."

Even Cameron seemed taken aback by her ruthlessness, but there was also a glint of admiration in his eyes. Aye, the man would appreciate the same dishonorable qualities in others he himself possessed.

"Very well, my lady. His sentence will be carried out in the morn."

He motioned his men to take Caelen away and then he turned back to Rionna. "Would you like refreshment? 'Tis a long way you've journeyed and you must be fatigued."

As Caelen was pulled from the hall, he watched as his wife smiled up at the man he hated most in the world.

Rionna glanced up at the last moment and caught his gaze. A shadow crossed over her eyes and then she looked quickly away.

Rionna stood by the window of her chamber, staring out at the snow-covered landscape. She was exhausted to the bone, but she would not sleep this night. Not when she imagined Caelen below in the dungeon, enduring unspeakable conditions.

She closed her eyes and replayed the look on his face, his angry words, and finally his acceptance that she had betrayed him. More than ever she was determined not to fail in her quest, for she would not have her husband die thinking she'd played him false.

She cupped her hands over her belly and rubbed just as she felt a faint quickening deep in her womb. Tears sprang to her eyes as she realized that her babe had chosen this moment to move, as if reaffirming his mother's vow that his father would be saved at all costs.

"You are my future, Caelen McCabe. The future of my clan. Our son or daughter's future," she whispered fiercely. "I'll not let you die in some dark hole where you're tethered like an animal."

She retreated to her bed and sank down onto the edge. Cameron had provided her adequate accommodations. He'd even had one of his men lay a fire in the hearth. As soon as she was alone, though, she closed and barred the door with a heavy chair she dragged from the window.

She would take no chances. Cameron was an arrogant bastard of the first order. He believed that whatever he looked upon was his for the taking. She didn't imagine for a moment that he was overcome by her beauty. She'd purposely downplayed her features and her body so that she looked like the lad she mimicked, but she'd seen the curiosity and lust in the laird's eyes.

She lay back on the mattress still fully clothed and closed her eyes for a brief moment of rest. She willed the hours to pass so she could end this once and for all.

Even now, her men would be taking position along the walls. Waiting for her cry to arms.

She alternated pacing and resting on the various pieces of furniture in the chamber until the knock came at her door the next morning. She took her time and even called out that she'd be a moment, wanting to give the appearance that she'd slept and was now dressing.

She pulled back the furs and cast them this way and

that and then pulled her hair over her shoulder to plait as she went to the door.

Shoving the chair to the side, she opened it to find her father standing in the hallway. She let her hands drop from the braid and stood there regarding him in silence.

"The laird bade you to come to the courtyard."

She nodded and waited for him to precede her down the hallway but he hesitated and fixed her with his stare. "What did McCabe really do to gain your ire? You turned from me in favor of him, refusing to back me as laird and now you welcome me back with open arms?"

Knowing he wouldn't believe a sudden change of heart, she instead spoke the truth.

"I would not have you as laird either. You, Caelen McCabe, 'tis a matter of choosing the lesser of two evils."

Gregor McDonald's gaze narrowed and he glared at his daughter. "You still haven't learned to control your tongue or address your betters with a civil tongue."

"'Tis not my better I address, and if you think to strike me as you did the last time we had this conversation, I'll make good on my threat and the McDonalds will seek a new laird this day."

"I'll deal with you in time," he warned.

She shrugged as if she didn't place much importance on his threats.

As they stepped into the courtyard, she pulled her cloak tighter around her to ward off the chill. Her heart nearly stopped when she saw that Caelen was already tied to a stake in the center. Wood was stacked in a circle around him, surrounding him on all sides.

He looked even more battered than he had the night before. New bruising was evident on his face and fresh blood streamed down his side.

Her teeth ached from clenching her jaws and she blinked back tears of rage. Never had she hated someone as much as she hated her father and Duncan Cameron. 'Twould be so simple to draw her sword now and end her father's miserable life, but she must be patient, for Caelen would be killed before her father fell to the ground.

Cameron stood several paces in front of Caelen, surrounded by his men, all bearing torches. When she neared Cameron, he reached for one of the torches and handed it to her.

"If you'll do the honors," he said. "Be quick about it. I find the smell of burning flesh to be distasteful and I've other matters to attend to."

Her hand shook as she took the torch and turned to face her husband. She took a step forward, sucking in deep breaths as she mentally prepared herself for what was to come.

Their gazes met and held. His clear green eyes were pain-filled and dulled. He didn't seem entirely aware of his surroundings. She silently cursed, for she needed her husband's might this day.

CHAPTER 32

Caelen watched as Rionna took the torch from Cameron's hand. Pain whipped and coiled through his body. He was racked by chills and he burned with fever. But he kept his gaze on his wife as she stared into his eyes.

Something had bothered him the entire night as he'd lain awake, huddled on the wet, cold floor of the dungeon. It had bothered him ever since he'd seen the shadow cross her eyes when he'd been dragged away the evening before.

And now his gut was screaming at him that nothing was as it seemed. He battled with himself, for he'd vowed to never again doubt what stared him in the face. The evidence didn't lie.

But. But, but, but, he couldn't accept that Rionna had coldly betrayed him. In the heat of the moment, his surprise over seeing her and the shock of all that had transpired had rendered him unable to think.

But now when he thought back over the last months, he couldn't accept that Rionna had turned against him. Too much didn't make sense. She hated her father. She feared him. Why then would she support his return to her clan?

She'd stood with him against her kin. She'd supported him at the risk of alienating her people. Those were not the actions of a woman who'd lied about everything.

Nay, 'twas not possible. Even if it made him a fool for once again trusting his heart and not his head. This time . . . This time his heart wasn't wrong. He'd wager his life on it.

Which meant that his wife was in a dangerous situation and he was helpless to protect her.

What was her aim? What purpose did this pretense of hers serve?

She gripped the torch and then he saw her free hand slide carefully into her cloak. And there, in her eyes, a plea. A plea for help. A plea for understanding. It was gone before he could blink but he hadn't mistaken it. Or maybe 'twas what he wanted to see. But his pulse ratcheted up and he tensed in anticipation.

He wanted to yell at her to get the hell away, to protect herself and their bairn. He wanted to tell her that whatever she planned, it wasn't worth her life. Not in trade for his.

But he remained silent, knowing his cry would mean her quick death.

Then she made her move. She turned abruptly and thrust the torch into Cameron's face. His howl of pain was instantaneous. At the exact moment of his cry, Rionna let out a war cry that rivaled any Caelen had ever heard.

She drew her sword, tore off her cloak, and ran for the stake. Caelen stared in disbelief as McDonald soldiers swarmed over the walls, dropping down, swords in hands.

The wife and clan he'd vowed was not his own had come to save him.

"Are you strong enough to fight?" Rionna yelled as she slashed at the bonds securing him to the stake.

"Aye, I can fight." He wasn't dead yet and he'd be damned if he let his wife risk everything for naught.

She disappeared before he had fully loosened himself from the ropes. He caught sight of her engaged in battle a short distance away but before he could think to aid her, he dodged a sword and rolled away, barely surviving with his head.

The first order of business was to find a sword. Caelen dodged again when one of Cameron's men slashed his blade mere inches from his face. Bending low, he rammed into the warrior's legs, knocking them both to the ground.

The sword went sliding through the snow and Caelen slammed his fist into the man's face until blood sprayed onto the snow. He rolled away and lunged for the sword. He gripped the hilt and yanked it to him just as another man appeared above him, sword over his hand as he slashed downward.

Caelen rolled, swinging his sword as he went. The blade cut through the warrior's leg. Caelen jumped to his feet, his pain and fever forgotten. All that occupied his mind was finding his wife and hunting Duncan Cameron.

He fought his way to the wall, his gaze scanning left and right. Only by sheer will was he even standing. What he saw as he surveyed the courtyard made his heart sink.

While fighting valiantly and with more fire than he'd ever witnessed in the McDonald soldiers, they were vastly outnumbered, and they were tiring quickly.

He finally spotted Rionna again. She was backing a Cameron warrior to the wall. She quickly dispatched him by thrusting her sword in his chest, then yanked it away and turned, only to find another soldier in his place.

That was the problem. For every Cameron soldier felled, there was another right behind.

Caelen began to work his way in his wife's direction, determined to get her to safety, when he heard a chilling war cry so achingly familiar that he nearly went to his knees in relief.

He rallied his strength, threw back his head, and uttered a harsh call in return. Then he shouted to the McDonald soldiers. "Reinforcements are here! Hold your ground!"

Caelen turned in time to see his brothers charge through the gates. Hundreds of McCabe warriors swarmed from every direction. 'Twas the most magnificent thing he'd ever viewed. If he lived to be a hundred, he'd never forget the sight.

The tide had swung decidedly in favor of the McDonalds. Where before they'd looked haggard and near the end of their strength, they suddenly began fighting as though God himself had given then renewed strength.

Ewan, who'd led the charge through the gate, slid from his horse a few feet from Caelen, sword in hand. Alaric rode up a moment later and did the same until Caelen was flanked by his brothers.

"How bad is it?" Ewan yelled as he looked at the blood running down his brother's side.

"I'll survive."

The brothers cut a vicious path through Cameron warriors. They fought with determination, their attack fueled by rage and an overwhelming desire for revenge.

"Where's Rionna?" Alaric shouted when they reached the middle of the courtyard.

Caelen glanced around before ducking a blow from

an advancing warrior. "I know not. I lost sight of her when you came through the gates."

"Your wife has lost her mind," Ewan said as he cut through another soldier. "She has to be the most daft, infuriating, *brave* lass I've ever had the occasion to meet."

"Aye, she is all that," Caelen agreed. "And she's mine."

Alaric grinned then pivoted and delivered a death blow, his sword coming away bright with blood. "You're a most fortunate man, Caelen. Clearly your wife is too stubborn to let you die."

"Where is Cameron?" Ewan shouted in frustration. "I'll not let that bastard escape me yet again."

"Rionna thrust a torch in his face. I've not seen him since she freed me."

They quieted as they greeted another onslaught of attacks. They came from every angle and it took all of Caelen's skill and concentration to block the agonizing pain and focus on the matter at hand.

His concern wasn't for Duncan Cameron. He searched for Rionna. He feared for her more than he'd feared anything else in his life.

"They're running!" Hugh McDonald shouted. "Close in! Close in! Don't let them escape!"

The courtyard was littered with bodies, and what was once a pristine covering of snow was now bathed in scarlet. The blood shone in the sun, stark against the white, and the acrid smell rose and scattered with the wind.

The ranks had thinned enough that Caelen could see more than a few paces and he frantically searched for sign of his wife. When he saw her, his blood froze in his veins.

She was battling her father, and the man fought wildly,

with no discipline of a seasoned warrior. He fought like a man who knew he was going to die.

Her back was to Caelen, and she fought valiantly, holding off the frantic blows with her sword, but each forward attack backed her up and her strength was waning.

Caelen broke into a run, ignoring his own pain and overwhelming exhaustion. He was halfway across the courtyard when he caught sight of Duncan Cameron.

Typical of the coward he was, he'd positioned himself behind a wall of his men, but now most had fallen and he was vulnerable to attack.

The left side of his face was blistered and smeared with blood from the burn Rionna had inflicted on him. He had a sword in one hand and a dagger in the other.

Before Caelen realized what he was doing, Cameron took aim and hurled the dagger in Rionna's direction.

"Nay!" Caelen roared.

But it was too late. Cameron's aim was true and the dagger struck Rionna just inside her right shoulder blade. She staggered, deflected a blow delivered by her father, and then went down on one knee.

Gregor raised his sword again to deliver the killing blow when an arrow struck him in the chest. Caelen never turned to see who'd let the arrow fly. His focus was solely on Rionna.

Rage like he'd never known gave him the strength of a hundred men. He roared Cameron's name and launched himself at the man who'd felled Rionna.

The two men met with a clash of swords, the sound of metal ringing throughout the courtyard. Caelen fought like a man possessed. He could taste Cameron's blood. He wanted to bathe in it right after he carved the bastard's heart from his chest.

But Cameron also fought like a man who knew he

was marked for death. Much of the arrogance that Cameron wore like a cloak had disappeared. It was as if for the first time he sensed his own mortality and was desperate to survive.

Weakened by fever and blood loss and the ferocity of the battle thus far, Caelen stumbled back under the force of Cameron's attack. He dug in his heels and met Cameron's sword with his own, the impact jarring his shoulders.

With the blades kissing, Caelen thrust his boot into Cameron's midsection, knocking him back. He followed, pressing his momentary advantage by launching a series of blows that had Cameron retreating.

The insistent clang of metal rang in his ears. Around him the smell of death was thick and cloying. Much of the roar had faded, as McCabes and McDonalds alike worked to dispatch the men who'd sworn their loyalty to a man with no honor.

All Caelen could see over and over was Rionna staggering to her knees before pitching forward to the ground. A sound much like that of a wounded animal bellowed from his throat.

For all Cameron's cowardice, he was a skilled warrior, and he was fighting for his life. He knocked Caelen back and swung his sword. Caelen went to his knees and jerked his head back so the blade cut through empty air just an inch from his throat.

His shoulder burned, stinging from sweat and slick with blood. His strength was fast ebbing and he had to end this quickly. His brothers were occupied with their own battle across the courtyard. There was no one to aid Caelen. He had no reserves to draw on.

He staggered to his feet after deflecting yet another blow and prepared to launch himself directly at his enemy. Cameron raised his sword over his head and, with a snarl, started to leap forward to meet Caelen's attack, when suddenly a sword thrust through Cameron's chest.

He was completely impaled on the length. The point sliced through the front, bathed in crimson. Cameron looked down in complete befuddlement, his eyes glassy as death crept over him.

As his knees buckled and he slipped to the ground, Rionna came into view. She gripped the hilt of her sword with both hands, her face as pale as death. When she lifted her gaze from Cameron's lifeless body to Caelen, her eyes were cloudy with pain and as dull and glassy as Cameron's had looked when he drew his last breath.

"He didn't deserve to die with honor," she whispered. "He has none."

She took one step forward then bobbled and put her other foot back to steady herself. Then she sagged and went to her knees in the snow.

All Caelen could see was the blood that soaked her tunic.

"Rionna!" he cried.

He dropped his sword and ran forward, catching her as she pitched sideways. He gathered her close to his chest and gently lowered her to her side, mindful of the dagger still deep within her flesh.

"Thank God," she whispered as she stared up at him, her eyes so dim that it was like all the life had leeched right out of them. The usual wash of gold and amber, so warm and vibrant, was a dull shade of brown, like trees in winter. "I worried so. I couldn't find you during battle. I worried you'd been killed."

A spasm of pain crossed her face and she gave a soft sigh as she closed her eyes.

He touched her cheek, her mouth, her eyes, and even her ears. "Don't you die, Rionna. Do you hear me?

Don't you dare die on me. You'll live. I command it. Oh God," he said brokenly. "Please don't die, lass. You can't leave me."

He lifted her against his chest and rocked back and forth, grief so thick in his heart that he couldn't breathe.

"I love you," he said fiercely. "'Tis not true that I kept a part of my heart locked away from you. You own all of it, lass. You've always owned it. I didn't give it to you. You took it from the very start."

He touched her cheek again, willing her to open her eyes, and as if she answered his unspoken demand, her eyelids fluttered and opened, but it was evident it cost her dearly.

She smiled faintly. "'Tis glad I am to hear it, husband, for 'tis the truth I despaired of you ever giving me the words I most wanted to hear."

"You stay with me and you'll hear them every day for the rest of our lives," he said in a harsh tone that was rife with grief and desperation. "Ah, lass, I don't deserve you. 'Tis God's truth, I don't, but I want you all the same and I'll not live a single day without you."

"What a pair we are," she whispered. "Battered, bruised, and bloody. Too weak to help the other to our deathbed. 'Tis the truth we'll have to die here because I lack the strength to carry you."

The teasing in her tone was his undoing. The knot swelled in his throat and tears burned his eyes, crowding in until his vision went wet and blurry.

"Aye, lass, you have the right of it. Perhaps my brothers will come along and carry the both of us to our sick beds. But if you think you get your own bed, you're sorely mistaken."

"I've never before seen such a pitiful sight. What say you, Alaric?"

Caelen looked up to see Ewan and Alaric standing

over him and Rionna. Worry burned bright in their gazes but Ewan's tone was light and jesting, as if he was loathe to let his fear bleed over into his words.

"Methinks marriage has made my brother soft," Alaric replied. "'Tis a shame when a puny lass has to save his arse."

"Come down here and I'll show you puny," Rionna grumbled.

Caelen didn't know whether to laugh or cry so he sat there, with Rionna gathered tight in his grasp, and buried his face in her hair. He shook from head to toe as it sank in just how close he'd come to losing her, and in fact, he could lose her still.

"How is she?" Gannon demanded as he ran up.

"Gannon," she said in weak delight. "So glad you made it. I owe you my thanks. We couldn't have done it without you."

Gannon looked much the same as Caelen felt. Awed. Scared. Mystified.

"Nay, my lady. I have no doubt you and your men would have taken on the whole of Duncan Cameron's army and dragged Caelen home to McDonald keep."

He knelt beside Caelen in the snow and feathered a hand over Rionna's forehead. "'Tis God's truth, my lady. Never have I met a lass as brave and as fierce as you. I'm honored to serve you. I'm grateful you were able to save our laird's life. I've grown used to serving with the grumpy bastard."

Rionna laughed and then promptly broke off with a groan, as pain wracked her small frame. "He is grumpy, but I'm going to work on that."

Ewan laid a hand on Caelen's shoulder when another spasm of pain crawled over Rionna's face. "Let her go, Caelen. Let Alaric carry her back into the keep. The battle is over. Cameron is dead, and the few men who still live are scattered and running. We must see to both of your wounds."

"Caelen?"

Caelen looked down and brushed away the hair from her eyes. "Aye, lass."

Her unfocused gaze found his and she licked her lips. "I seem to have a dagger in my back. Could you take it out for me?"

CHAPTER 33

"If you don't let me tend your wounds, you'll die, and what good will you be to Rionna then?" Ewan demanded in exasperation.

Caelen snarled back at his brother, his impatience simmering like a cauldron. "You should be with Rionna. *She* is who needs tending. If she dies because we stand here arguing, I'll make Mairin a widow, I swear it."

Ewan blew out his breath in frustration. "If I have to sit on you and have Alaric clean your wound, I'll do it. The sooner you allow me to tend you, the sooner Rionna will get the care she needs."

Caelen swore viciously. "Would you allow me to tend you if Mairin had suffered as Rionna has? Nay, you would insist that Mairin be taken care of first."

"Gannon is with Rionna. He'll call if he has need of me. Rionna's wound is fresh. Yours is not and it has already begun festering. Damn it, Caelen, give over so that you can rest beside Rionna."

'Twas the mention of being able to be with Rionna that made Caelen yield. While they stood arguing, Rionna was alone and without comfort and it twisted Caelen's stomach into knots. He still remembered his harsh words, the fact that he had at first believed the worst of her. He would not have her believe he thought ill of her any longer.

"You burn with fever," Ewan said grimly when Caelen was laid on the bed in one of the chambers. "You worry for Rionna, but 'tis the truth you are far more seriously wounded."

"She's with child," Caelen said in a low voice. "I know not even if you were aware of it yet. She was out fighting for my life when she carries a child. She had to have ridden nonstop to arrive here when she did. God's teeth, Ewan, but it makes me want to weep like a babe."

"Aye, I know it," Ewan said. "But Rionna is a strong-willed lass. I don't see her giving up without a fight. She was hell-bent on saving you, damn king and country and whether I agreed or not. Gannon rode into Neamh Álainn and delivered her orders as imperiously as a man ever did."

"She's one of a kind," Caelen murmured. "And I didn't appreciate her for the wonder she is. I tried too hard to change her and mold her into what I thought I wanted."

Ewan chuckled. "I don't imagine she put up with that."

Caelen smiled ruefully then swore when Ewan began cleaning the arrow wound. "Nay, she didn't. She's a fierce lass. I . . ." He broke off, unable to voice the words. Nay, he wouldn't speak them here. 'Twas not for his brother to hear, but for Rionna, and he wouldn't give them to anyone but her. She'd fought for them. She'd demanded them. She'd bloody well have them.

"Tell me of Neamh Álainn," Caelen said through gritted teeth, as pain swamped over him.

"'Tis the most beautiful place I've ever seen," Ewan said quietly. "The keep has existed for over a century and it looks as though it were constructed yesterday. The king's men have guarded it well since Alexander's passing. He provided well for Mairin and her firstborn. 'Tis a fine legacy bestowed upon Isabel."

"Men will seek Isabel as they did Mairin," Caelen said grimly. "'Tis a fine legacy, aye, but it won't be an easy burden for the lass."

"She'll have protection that Mairin didn't," Ewan said. "Mairin was left without someone to guard her until she married. It won't be the same for Isabel. I'll watch over her well until she decides who she'll marry."

Caelen smiled at the edge in his brother's voice. "You'll give her a choice then."

"Aye. She'll have better than Mairin had. I never want her to feel as desperate as Mairin felt or be forced to choose the lesser of two evils because she's backed into a corner."

"'Tis a good thing. We've brought exceptional women into the McCabe clan. We'll breed little warriors with the fire and intelligence of their mothers for sure."

Ewan chuckled. "Aye. That we will."

Caelen winced again when Ewan poked at the wound. "God's teeth, Ewan, are you done yet?"

"It needs stitching and you'll lie there and allow it or so help me I'll sew your mouth shut."

"Just get on with it. I want to get back to Rionna. I'll not have her think the worst when she doesn't see me."

"I've sent Alaric to tell her that you're carrying on as usual and making threats. She'll know you're fine when she hears that."

"If I didn't hurt so badly, I'd hit you for that."

Ewan grinned. "You can try. You're as weak as a newborn babe at the moment. I think Rionna could take you even with a dagger in her back."

Caelen sobered. "She amazes me, Ewan. I don't even know how to act around her. How can I ever go beyond the fact that she risked all for me?"

"You'd do the same for her," Ewan said bluntly. "It

stands to reason she'd stand up for you as well. They broke the mold when they made her. You're well blessed, Caelen. I hope you know it."

"Aye, I do," he murmured.

"There," Ewan said as he sat back. "'Tis stitched and the bleeding has stopped."

Caelen tried to rise but he fell back on his side, every bit of his strength gone. His muscles felt like mush, and he was so weak he could barely lift his arm.

He cursed and struggled to rise again. "Help me up, damn it."

"I'll help you to the chamber where Rionna is if you swear to stay abed."

"I'll not bargain with you over Rionna," Caelen growled. "I'll not leave her even for a moment."

"'Tis a serious wound, Caelen. You're fevered and your strength is gone. You could die if you won't have a care."

"Help me up," he said again.

Ewan shook his head and pulled Caelen to a sitting position. "I swear I have no idea whose loins you sprang from. I'm convinced you were left on the steps to the keep when you were a wee bairn."

Caelen sobered as he struggled to his feet. Cameron's words about their father drifted back into his hazy consciousness. He would never know if there was any truth to Cameron's rantings. But he wouldn't relate the story to his brothers. There was no need to plant any doubt in their minds. Cameron had existed on hatred and revenge for years and it had brought him nothing. In the end, he'd brought dishonor on himself and the father he claimed to avenge.

"'Tis over, Ewan," he said quietly as they hobbled down the hallway. "After eight years, 'tis over. Cameron is dead and neither of us dealt the killing blow."

"Aye," Ewan murmured. "Our father can rest now. He has been avenged."

"Nay," Caelen said swiftly. "'Tis not about vengeance. 'Tis about what is honorable and just. Cameron acted without honor. He died without honor. 'Tis enough."

Ewan's brow furrowed as he cast a sideways glance at his brother. "I owe your wife a debt I can never repay. She not only saved your life, but she killed a man who has caused much grief to my wife and who threatened my daughter."

"'Twould seem there are many of us indebted to my wife," Caelen said dryly.

Ewan knocked at the chamber door and Caelen pushed impatiently in before the summons was issued. His heart nearly stopped when he saw Rionna sprawled facedown on the bed, face turned to the side and eyes closed.

Gannon immediately put up a hand. "She passed out awhile ago, but she's breathing. The pain became too much for her."

"Can't we give her a potion? Is there a healer in this clan?" Caelen demanded. "I'll not have her suffer unnecessarily."

"Be at ease," Alaric said. "You don't want to frighten Rionna if she awakens. We've convinced her 'tis a minor wound and nothing to worry over. She fears more for you than for herself and 'tis better that way. 'Twill give her something to fight for."

Caelen went to her bedside, battling pain and the mugginess of fever. His head swam and it felt as though he walked through a bog, but he was determined that he'd remain by her side.

"The dagger is deep, Ewan."

"Aye. It's going to bleed more freely once the blade is out. I'll have to work fast to stop it and stitch the wound."

"She's a fighter," Gannon said gruffly. "This is naught for her."

Caelen had never seen his commander so pale. He hovered over Rionna, clenching and unclenching his fists as if he had no idea what to do.

"Has there been other bleeding?" Caelen asked fearfully. "She carries a babe."

Alaric shook his head. "None that I've been able to see. She's complained of no pain in her stomach. Just in her back."

"Get on the bed with her before you fall over," Ewan said crossly. "Get to one side so that when you finally pass out, you won't be in the way."

A knock sounded at the door and Gannon and Alaric both drew their swords. Gannon hurried to answer, opening it just a crack. Then he opened it wider to admit a gray-haired woman who looked to be as old as Methuselah.

She looked extremely agitated and she wrung her hands in front of her.

"Begging your pardon, Laird McCabe, but I was told you had need of a healer."

Ewan gazed sharply at the old woman. "Have you skill?"

The woman drew herself up and pinned Ewan with a beady stare. "I was versed in the healing arts long afore you were born, laddie."

"I need a drought for pain and a poultice to rub on the wound after it's been stitched."

She nodded. "Aye, I have those things. Would you be needing a steady hand to do the stitching? I'm old, aye, but my hand hasn't wavered in all my sixty years."

"Nay," Caelen interjected. He turned to Ewan. "You do it. I trust you."

Ewan nodded then gestured toward the older woman. "Fetch the items I requested."

She nodded and backed from the room.

"I'll need help to pull the dagger from her back," Ewan said with a grimace. "'Twill have to be done quickly, and then we have to stop the bleeding. Caelen, lie down. If she awakens, it will soothe her to have you near."

Caelen crawled onto the bed and collapsed next to her, as his strength finally gave out. His smoothed his hand over the back of her head, stroking her hair that was matted with blood at the ends.

"When 'tis done, I'll bathe you as you once bathed me," he murmured close to her ear. "We'll sit by the fire and I'll brush your hair and then feed you by my hand. I'll read you all the thoughts I've written down since the day I first laid eyes on you. 'Tis the truth I wanted you even then. Even when you belonged to my brother."

He touched her cheek, trying to infuse some color. It was pale and cool.

"Build up the fire," he said to Gannon. "I don't want her to be cold. I'd have her as comfortable as possible."

"Place your hands on either side of the dagger," Ewan instructed Alaric. "I want you to push down when I pull. As soon as the dagger is free, press your hands firmly over the wound."

Alaric nodded and Caelen moved in close until his lips brushed her temple.

"Be brave, lass," he whispered. "As brave as you've been through everything else. I'm here. I'll not leave you."

Ewan nodded at Alaric and then took hold of the dagger and pulled. Rionna jerked. Her eyes flew open, panic flaring in their depths. She cried out and began to struggle.

The knife came free, bathed in blood, and Alaric pressed down on the wound as Rionna writhed beneath him.

"Shh, Rionna, 'tis I, Caelen. Be at ease, lass. We're helping you. 'Tis Ewan my brother who has pulled the dagger from your back."

Ewan cut impatiently at her tunic until her back was bare. Caelen closed his eyes as he saw blood stream from underneath Alaric's palms.

Rionna whimpered as Alaric pressed harder, and Caelen reached for her hand.

Her fingers bit into his palm, her nails digging deep. He didn't mind the pain for if it helped her to bear hers, he'd do anything.

"'Tis like fire," Rionna gasped. "Oh God, it burns."

"I know it, lass. It will be over soon. I swear it. Breathe for me. Look at me. Only at me and put this from your mind."

Her gaze found his, her eyes wide and panicked.

"He's going to stitch the wound," Caelen said calmly. "I want you to focus on me. Push the pain from your mind and imagine holding our bairn."

Some of the wildness eased from her eyes and soft joy replaced the pain.

The next hour was a test of Caelen's endurance. Weakened from his own injuries, fevered, and in a great deal of pain himself, he coaxed Rionna through every stitch that Ewan set. When her face went gray with pain, he kissed her and talked of their child. When she was near to passing out, he stroked her cheek and told her he loved her.

By the time Ewan was done with the last of it, Caelen was barely conscious himself.

Ewan stepped back from the bed and wiped his brow with the back of his arm. "'Tis done, Caelen. 'Tis in God's hands now."

Caelen didn't respond.

"Caelen?"

Ewan bent over the bed to see that his brother had finally succumbed to unconsciousness. He glanced up at Alaric and Gannon.

"I'm worried for them both. They both have grievous wounds and have lost a lot of blood. But 'tis Caelen's that went the longest without care and they'd already began to fester. He has a fever already."

"What do we do?" Gannon asked quietly.

"We bear them back home and pray that God is merciful."

CHAPTER 34

Rionna woke, awash in pain. Her entire body felt stretched and tight as if her skin fit too snugly. Her lips were dry and cracked and she'd sell her soul for just a taste of water.

"Ah, there you are," a sweet voice soothed.

"Oh God, I've died, haven't I?" Rionna said in disgust.

There was a light chuckle. "Now why would you think that?"

"Because you have the voice of an angel."

Rionna pried open one eye, never imagining it could hurt so much to do something so insignificant.

"Keeley," she breathed. "You're here." Then she frowned because she wasn't sure where here was. She looked around to see that she was in her old chamber at McDonald keep.

"Aye, I'm here. Would I be anywhere else when those I love are in need of my skills?"

Keeley eased onto the bed beside Rionna, holding a goblet of water. "Would you like a drink?"

"More than I want to breathe."

Keeley laughed again. "Not dramatic, are you?"

Rionna sucked thirstily at the liquid, ignoring the pain that her movement caused. When she was done, she eased back down onto the pillow and closed her eyes to ward off the spasm of discomfort that gripped her.

"Why am I in here?" she asked. She didn't want to read too much into why she wasn't in Caelen's chamber—the chamber they'd shared ever since Caelen had fetched her from this very room.

Keeley placed a cool hand on Rionna's forehead and rubbed soothingly.

"I wanted you in a room with no windows. You burned with fever for so many days. The draft from the windows was too cold and yet I didn't want a fire to keep you overwarm."

"That made no sense to me," Rionna said tiredly.

Keeley smiled down at her as Rionna opened her eyes again.

"Where is Caelen?" she asked, voicing the question that had burned in her mind from the moment she woke up.

"He hasn't yet awakened."

Rionna struggled up, nearly fainting from the red-hot pain that lanced through her back. "How long have I lain here?" she asked hoarsely, ignoring Keeley's attempts to make her lie back down.

"The journey back here took two days and you've been insensible with fever for the last seven."

Panic gripped Rionna by the throat. It took every bit of her strength, but she pushed Keeley aside and forced herself up from the bed.

"Where is he?" she demanded, even as she staggered toward the door.

"Where is who? Rionna, stop at once. You're too weak and you've still got a fever."

She threw open the door. "Caelen," she replied. "Where is he?"

"In his chamber, of course. Now come back. For God's sake, you've naught on but your nightdress."

Rionna warded off Keeley's grasp and strode down the hallway and around the bend. Gannon stood outside Caelen's door and he didn't look at all happy to see her.

He rushed to catch her before her knees gave out. "Sweet Jesu, my lady. What are you thinking?"

Keeley caught up to Rionna just as she tried to shake off Gannon's grasp.

"Move out of my way," she gritted out. "I would see my husband for myself."

Gannon's eyes softened and he wrapped a strong arm around her waist. "If I let you inside, you have to swear you'll return to your bed. 'Tis the truth you look like death."

"Thanks," Rionna grumbled. "You flatter me so."

Keeley turned her lips in to hide the smile. "I'll wait out here, Rionna. But I'm coming in to get you after a moment. Don't think I won't."

"It might take more than a moment to convince my stubborn husband he's not going to die," Rionna bit out as she walked through the door.

Gannon and Keeley exchanged puzzled glances but Rionna was already gone.

Rionna barely made it to Caelen's bed before her legs gave out. She perched herself on the edge and looked upon her husband's face. He looked at peace. No lines carved across his forehead. He lay so still that it frightened her.

Then anger consumed her and she leaned forward so that she was close to his face and there was no chance he couldn't hear her. She'd make him hear her, by God.

"Listen to me, husband, and listen well," she all but shouted at him. "You'll not die on me. Not after all I did to save your sorry hide. Is this how you show your gratitude? By dying on me after all? 'Tis a disgrace, that's what it is."

She framed his face in her hands and leaned farther down.

"You'll fight, damn it. You'll not give over this easily. God is not ready for you yet because I am not through with you. You're going to wake up and you're going to give me the words I've waited on for so long. Telling me you love me on the battlefield as we both lay dying doesn't count. You'll give them to me and mean them or so help me I'll bury you in unconsecrated ground so that you never rest and you'll be forced to dwell in this keep with me for eternity."

To her complete surprise, his eyes opened and a smile curved his lips upward. Warmth gleamed in those beautiful green eyes as he stared up at her.

"I love you."

Tears filled her eyes until she could no longer even see his face. Relief was so sweet and so overwhelming that she couldn't hold herself up. He gripped her arms and lowered her to his chest as she lay exhausted over him.

"Is that what you woke me for, wife? To beat the words from me? I would have gladly given them to you except you've been unconscious the last days and I grew tired of saying them to a woman who couldn't hear me."

She pushed herself off his chest and glared down at him. "What? But I thought you hadn't yet awakened. I thought you were dying. Keeley said you hadn't yet awakened."

"Aye, I hadn't," he said in an amused voice. "'Tis the truth it was late when I took to my bed and I only did so because Gannon threatened to knock me over the head to force me to sleep if I didn't leave your bedside."

Weak tears slid down her cheeks. She could barely breathe for the relief beating in her chest. "You weren't dying. You're going to be all right. You won't die."

"I have no intention of leaving you, lass."

Then he fixed her with a stern scowl.

"You, however, are not so assured of glowing health. You should not be out of bed. 'Tis the truth you look like you're but a few steps out of the grave."

Even as he spoke, he ran trembling hands over her arms and then up to her face.

"How typical that you spring from your deathbed to prevent me from going to mine," he murmured. "You worried me, lass. The last days have been the longest of my life."

"I'll not go back to that chamber," she said stubbornly. "When I woke, I worried that you were still angry with me and that I'd been banished from our chamber. 'Tis not a feeling I ever want to experience again."

His eyes went soft and he gently rolled her so that she lay beside him on the bed. He fussed and rearranged the furs, making sure she was comfortable and without pain. How could she think of pain when the husband she thought lay dying was staring at her with love in his eyes?

"If I have my way, we'll never be separated again," he said. "God's teeth, Rionna. You frightened at least a decade from my life. I was so worried for you and our babe."

Rionna's hand went automatically to her stomach, her expression panicked.

Caelen laid his hand over hers and she calmed. "Aye, our bairn is still there, wedged in his mother's womb. I've no doubt that he or she is every bit the fierce warrior that their mother is."

"Tell me what happened," she said, as he turned on his side next to her. "So much is a blur. I don't remember much of the battle. I was so terrified."

He stroked her hair and kissed her forehead as if he couldn't bear not to touch her.

"You were magnificent. You saved me. 'Tis a fact I'll not forget in this lifetime. You led our clan into battle. You were the fiercest warrior princess that ever was."

She frowned and looked suspiciously up at him. "How came you by that term?"

He smiled. "Keeley told me of your childhood dreams. Aye, Rionna, you're my warrior princess."

Her heart melted and she sighed at the adoration in her warrior's eyes.

"I'm ashamed that for so long I tried to mold you into someone else," he said with a grimace. "But 'tis the truth, from the first day I saw you attired in those trews and a man's tunic, wielding a sword as deftly as any warrior, I wanted you so badly I ached with it. I thought if I forced you to be something you were not, 'twould temper my fierce need for you."

"Perhaps you recognized in me the mirror of yourself. Your other half," she whispered.

"Aye, I did, but I fought it. But no more."

"Then you'll let me fight alongside you?" she asked with a raised eyebrow.

He leaned down to kiss her. His breath stuttered out unevenly and it took him a moment to respond. "I'll not lie. 'Tis my wish to forever keep you here and under my protection. I died a thousand deaths watching you in battle. Part of me was so proud. I wanted to shout to the world, Look at her! She is mine! The other part of me wanted to drag you as far from danger as I could and keep you from harm all the days of your life. I can only promise not to be so rigid in the future. I'll not ever be accepting of anything that puts you in danger."

She smiled and laid her head on his shoulder. "'Tis enough you love me and accept what I am, faults and all."

"I'll love you well, lass. 'Tis one promise I can make and vow to keep. I'll love you until I draw my last breath and beyond. You were made for me. I cannot imagine a more perfect mate."

The door opened and Keeley stormed in, Gannon on her heels. Behind them, Alaric and Ewan crowded in.

"You've had long enough," Keeley said. "'Tis time to return to your bed. You're not well, Rionna."

Caelen turned and smiled. "She'll remain here where she belongs. Her fever has broken and I'll be sure to keep the furs tight over the windows so no draft blows in."

Ewan walked farther into the room and then came to stand over the bed where Rionna and Caelen lay.

"'Tis relieved I am to hear you've awakened, Rionna. For I would offer you my deepest gratitude before I return to Mairin and Isabel."

Her brows knit together in confusion. Caelen chuckled softly.

"She doesn't even realize all she has done. It would appear her sole aim was to save her husband's worthless hide."

"You have my thanks for saving my brother. He's difficult and grumpy, but a more loyal man I'll never find. He's suffered for the sins of others for far too long."

Rionna smiled as Ewan continued.

"And as much as I wanted the duty myself, I would also thank you for ridding the world of Duncan Cameron. I have it on good authority the king will bestow his gratitude on you personally. Without the support of Cameron, Malcolm's rebellion is dead. He hasn't the resources or the support to launch a bid for the throne. Indeed, the whole of the highlands is in your debt."

"I wish I could say I thought of all that just before I thrust my sword through Cameron's back, but 'tis the truth, my only aim was to prevent him from killing my husband," she said ruefully.

The others laughed and Caelen squeezed her to him as

he kissed her forehead. "You'll rest now," he murmured. "Here in my arms where I know you're safe and I can watch over you and our babe."

She sighed and closed her eyes. "Aye. 'Tis where I want to be most."

Never looking away from his wife or moving his lips from her temple, he raised his hand and waved the others away.

Keeley's gaze was misty as she stared at the two entwined on the bed. Alaric chuckled softly and pulled her into his side.

Even Gannon and Ewan wore soft smiles as they tiptoed quietly from the room.

CHAPTER 35

"Ouch!" Rionna yelped when Mairin stuck another pin in her hair. She tried to rub at the spot, but Keeley grabbed her hand and forced it away from her hair.

"'Tis important you look perfect this day," Mairin said.

"I don't see why," Rionna muttered. "If the king wanted to thank me, a private word would be sufficient. All this pomp makes me nervous."

Keeley and Mairin exchanged conspiratorial glances and Rionna was quick to latch on.

"What? What mischief are you two brewing? I saw that look."

Keeley rolled her eyes. "We just want you to look stunning. You're recovery has been long. The weather is beautiful today. You should shine as marvelously as the sun."

"You've a silver tongue, Keeley McCabe. I see your aim. Ply me with flattery so I'll forget that look between the two of you."

Mairin laughed. "Oh, Rionna, do stop. Now let me look at you."

She stepped back and Rionna ran a nervous hand over the burgeoning swell of her belly. Keeley and Mairin had worked to let out the waist so that it wouldn't be too constricting. The result, Rionna had to admit, was wonderful.

The dress flowed to her ankles and hid the evidence of her pregnancy. Only a slight distension at the waist hinted at her condition. And the dress itself was a masterpiece. Rionna could scarcely believe such a creation belonged to her.

Miles and miles of amber velvet trimmed with golden threads and russet embroidery. It was a tribute to her hair and all the varying shades of the sunset it embodied.

For all her grumblings, Rionna wanted to look stunning. Aye, she wanted her husband to look upon her and see naught else. It hadn't occurred to her to be nervous over the king's visit or his tribute to her. Nay, she worried only over her husband's reaction to her appearance.

"'Tis time," Mairin said.

"'Tis time for what?" Rionna asked in exasperation. "The two of you are acting so secretive."

Keeley smiled mysteriously and took Rionna's arm to guide her from the chamber. "We are to deliver you to the balcony overlooking the courtyard."

The two women tucked their arms through Rionna's and walked her out of the chamber and to the doorway leading outside to the balcony.

Rionna squinted at the sudden wash of sunshine but then closed her eyes and allowed the warmth to pour over her. It felt so good to be outside again. She inhaled deeply the sweet-scented air. Spring had at long last arrived and the earth burst with green, the snows long since melted and replaced by vibrant carpets of color.

She opened her eyes and glanced down to see all the McDonald warriors assembled in the courtyard. To the right, Caelen's two brothers stood and beside them was seated the king, surrounded by his guard.

Rionna looked back to comment to Mairin and Keeley

but found them gone. Befuddled, she turned her attention back to the courtyard in time to see her husband stride out to stand in front of the assembled men.

But it wasn't them he faced or them he addressed. He turned and stared up at her. Quiet descended on the courtyard and Rionna swallowed, suddenly nervous and unsure of what was happening.

And then Caelen's voice rang out over the courtyard: "Rionna McDonald, I stand here today because you assembled your warriors and came for me with a plan so crazed that it was brilliant. You risked your life because you loved me. I have not a gesture so grand as yours to prove my love and regard. You once told me you demanded the words and you demanded the part of my heart you swore I locked away from you. 'Tis the truth that no part of me was safe from your possession."

Rionna gripped the stone edge of the curved balcony wall and leaned forward as she drank in her husband's appearance and let his words slide like silk over her ears.

"Nay, my gesture is not as grand as yours. You were willing to sacrifice all because you considered me yours and were unwilling to let me go.

"I once made the mistake of trying to change who you were. I tried to take a bold, courageous woman and make her into a meek, mild-mannered genteel lady because I thought I would be safe from her. 'Twas the biggest mistake I've ever made and one I'll regret all my days.

"I offer you the words now, wife. I love you. I love my warrior princess. I say it in front of my king, my clan. *Our* clan. So that you'll know how very loved and cherished you are."

A roar of approval went up from the men. They raised their swords and whoops and whistles rose sharply through the air.

She pressed her fist to her mouth so she wouldn't embarrass herself or Caelen by bursting into tears. "I love you, too, my gruff warrior," she whispered.

"I gathered my king and my family today to rectify a wrong," Caelen continued when the cheers diminished. He turned then, partly to include the McDonald men in his address. "The McDonalds deserve to have their name live on. 'Tis a noble and courageous thing they did for the laird who bore not their name and for the king who divided their clan."

Slowly he raised his gaze once more to find Rionna's. His love was a tangible warmth crowding his clear green eyes.

"Henceforth I will no longer be known as Caelen McCabe. From this day forward I take the name of Caelen McDonald. May our clan live long, and the glory of the day a golden-haired warrior princess led them into battle be retold for many years to come."

Rionna's mouth dropped open. Stunned silence settled over the courtyard as the warriors all stared at Caelen. The women who'd gathered to hear the address put their hands to their mouths. Some openly wept and others brought their aprons to their eyes.

Ewan stared at his brother with pride while Mairin, who'd gone to join her husband, wiped tears from her face.

And then Rionna was running. She flew into the keep and down the stairs, grasping her skirts in tight fists so she didn't fall. She burst out of the door of the keep and there was Caelen, standing before her, the king, his brothers, and their clan.

She stopped before she hurled herself into his arms, remembering his admonishment so many months earlier about showing affection in front of his men.

"If you wait any longer to come to me, I'll tackle you here in front of everyone," Caelen said in a low voice.

With a cry she launched herself into his arms and he

caught her against him as she fused her mouth to his in a kiss that her clansmen would talk about years later.

He spun her around and around as her laughter filled the air. Around them their clan gathered, joyous and celebrating. When he finally lowered her to the ground, he kept her pressed to his chest as he stared into her eyes.

"I love you, lass. There is not a single part of my heart or soul that you do not own."

"I'm glad of that, Caelen McDonald, for I am a possessive woman and I'll not be content with anything less than the whole of you."

He grinned and lowered his mouth to kiss her again. "You are a greedy lass. I like it."

EPILOGUE

Caelen quietly let himself into his chamber, his newborn son nestled in his arms. A few feet away, Rionna slept, exhausted from the birth.

Carefully, so as not to awaken her, he lay the babe next to her and stood looking down on the most precious things in his life.

The celebration was still ongoing below. His brothers and their wives had traveled to McDonald keep for the birth, and Caelen had gone down to present his son to his clan.

He could go back down and leave Rionna to rest, but he found himself going to his desk and taking out his scrolls, quill, and inkwell.

As he'd told Rionna, he wasn't an eloquent man and could oft express himself better in writing than he could aloud. Today was such a day, for his heart was so full he could never hope to fully put into speech all that he felt.

He opened the scroll and hastily scrawled the year and the day, for this was an important entry. The day that marked the birth of his son.

But 'twas his wife he found himself thinking on as he sat writing by the light of a candle. Every once in awhile he looked up and smiled a contented smile as he watched his wife and child sleep.

When he'd finished the last of his entry, he scattered sand to dry the ink and then looked one last time at all he'd written.

Today will long be a day that lasts in my memory. I was sore afraid as Rionna struggled to bring forth life from her womb, but I needn't have worried, for my warrior princess was as fierce as ever. And indeed she presented me a fine, squalling son, with a satisfied smile upon her face. She informs me that my son will bear my green eyes and dark hair because she commands it. I'll not gainsay her, for 'tis widely known that I cannot deny her anything.

She rests now and I cannot help but stare and marvel at the miracle she represents. I'll never forget the day I first saw her and how she fascinated me with her mannish attire, the sword she wielded with the skill of a warrior, and the challenge in her beautiful eyes. She's spoken before of a time when part of my heart was withheld from her because it belonged to another, but from the moment I laid eyes on her, I belonged solely to her.

Ah, lass, I think I have always loved you, for 'tis the truth I cannot ever remember a time I didn't.

Caelen McDonald, Laird of the McDonald clan

ACKNOWLEDGMENTS

I owe so much to my family and, in particular, my husband, who's taken over laundry, cooking, and most of the house stuff so that I can meet my deadlines.

My agent, Kim Whalen, is an invaluable business partner who never hesitates to keep me straight and motivated and doesn't mind my meltdowns.

And people like Jaci Burton, Laurie K., Vicki L., and Shannon Stacey keep me going and provide an invaluable, priceless thing: friendship. Thank you.

Writing may well be a very solitary endeavor, but the people in my life make my job easier and more rewarding. I wouldn't want to do it without them.

Read on for previews of the first two exciting books
in the McCabe trilogy

IN BED WITH A HIGHLANDER

Mairin Stuart knelt on the stone floor beside her pallet
and bowed her head in her evening prayer. Her hand
slipped to the small wooden cross hanging from a bit of
leather around her neck, and her thumb rubbed a familiar path over the now smooth surface.

For several long minutes, she whispered the words
she'd recited since she was a child, and then she ended it
as she always did. *Please, God. Don't let them find me.*

She pushed herself from the floor, her knees scraping
the uneven stones. The plain, brown garb she wore sig-
naled her place along the other novices. Though she'd
been here far longer than the others, she'd never taken
the vows that would complete her spiritual journey. It
was never her intention.

She went to the basin in the corner and poured from
the pitcher of water. She smiled as she dampened her
cloth, and Mother Serenity's words came floating to
mind. *Cleanliness is next to Godliness.*

She wiped her face and started to remove her gown to
extend her wash when she heard a terrible crash. Startled,
she dropped the cloth and whirled around to stare at
her closed door. Then galvanized to action, she ran and
flung it open, racing into the hall.

Around her, the other nuns also filled the hall, their

dismayed murmurs rising. A loud bellow echoed down the corridor from the abbey's front entrance. A cry of pain followed the bellow, and Mairin's heart froze. Mother Serenity.

Mairin and the rest of the sisters ran toward the sound, some lagging back while others shoved determinedly ahead. When they reached the chapel, Mairin drew up short, paralyzed by the sight before her.

Warriors were everywhere. There were at least twenty, all dressed in battle gear, their faces unwashed, sweat drenching their hair and clothing. But no blood. They hadn't come for sanctuary or aid. The leader held Mother Serenity by the arm, and even from a distance, Mairin could see the abbess's face drawn in pain.

"Where is she?" the man demanded in a cold voice.

Mairin took a step back. He was a fierce-looking man. Evil. Rage coiled in his eyes like a snake waiting to strike. He shook Mother Serenity when she didn't respond, and she warbled in his grasp like a rag doll.

Mairin crossed herself and whispered an urgent prayer. The nuns around her gathered in a close ball and also offered their prayers.

"She is not here," Mother Serenity gasped out. "I've told you the woman you seek is not here."

"You lie!" he roared.

He looked toward the group of nuns, his gaze flickering coldly over them.

"Mairin Stuart. Tell me where she is."

Mairin went cold, fear rising to a boil in her stomach. How had he found her? After all this time. Her nightmare wasn't over. It was, indeed, just beginning.

Her hands shook so badly that she had to hide them in the folds of her dress. Sweat gathered on her brow, and her gut lurched. She swallowed, willing herself not to be sick.

When no answer was forthcoming, the man smiled,

and it sent a chill straight down Mairin's spine. Still staring at them, he lifted Mother Serenity's arm so that it was in plain sight. Callously, he bent her index finger until Mairin heard the betraying pop of bone.

One of the nuns shrieked and ran forward only to be backhanded down by one of the soldiers. The rest of the nuns gasped at the bold outrage.

"This is God's house," Mother Serenity said in a reedy voice. "You sin greatly by bringing violence onto holy ground."

"Shut up, old woman," the man snapped. "Tell me where Mairin Stuart is or I'll kill every last one of you."

Mairin sucked in her breath and curled her fingers into balls at her sides. She believed him. There was too much evil, too much desperation, in his eyes. He had been sent on a devil's errand, and he wouldn't be denied.

He grasped Mother Serenity's middle finger, and Mairin rushed forward.

"Charity, nay!" Mother Serenity cried.

Mairin ignored her. "I'm Mairin Stuart. Now let her go!"

The man dropped Mother Serenity's hand then shoved the woman back. He stared at Mairin with interest, then let his gaze wander suggestively down her body and back up again. Mairin's cheeks flamed at the blatant disrespect, but she gave no quarter, staring back at the man with as much defiance as she dared.

He snapped his fingers, and two men advanced on Mairin, grabbing her before she could think to run. They had her on the floor in a split second, their hands fumbling with the hem of her gown.

She kicked wildly, flailing her arms, but she was no match for their strength. Would they rape her here on the chapel floor? Tears gathered in her eyes as they shoved her clothing up over her hips.

They turned her to the right and fingers touched her hip, right where the mark rested.

Oh nay.

She bowed her head as tears of defeat slipped down her cheeks.

" 'Tis her!" one of them said excitedly.

He was instantly shoved aside as the leader bent over to examine the mark for himself.

He, too, touched it, outlining the royal crest of Alexander. Issuing a grunt of satisfaction, he curled his hand around her chin and yanked until she faced him.

His smile revolted her.

"We've been looking for you a long time, Mairin Stuart."

"Go to hell," she spat.

Instead of striking her, his grin broadened. "Tsk-tsk, such blasphemy in the house of God."

He stood rapidly, and before Mairin could blink, she was hauled over a man's shoulder, and the soldiers filed out of the abbey and into the cool night.

They wasted no time getting onto their horses. Mairin was gagged then trussed hand and foot and tossed over the saddle in front of one of the men. They were away, the thunder of hooves echoing across the still night, before she had time to react. They were as precise as they were ruthless.

The saddle dug into her belly, and she bounced up and down until she was sure she was going to throw up. She moaned, afraid she'd choke with the gag so securely around her mouth.

When they finally stopped, she was nearly unconscious. A hand gripped her nape, the fingers easily circling the slim column. She was hauled upward and dropped unceremoniously to the ground.

Around her, they made camp while she lay shivering in the damp air. Finally she heard one say, "You best be seeing to the lass, Finn. Laird Cameron won't be happy if she dies of exposure."

An irritated grunt followed, but a minute later, she was untied and the gag removed. Finn, the apparent leader of this abduction, leaned down over her, his eyes gleaming in the light of the fire.

"There's no one to hear you scream, and if you utter a sound, I'll rattle your jaw."

She nodded her understanding and crawled to an up-right position. He nudged her backside with his boot and chuckled when she whirled around in outrage.

"There's a blanket by the fire. Get on it and get some sleep. We leave at first light."

She curled gratefully into the warmth of the blanket, uncaring that the stones and sticks on the ground dug into her skin. Laird Cameron. She'd heard talk of him from the soldiers who drifted in and out of the abbey. He was a ruthless man. Greedy and eager to add to his growing power. It was rumored that his army was one of the largest in all of Scotland and that David, the Scottish king, feared him.

Malcolm, bastard son of Alexander—and her half brother—had already led one revolt against David in a bid for the throne. Were Malcolm and Duncan Cameron to ally, they would be a near unstoppable force.

She swallowed and closed her eyes. The possession of Neamh Álainn would render Cameron invincible.

"Dear God, help me," she whispered.

She couldn't allow him to gain control of Neamh Álainn. It was *her* legacy, the only thing of her father's that she had.

It was impossible to sleep, and so she lay there huddled in the blanket, her hand curled around the wooden cross as she prayed for strength and guidance. Some of the soldiers slept while others kept careful watch. She wasn't fool enough to think she'd be given any opportunity to escape. Not when she was worth more than her weight in gold.

But they wouldn't kill her either, which granted her an advantage. She had nothing to fear by trying to escape and everything to gain.

An hour into her vigil of prayer, a commotion behind her had her sitting straight up and staring into the darkness. Around her, the sleeping soldiers stumbled upward, their hands on their swords when a child's cry rent the night.

One of the men hauled a kicking, wiggling child into the circle around the fire and dropped him on the ground. The child crouched and looked around wildly while the men laughed uproariously.

"What is this?" Finn demanded.

"Caught him trying to sneak one of the horses," the child's captor said.

Anger slanted Finn's features into those of the devil, made more demonic by the light of the fire. The boy, who couldn't be more than seven or eight years old, tilted his chin up defiantly as if daring the man to do his worst.

"Why you insolent little pup," Finn roared.

He raised his hand, and Mairin flew across the ground, throwing herself in front of the child as the fist swung and clipped her cheek.

She went reeling but recovered and quickly threw herself back over the child, gathering him close so she could cover as much of him as possible.

The boy struggled wildly under her, screeching obscenities in Gaelic. His head connected with her already aching jaw, and she saw stars.

"Hush now," she told him in his own language. "Be still. I won't let them hurt you."

"Get off him!" Finn roared.

She tightened around the little boy who finally stopped kicking and flailing. Finn reached down and curled his hand into her hair, yanking brutally upward, but she refused to let go of her charge.

"You'll have to kill me first," she said cooly when he forced her to look at him.

He dropped her hair with a curse then reared back and kicked her in the ribs. She hunched over in pain but was careful to keep the child shielded from the maniacal brute.

"Finn, enough," one man barked. "The laird wants her in one piece."

Muttering a curse, he backed away. "Let her keep the dirty beggar. She'll have to turn loose of him soon enough."

Mairin snapped her neck up to glare into Finn's eyes. "You touch this boy even once and I'll slit my own throat."

Finn's laughter cracked the night. "That's one crazy bluff, lass. If you're going to try to negotiate, you need to learn to be believable."

Slowly she rose until she stood a foot away from the much larger man. She stared up at him until his eyes flickered and he looked away.

"Bluff?" she said softly. "I don't think so. In fact, if I were you, I'd be guarding any and all sharp objects from me. Think you that I don't know what my fate is? To be bedded by that brute laird of yours until my belly swells with child and he can claim Neamh Álainn. I'd rather die."

Finn's eyes narrowed. "You're daft!"

"Aye, that might be so, and in that case I'd be worried one of those sharp objects might find its way between your ribs."

He waved his hand. "You keep the boy. The laird will deal with him and you. We don't take kindly to horse thieves."

Mairin ignored him and turned back to the boy who

huddled on the ground, staring at her with a mixture of fear and worship.

"Come," she said gently. "If we snuggle up tight enough, there's plenty of blanket for the both of us."

He went eagerly to her, tucking his smaller body flush against hers.

"Where is your home?" she asked when he had settled against her.

"I don't know," he said mournfully. "It must be a ways from here. At least two days."

"Shh," she said soothingly. "How did you come to be here?"

"I got lost. My papa said I was never to leave the keep without his men, but I was tired of being treated like a baby. I'm not, you know."

She smiled. "Aye, I know. So you left the keep?"

He nodded. "I took a horse. I only meant to go meet Uncle Alaric. He was due back and I thought to wait near the border to greet him."

"Border?"

"Of our lands."

"And who is your papa, little one?"

"My name is Crispen, not 'little one.'" The distaste was evident in his voice, and she smiled again.

"Crispen is a fine name. Now continue with your story."

"What's your name?" he asked.

"Mairin," she answered softly.

"My papa is Laird Ewan McCabe."

Mairin struggled to place the name, but there were so many clans she had no knowledge of. Her home was in the highlands, but she hadn't seen God's country in ten long years.

"So you went to meet your uncle. Then what happened?"

"I got lost," he said mournfully. "Then a McDonald

soldier found me and intended to take me to his laird to ransom, but I couldn't let that happen. It would dishonor my papa, and he can't afford to ransom me. It would cripple our clan."

Mairin stroked his hair as his warm breath blew over her breast. He sounded so much older than his tender years. And so proud.

"I escaped and hid in the cart of a traveling merchant. I rode for a day before he discovered me." He tilted his head up, bumping her sore jaw again. "Where are we, Mairin?" he whispered. "Are we very far from home?"

"I'm not sure where your home is," she said ruefully. "But we are in the lowlands, and I would wager we're at least a two days' ride from your keep."

"The lowlands," he spat. "Are you a lowlander?"

She smiled at his vehemence. "Nay, Crispen. I'm a highlander."

"Then what are you doing here?" he persisted. "Did they steal you from your home?"

She sighed. " 'Tis a long story. One that began before you were born."

When he tensed for another question, she hushed him with a gentle squeeze. "Go to sleep now, Crispen. We must keep our strength up if we are to escape."

"We're going to escape?" he whispered.

"Aye, of course. That's what prisoners do," she said in a cheerful tone. The fear in his voice made her ache for him. How terrifying it must be for him to be so far from home and the ones who love him.

"Will you take me back home to my papa? I'll make him protect you from Laird Cameron."

She smiled at the fierceness in his voice. "Of course, I'll see to it that you get home."

"Promise?"

"I promise."

* * *

"Find my son!"

Ewan McCabe's roar could be heard over the entire courtyard. His men all stood at attention, their expressions solemn. Some were creased in sympathy. They believed Crispen to be dead, though no one dared to utter that possibility to Ewan.

It wasn't something Ewan hadn't contemplated himself, but he would not rest until his son was found—dead or alive.

Ewan turned to his brothers, Alaric and Caelen. "I cannot afford to send every man in search of Crispen," he said in a low voice. "To do so would leave us vulnerable. I trust you two with my life—with my son's life. I want you each to take a contingent of men and ride in different directions. Bring him home to me."

Alaric, the second oldest of the McCabe brothers, nodded. "You know we won't rest until he is found."

"Aye, I know," Ewan said.

Ewan watched as the two strode off, shouting orders to their men. He closed his eyes and curled his fingers into fists of rage. Who dared take his son? For three days he'd waited for a ransom demand, only none had been forthcoming. For three days he'd scoured every inch of McCabe land and beyond.

Was this a precursor to an attack? Were his enemies plotting to hit him when he was weak? When every available soldier would be involved in the search?

His jaw hardened as he gazed around his crumbling keep. For eight years he'd struggled to keep his clan alive and strong. The McCabe name had always been synonymous with power and pride. Eight years ago they'd withstood a crippling attack. Betrayed by the woman Caelen loved. Ewan's father and young wife had been killed, their child surviving only because he'd been hidden by one of the servants.

Almost nothing had been left when he and his brothers had returned. Just a hulking mass of ruins, his people scattered to the winds, his army nearly decimated.

There had been nothing for Ewan to take over when he became laird.

It had taken this long to rebuild. His soldiers were the best trained in the highlands. He and his brothers worked brutal hours to make sure there was food for the old, the sick, the women, and the children. Many times the men went without. And silently they grew, adding to their numbers until, finally, Ewan had begun to turn their struggling clan around.

Soon, his thoughts could turn to revenge. Nay, that wasn't accurate. Revenge had been all that sustained him for these past eight years. There wasn't a day he *hadn't* thought about it.

"Laird, I bring news of your son."

Ewan whipped around to see one of his soldiers hurrying up to him, his tunic dusty as though he'd just gotten off his horse.

"Speak," he commanded.

"One of the McDonalds came upon your son three days ago along the northern border of your land. He took him, intending to deliver him to their laird so he could ransom the boy. Only, the boy escaped. No one has seen him since."

Ewan trembled with rage. "Take eight soldiers and ride to McDonald. Deliver him this message. He will present the soldier who took my son to the entrance of my keep or he signs his own death warrant. If he doesn't comply, I will come for him myself. I will kill him. And it won't be quick. Do not leave a word out of my message."

The soldier bowed. "Aye, Laird."

He turned and hurried off, leaving Ewan with a mix of relief and rage. Crispen was alive, or at least he had been. McDonald was a fool for breaching their tacit peace agreement. Though the two clans could hardly be considered allies, McDonald wasn't stupid enough to incite the wrath of Ewan McCabe. His keep might be crumbling, and his people might not be the best-fed clan, but his might had been restored twofold.

His soldiers were a deadly fighting force to be reckoned with, and those close enough to Ewan's holdings realized it. But Ewan's sights weren't on his neighbors. They were on Duncan Cameron. Ewan wouldn't be happy until the whole of Scotland dripped with Cameron's blood.

SEDUCTION
OF A HIGHLAND LASS
❧ ❦

Alaric McCabe looked out over the expanse of McCabe land and grappled with the indecision plaguing him. He breathed in the chilly air and looked skyward. It wouldn't snow this day. But soon. Autumn had settled over the highlands. Colder air and shorter days had pushed in.

After so many years of struggling to eke out an existence, to rebuild their clan, his brother Ewan had made great strides in restoring the McCabes to their former glory. This winter, their clan wouldn't go hungry. Their children wouldn't go without proper clothing.

Now it was time for Alaric to do his part for his clan. In a short time, he would travel to the McDonald holding where he would formally ask for Rionna McDonald's hand in marriage.

It was pure ceremony. The agreement had been struck weeks earlier. Now the aging laird wanted Alaric to spend time among the McDonalds, a clan that would one day become Alaric's when he married McDonald's daughter and only heir.

Even now the courtyard was alive with activity as a contingent of McCabe soldiers readied to make the journey with Alaric.

Ewan, Alaric's older brother and laird of the McCabe

clan, had wanted to send his most trusted men to accompany Alaric on his journey, but Alaric refused. There was still danger to Ewan's wife, Mairin, who was heavily pregnant with Ewan's child.

As long as Duncan Cameron was alive, he posed a threat to the McCabes. He coveted what was Ewan's— Ewan's wife and Ewan's eventual control of Neamh Álainn, a legacy brought through his marriage to Mairin, the daughter of the former king of Scotland.

And now because of the tenuous peace in the highlands and the threat Duncan Cameron posed not only to the neighboring clans, but to King David's throne, Alaric agreed to the marriage that would cement an alliance between the McCabes and the only clan whose lands rested between Neamh Álainn and McCabe land.

It was a good match. Rionna McDonald was fair to look upon, even if she was an odd lass who preferred the dress and duties of a man over those of a woman. And Alaric would have what he'd never have if he remained under Ewan: his own clan to lead. His own lands. His heir inheriting the mantle of leadership.

So why wasn't he more eager to mount his horse and ride toward his destiny?

He turned when he heard a sound to his left. Mairin McCabe was hurrying up the hillside, or at least attempting to hurry, and Cormac, her assigned guard for the day looked exasperated as he followed in her wake. Her shawl was wrapped tightly around her, and her lips trembled with the cold.

Alaric held out his hand, and she gripped it, leaning toward him as she sought to catch her breath.

"You shouldn't be up here, lass," Alaric reproached. "You're going to freeze to death."

"Nay, she shouldn't," Cormac agreed. "If our laird finds out, he'll be angry."

Mairin rolled her eyes and then looked anxiously up

at Alaric. "Do you have everything you require for your journey?"

Alaric smiled. "Aye, I do. Gertie has packed enough food for a journey twice as long."

She alternated squeezing and patting Alaric's hand, her eyes troubled as she rubbed her burgeoning belly with her other hand. He pulled her closer so she'd have the warmth of his body.

"Should you perchance wait another day? It's near to noon already. Maybe you should wait and leave early on the morrow."

Alaric stifled his grin. Mairin wasn't happy with his leaving. She was quite used to having her clan right where she wanted them. On McCabe land. And now that Alaric was set to leave, she'd become increasingly more vocal in her worry and her dissatisfaction.

"I won't be gone overlong, Mairin," he said gently. "A few weeks at most. Then I'll return for a time before the marriage takes place and I reside permanently at McDonald keep."

Her lips turned down into an unhappy frown at the reminder that Alaric would leave the McCabes and, for all practical purposes, become a McDonald.

"Stop frowning, lass. It isn't good for the babe. Neither is you being out here in the cold."

She sighed and threw her arms around him. He took a step back and exchanged amused glances with Cormac over her head. The lass was even more emotional now that she was swollen with child, and the members of her clan were becoming increasingly more familiar with her spontaneous bursts of affection.

"I shall miss you, Alaric. I know Ewan will as well. He says nothing, but he's quieter now."

"I'll miss you, too," Alaric said solemnly. "Rest assured, I'll be here when you deliver the newest McCabe."

At that, her face lit up and she took a step back and reached up to pat him on the cheek.

"Be good to Rionna, Alaric. I know you and Ewan feel she needs a firmer hand, but in truth, I think what she most needs is love and acceptance."

Alaric fidgeted, appalled that she'd want to discuss matters of love with him. For God's sake.

She laughed. "All right. I can see I've made you uncomfortable. But heed my words."

"My lady, the laird has spotted you and he doesn't look pleased," Cormac said.

Alaric turned to see Ewan standing in the courtyard, arms crossed over his chest and a scowl etched onto his face.

"Come along, Mairin," Alaric said as he tucked her hand underneath his arm. "I better return you to my brother before he comes after you."

Mairin grumbled under her breath, but she allowed Alaric to escort her down the hillside.

When they reached the courtyard, Ewan leveled a glare at his wife but turned his attention to Alaric. "Do you have all you need?"

Alaric nodded.

Caelen, the youngest McCabe brother, came to stand at Ewan's side. "Are you sure you don't want me to accompany you?"

"You're needed here," Alaric said. "More so as Mairin's time draws nigh. Winter snows will be upon us soon. It would be just like Duncan to mount an attack when he thinks we least expect it."

Mairin shivered at Alaric's side again, and he turned to her. "Give me a hug, sister, and then go back into the keep before you catch your death of cold. My men are ready, and I won't have you crying all over us as we try to leave."

As expected, Mairin scowled but once again threw her arms around Alaric and squeezed tight.

"God be with you," she whispered.

Alaric rubbed an affectionate hand over her hair and then pushed her in the direction of the keep. Ewan reinforced Alaric's dictate with a ferocious scowl of his own.

Mairin stuck her tongue out and then turned away, Cormac following her toward the steps of the keep.

"If you have need of me, send word," Ewan said. "I'll come immediately."

Alaric gripped Ewan's arm and the two brothers stared at each other for a long moment before Alaric released him. Caelen pounded Alaric on the back as Alaric went to mount his horse.

"This is a good thing for you," Caelen said sincerely once Alaric was astride his horse.

Alaric stared down at his brother and felt the first stirring of satisfaction. "Aye, it is."

He took a deep breath as his hands tightened on the reins. His lands. His clan. He'd be laird. Aye, this was a good thing.

Alaric and a dozen of the McCabe soldiers rode at a steady pace throughout the day. Since they'd gained a late start, what would normally be a day's ride would now require them to arrive on McDonald's land the next morning.

Knowing this, Alaric didn't press, and actually halted his men to make camp just after dusk. They built only one fire and kept the blaze low so it didn't illuminate a wide area.

After they'd eaten the food that Gertie had prepared for the journey, Alaric divided his men into two groups and told the first of the six men to take the first watch.

They stationed themselves around the encampment,

providing protection for the remaining six to bed down for a few hours' rest.

Though Alaric was scheduled for the second watch, he couldn't sleep. He lay awake on the hard ground, staring up at the star-filled sky. It was a clear night and cold. The winds were picking up from the north, heralding a coming change in the weather.

Married. To Rionna McDonald. He tried hard but could barely conjure an image of the lass. All he could remember was her vibrant golden hair. She was quiet, which he supposed was a good trait for a woman to have, although Mairin was hardly a quiet or particularly obedient wife. And yet he found her endearing, and he knew that Ewan wouldn't change a single thing about her.

But then Mairin was all a woman should be. Soft and sweet, and Rionna was mannish in both dress and manner. She wasn't an unattractive lass, which made it puzzling that she would indulge in activities completely unsuitable for a lady.

It was something he'd have to address immediately.

A slight disturbance of the air was the only warning he had before he lunged to the side. A sword caught his side, slicing through clothing and flesh.

Pain seared through his body, but he pushed it aside as he grabbed his sword and bolted to his feet. His men came alive and the night air swelled with the sounds of battle.

Alaric fought two men, the clang of swords blistering his ears. His hands vibrated from the repeated blows as he parried and thrust.

He was backed toward the perimeter set by his men and nearly tripped over one of the men he'd posted as guard. An arrow protruded from his chest, a testimony to how stealthily the ambush had been set.

They were sorely outnumbered, and although Alaric

would pit the McCabe soldiers against anyone, anytime, and be assured of the outcome, his only choice was to call a retreat lest they all be slaughtered. There was simply no way to win against six-to-one odds.

He yelled for his men to get to their horses. Then he dispatched the man in front of him and struggled to reach his own mount. Blood poured from his side. The acrid scent rose in the chill and filled his nostrils. Already his vision had dimmed, and he knew if he didn't get himself on his horse, he was done for.

He whistled and his horse bolted forward just as another warrior made his charge at Alaric. Weakening fast from the loss of blood, he fought without the discipline Ewan had instilled in him. He took chances. He was reckless. He was fighting for his life.

With a roar, Alaric's opponent lunged forward. Gripping his sword in both hands, Alaric swung. He sliced through his attacker's neck and completely decapitated him.

Alaric didn't waste a single moment savoring the victory. There was another attacker bearing down on him. With the last of his strength, he threw himself on his horse and gave the command to run.

He could make out the outline of bodies as his horse thundered away, and with a sinking feeling, Alaric knew that they weren't the enemy. He'd lost most, if not all, of his soldiers in the attack.

"Home," he commanded hoarsely.

He gripped his side and tried valiantly to remain conscious, but with each jostle as the horse flew across the terrain, Alaric's vision dimmed.

His last conscious thought was that he had to get home to warn Ewan. He just hoped to hell there hadn't been an attack on the McCabe holding as well.

Sad cypress   22396
Christie, Agatha   FIC C555s

Walsh Jesuit Student Library

A PRETTY PAIR
OF CORPSES

A delicately lovely old woman of wealth and
refinement . . . a sensually beautiful young
girl from the wrong side of the tracks . . .
There seemed nothing in common between
them, except for the mysterious link that
bound them together in life—and the identical
manner of their murders. . . .

On a secluded estate, amid a bitter struggle
over a fortune left up for grabs, Hercule Poirot
had to unlock the baffling secrets of the past
—and catch a killer willing to stop at nothing
to lead the great detective up the garden path
and into the grave. . . .

DISCARDED